A TANGLED WEAVE:
DEATH OF A CHILD

K.R. SOMO

KRS

www.krsomo.com

A TANGLED WEAVE: Death of a Child

Copyright © 2023 K.R. SOMO

All rights reserved.

ISBN: 9798862464580

A Tangled Weave-Death of a child is a work of fiction. Names, characters, places, and incidents are the product of the author's imagination or are used fictitiously. Any resemblance to actual events, locales, or persons, living or dead, is purely coincidental.

All rights reserved. No part of this book may be reproduced or transmitted in any form or by means, electronic or mechanical, including photocopying, recording, or by any informational storage and retrieval system, without the author's permission.

A TANGLED WEAVE: Death of a Child

DEDICATION

To my children, growing up you always enjoyed fantasy, horror, and supernatural stories. You made Halloween and Friday the 13th fun.

To my Aunt Annie, your jest for life and constant humor will follow me forever.

Death ends a life, not a relationship. All the love you created is still there. All the memories are still there. You live on- in the hearts of everyone you have touched and nurtured while you were here.

Mitch Albom

CHAPTER 1

The sun's first rays pierced the bedroom curtains, casting a golden glow upon Lucy's face. The 12-year-old stirred in her sleep, reluctant to leave the comfort of her dreams. But, as she had been taught, Lucy pushed herself out of bed and started her day. After dressing in her modest school uniform, she made her way downstairs to join her mother, Teresa, and stepfather, Steve, for breakfast.

"Morning, sweetheart," Teresa greeted Lucy warmly, her eyes filled with love. "Morning, sweetheart," Teresa greeted Lucy warmly, her eyes filled with love. As Lucy sat down for breakfast, Teresa put a bowl of cereal in front of her daughter and smiled. Teresa was a resilient and loving mother in her mid-30s with wavy blonde hair and soft blue eyes. She worked tirelessly to provide for her family, despite the challenges she faced in her personal life. She had worked late at the hospital but would never show the aches in her back and feet. She was a woman determined to provide a good and loving home to her daughter.

After the tragic accident of Lucy's father, she had been more determined than ever to keep her home even marrying a man she did not love for the stability. Teresa treasured every moment with Lucy, knowing that each day might be their last together as a family unit. But Teresa kept smiling because it was all worth it; through all the struggles and heartache, Teresa still believed that one day life would be better for them all, if they just held on long enough for things to get better.

"Eat up," Teresa said softly with a gentle smile, before turning away to prepare breakfast for Steve. Lucy smiled back at her mother before taking her first bite of breakfast with determination – just like her mother had taught her.

"Morning, Mom," Lucy replied, taking her seat at the table.

"Good morning, Lucy," Steve chimed in, his voice tinged with an edge of impatience.

"Hi, Steve," Lucy acknowledged, avoiding eye contact as she focused on the cereal before her. The trio ate together in silence, the room heavy with unspoken tension. Lucy's mind was elsewhere, lost in memories of her father, Tom, who had passed away four years ago. It seemed like the only way to find solace, especially when the air felt thick with resentment. As part of her daily routine, Lucy would spend her time after school sketching pictures of her father. Her memory of him was fading, but through her artwork, she kept him alive. With each stroke of her pencil, she could almost hear his laughter or feel the warmth of his embrace. It was a bittersweet connection, one that both comforted and pained her heart.

"Lucy, maybe you should put that drawing away," Steve suggested, annoyance creeping into his voice. Teresa shifted uncomfortably in her seat as she shot Steve a warning glance. But it was too late; the damage had already been done. Lucy glanced up in shock, taking in his words with hurt and confusion. She slowly rolled up the paper and tucked it away in her pocket without a word. She knew that Steve meant well—that he wanted to protect her from pain—but Lucy couldn't help feeling slighted. After all, the drawings were all she had left of her father.

Steve seemed like a kindhearted man, but there was something about him that just wasn't right. He tried hard to fit into the family, but he always fell short of Lucy's expectations of what a father should be like. While Teresa welcomed Steve into their lives with open arms, Lucy could not accept him as the father figure their family so desperately needed. Stillness filled the room once more, broken only by the sound of spoons scraping against the bottom of the bowls of cereal. Uncomfortable silence permeated the air as both adults pretended not to notice Lucy's distress.

"Lucy, come help me clean up the kitchen," Teresa called from the kitchen, pulling Lucy from her reverie. She complied; her fingers stained with graphite from her drawings. Together, they cleaned the kitchen while Steve sat drinking his coffee. While helping her mother, Lucy couldn't help but glance at her latest drawing of her father, which lay unfinished on the dining room table. She had drawn him standing in front of a towering oak tree, the sunlight filtering through its leaves and casting shadows on his face. She imagined him there, offering her words of encouragement and love.

"Your father would have been proud of you," Teresa said quietly, noticing Lucy's gaze. "He loved seeing your artwork."

"Thanks, Mom," Lucy replied, her green eyes shimmering with unshed tears. "I wish he were still here."

"Me too, sweetheart." Teresa embraced her daughter, their shared grief momentarily binding them together. Breakfast was a quiet affair, as usual. Steve ate quickly, focusing on his food and avoiding conversation. Lucy could feel his stare lingering on her drawing, and she knew that it bothered him. He longed to be seen as her father, but no matter how hard she tried, Lucy couldn't replace Tom in her heart.

The autumn sun hung low in the sky, casting long shadows beneath the towering oak tree. Lucy sat alone in the serene spot, her sketchbook resting on her lap. She had found solace in this secluded spot in their backyard, surrounded by nature's beauty, and it was here that she felt closest to her father's memory.

She prepared a pencil and drew with sure strokes as she recalled all of the stories, he used to tell her: stories of his childhood adventures, tales of brave knights and fierce dragons, and legends of brave heroes. He brought these stories to life with vivid descriptions and contagious enthusiasm.

Tears stung Lucy's eyes as she remembered how much she had looked up to him. She had wanted to be just like him - strong and brave - but now he was gone. His absence left a gaping hole in her heart that no one else could fill.

Lucy closed her eyes for a moment, allowing herself to drift away on a wave of memories and emotions. When she opened her eyes again, she focused on the intricate details of the tree before her - its gnarled branches reaching out for the sky, its leaves fluttering softly in the breeze. Her pencil moved swiftly across the page as she tried to capture every detail before it slipped away from her grasp.

"Lucy," called Teresa from the back porch, "Steve is home! Time to come inside."

"Coming, Mom!" Lucy replied, taking one last look at the landscape before gathering her pencils and charcoal sticks. With a heavy heart, she reluctantly made her way back inside – leaving behind an unfinished portrait of Tom beneath the oak tree – a reminder that love will never die. As she entered the cozy living room, Lucy could feel the familiar tension between her mother and stepfather. She looked over at Steve, who sat in his usual armchair, flipping through a magazine with a forced smile. Sensing his unease, Lucy hesitated before sitting down on the floor and opening her sketchbook.

"Coming, Mom!" Lucy replied, taking one last look at the landscape before gathering her pencils and charcoal sticks. As she entered the cozy living room, Lucy could feel the familiar tension between her mother and stepfather. She looked over at Steve, who sat in his usual armchair, flipping through a magazine with a forced smile. Sensing his unease, Lucy hesitated before sitting down on the floor and opening her sketchbook.

"Hey, kiddo," Steve said, trying to sound cheerful. "What are you working on today?"

"Another drawing of my dad," Lucy answered softly, her fingers tracing the lines of Tom's face in her sketch. She felt a pang of guilt as she glanced at Steve, wishing she could make him understand that her love for Tom didn't diminish her feelings for him.

"Lucy, I told you before," Steve began, his voice strained. "I want to be your dad, but it's hard when you keep holding onto the past like this."

"Steve," Teresa intervened, placing a hand on his shoulder, "she's just expressing her feelings. It's important for her to remember her father."

"Of course, but..." Steve trailed off, his jaw clenched as he tried to hide his frustration.

Lucy stared down at her sketch, biting her lip as she considered her stepfather's words. She knew he wanted to be a good father to her, but the memories of Tom were too precious to let go. The drawings were her way of preserving those memories, her connection to the man who had loved her unconditionally.

Steve felt the familiar sting of jealousy as he watched Lucy's face light up with joy. He clenched his fists at his sides, struggling to keep his emotions in check. The tension between them was palpable, like an invisible thread pulling them apart.

A TANGLED WEAVE: Death of a Child

The evening sun cast a golden glow on the kitchen walls as Teresa buttoned her coat, preparing to leave for work. Her soft blue eyes darted towards Steve and Lucy, who sat at the table in silence. The tension between them was intense.

"Lucy, remember to finish your homework before you go to bed, okay?" Teresa said gently, tucking a stray blonde curl behind her ear.

"Okay, Mom," Lucy replied, her green eyes meeting her mother's gaze briefly before dropping back down to her half-eaten plate of spaghetti.

"Steve, can you make sure she gets it done?" Teresa asked, her voice wavering slightly.

"Of course," Steve replied, his dark eyes narrow, betraying a hint of irritation. "You've got nothing to worry about."

Teresa hesitated, uncertainty flickering across her face, but ultimately sighed and nodded. She gave Lucy a quick hug, and then walked out the door, leaving her daughter alone with Steve.

As soon as the door clicked shut, the atmosphere in the room shifted, as though the air had been sucked from space. Steve's fingers drummed impatiently on the table, his brow creasing into a deep scowl. He glared at Lucy, who shrunk under his gaze.

"Didn't your mother tell you to finish your homework?" he snapped, his words like ice. "Why are you still sitting there?" He listened intently for Teresa's car to pull out of the drive, before walking to the back door. "I won't be home until late, do whatever you want, you will anyway." Lucy was relieved, she enjoyed this time to herself.

A gentle breeze whispered through the trees, carrying with it a chill that hinted at the coming winter. Inside, Lucy sat at the kitchen table, her sketchbook open before her as she drew another picture of her father. The soft scratch of her pencil mingled with the distant hum of the wind; she couldn't help but smile as she worked.

After her mother went off to work and Steve headed to the local bar, Lucy found herself all alone in their large house. This was a scene she was accustomed to, and Lucy never minded having the house to herself. Her mom had no clue her stepdad would abandon her when she worked night shifts at the hospital. If Teresa knew, she wouldn't allow it. But Lucy wasn't a child anymore; she was 12 years old and capable of taking care.

5

A TANGLED WEAVE: Death of a Child

Her pleasant thoughts were suddenly interrupted by a loud bang at the front door. Lucy jumped in her seat, her hand coming up to clutch at her chest as her heart raced in her chest. She waited for a moment, but the noise did not repeat itself. Cautiously, she rose from the table and made her way towards the front of the house. As she approached the door, she could feel her fear mounting. A sense of danger crept over her, and she felt a cold sweat break out across her skin.

But then she saw that the door was slightly ajar, and she could see a flash of movement just beyond it. Taking a deep breath, she pushed the door open and stepped outside. She immediately regretted it. Lucy opened her mouth to scream, but no sound came out. Suddenly, a figure lunged towards her, forcing her backwards. She stumbled and fell to the ground, her sketchbook tumbling from her hands.

The figure loomed over her, a chilling presence that suffocated her. Lucy tried to crawl away, but the figure grabbed her by the ankle and pulled her back. Its face was twisted into a horrifying grin, its eyes glinting with malice. Lucy again tried to scream for help, but nothing came out. She wished her dad were there, he would protect her. She closed her eyes, feeling the cold, sweating hands wrapped around her neck. The weight and pressure against her small body made it difficult to breathe.

Lucy struggled to move, scratching, and kicking at the figure that was holding her down. The tears and sweat running down her face from her fear and pain. She closed her eyes again, picturing what her father would do. "Help me," she cried, but no one was listening.

As Lucy's small, battered frame finally came to a rest, the house seemed to hold its breath, as if bearing witness to the unspeakable horror that had unfolded outside its walls. The wind whispered mournfully, the rustling leaves joining in a chorus of sorrow and despair. Within the clutches of darkness, the world watched as destiny's cruel hand reached out to claim another victim, snuffing out the light of innocence that had burned so brightly within her.

In the shadows, nature wept for the lost child, her dreams shattered like the fragile bones that now lay broken and twisted beneath her. The echoes of her laughter would soon be carried away in the winds, leaving behind only the cold silence of an empty house

A TANGLED WEAVE: Death of a Child

and the bitter sting of loss.

CHAPTER 2

Teresa was overwhelmed by the outpouring of love and support from her friends, family, and community members. In their presence, she could finally begin to process the depths of her grief. She spent most of her days in a fog, alternating between moments of overwhelming sadness and periods of strange calmness as she tried to make sense of it all.

The funeral was held several weeks after Lucy's body had been discovered. The entire town came together to say goodbye to such an amazing young child; they lit candles in her memory and shared stories about how wonderful a girl she was.

It was at this moment that Teresa realized just how loved and admired her daughter truly was. Despite the tragedy that had occurred, this day was marked with joy as everyone celebrated the life that Lucy had lived so passionately and with such enthusiasm. After the funeral, Teresa struggled to find her way back to some semblance of normalcy - but try as she might, things were never the same again. The days were long and filled with emptiness; the nights left her alone in bed facing questions for which there would never be answers. No matter how much time passed, Teresa could not seem to move on. She was stuck in a state of grief, unable to let go of the pain she felt from losing her daughter. Every day was a struggle and, despite all the wonderful people that offered their support and comfort, it still felt like there was a permanent void in her heart that would never be filled.

In an effort to cope with her loss more effectively, Teresa began attending grief counseling meetings as well as support groups for parents who have lost a child. Through these experiences she discovered that everyone grieved differently, and it was ok for her to take whatever amount of time she needed to heal.

The thought of putting her life back together was not possible for Teresa. She needed closure. She needed a chance to say good-bye, but most of all she needed to know who did this to her child. The people in Teresa's neighborhood continued to support her with organized weekly meetings at local churches where everyone gathered for prayer sessions devoted to keeping Lucy's memory alive. Even those who had never met her felt a deep sense of sorrow for her family; no one wanted them to bear this tragedy alone. Everyone was determined to make since of the tragedy.

Detective Samuel "Sam" Davis spent weeks going door to door, interviewing locals, and searching for any clues that could lead him closer to finding the person responsible for taking Lucy's life. Yet after all of his hard work and dedication nothing seemed to be working; no one had seen anything suspicious or out of the ordinary in the weeks leading up to Lucy's murder, which only made his job harder.

He felt discouraged by the lack of progress he was making with his investigation. He thought back to how he had first found out about the crime; a call from one of his colleagues who told him about Lucy's death and begged him to investigate further. Sam had been more than happy to take on this case as it reminded him of a similar tragedy that had happened years ago in another town.

He tried to stay positive but deep inside he knew that without any evidence, it would be almost impossible for him to find out what happened. He asked himself what else he could do, but there was simply nothing left except wait and hope that something new would come up soon.

Detective Samuel "Sam" Davis struggled to keep his focus on the case at hand, but his thoughts kept drifting off to the memory of his own daughter, Marie. She had been just a year older than Lucy when she died from cancer, and Sam could still remember the look of fear and desperation in her eyes when he'd taken her to visit different doctors in search of a cure. But it was a fruitless endeavor - no one could save them, and Marie succumbed to her illness in his arms.

Sam felt a deep sense of loss as he thought back on those heartbreaking memories; he knew that Teresa had suffered an even greater tragedy than his own, but he also knew that despite their differences, they shared a common pain of having lost their children too soon. In resolving to do all he could for Lucy's family, Sam worked tirelessly to find those responsible for taking her life away - doing whatever it took in order to provide Teresa with some kind of closure.

He studied every detail from the crime scene photos again and again until he realized that the crime had to be from someone she trusted. Lucy had to have known her killer. He began interviewing locals once more in hopes that someone would come forward with a new lead. Finally, after days spent investigating with little success, Sam knew he had to put an end to this hurtful family nightmare. He needs to start considering the people in her life.

Eventually Teresa mustered enough strength to return into society as she slowly started rebuilding the life she had before Lucy passed away; she began taking part in church activities once again, joined a local book club, and even attended memorial services dedicated solely towards remembering her lost daughter's spirit.

The desolate landscape seemed to mirror Teresa's own shattered world when she walked through the front door, her eyes red-rimmed from a day spent holding back tears at work. "Steve," she called out, her voice cracking with fatigue and grief. "I'm home."

"Hey, honey." Steve appeared in the doorway, his face a mask of practiced calm that belied the storm of guilt and fear churning within him. He forced a smile, though it never reached his eyes. "How was your day?"

"Difficult," Teresa admitted as she hung up her coat and crossed the room to embrace him. She could not know how much harder it was for Steve to return the gesture, to feel her warm body pressed against his, while the specter of Lucy's lifeless form haunted his every thought.

"Let me make you some tea," he suggested, pulling away from her gently. "You look like you could use something to help you relax."

"Thank you," she murmured, sinking into an armchair with a weary sigh. As Steve busied himself in the kitchen, his mind raced with panicked thoughts. How could leave the child alone in the house?

"Here you go," Steve said, handing Teresa a steaming cup of chamomile tea. She took it gratefully, sipping slowly as she stared vacantly at the flickering shadows cast by the fire.

"Lucy would have loved this weather," she whispered, her voice trembling with emotion. "She used to say that storms were nature's way of cleansing the earth, washing away the pain and sorrow of the past."

"Like the great flood in the old stories," Steve added, struggling to keep his voice steady. "A fresh start for all of creation."

A TANGLED WEAVE: Death of a Child

Teresa nodded, her eyes glistening with unshed tears. "I miss her so much, Steve. I can't believe she's really gone."

"Me too," he said softly, the words like rusty nails scraping against the raw wounds of his conscience.

The wind outside continued to howl, sending shivers down their spines as they sat together in the dimly lit room. It seemed as though the very air around them was thick with secrets and lies, suffocating them slowly as they tried to navigate the treacherous waters of grief and loss.

Just as the air could not get any thicker, a crash from the living room brought the two to attention. "What was that?" Teresa jumped out of her chair and her eyes jolted toward the living room.

"Stay here, I will take a look." Steve slowly and cautiously walked toward the sound of the crash.

Steve moved into the living room, dreading what he might find. His heart sank as soon as he saw it -- their family picture from the oak tree in the backyard. He carefully picked up the frame, it was unnaturally cold to the touch, and he felt a chill run down his spine. But as he looked around, nothing else seemed to have been disturbed, and a strange sense of relief washed over him. He returned to Teresa in the kitchen and held out the photo to her, "Nothing else there. Just this."

After examining it for a moment, Teresa glanced up at Steve with tears in her eyes and said "This was taken on Lucy's birthday last summer... I can't believe someone would do this."

Steve wrapped his arm around her shoulders and tightened his embrace while fighting back tears of his own. How could someone be so cruel? Still holding Teresa close, Steve vowed to himself that he would do whatever it took to bring those responsible for Lucy's death to justice.

"Maybe we should go away for a while," Teresa suggested after several minutes of silence. "Somewhere far from here, where we can try to heal and find some peace."

The rain fell relentlessly against the windows, casting a melancholic pall over the room. Teresa and Steve sat on opposite sides of the table, their hands wrapped around steaming mugs of tea, as if the warmth could somehow mend their shattered hearts. The silence between them was thick and heavy with unspoken words, each struggling to find a way to bridge the chasm that had grown in

A TANGLED WEAVE: Death of a Child

the wake of Lucy's death.

CHAPTER 3

The dimly lit living room cast shadows on the walls, as if whispering secrets that only the night could understand. Steve, a middle-aged man with a stern demeanor, stood by the window, his eyes narrowed as he watched Teresa move about the room. Her nervous disposition was clear in the way her hands trembled slightly while she arranged the cushions on the couch. The flickering flame of a solitary candle illuminated the tension between them, causing the darkness to hum with unspoken suspicions.

Steve's mind wandered to the mysterious package he had discovered in Teresa's room earlier that day. He couldn't shake the feeling that something was amiss, and for the past several days, he had been watching her behavior discreetly. The package weighed heavily on his thoughts, like an anchor dragging him into the depths of uncertainty. He yearned to confront her, to demand answers and unravel the truth hidden beneath the surface of their strained relationship.

As Teresa continued to busy herself in the living room, her wavy blonde hair cascading like a golden waterfall down her back, Steve clenched his fists, fighting the urge to challenge her directly. He knew that he needed solid evidence before making any accusations, but the gnawing curiosity clawed at his insides, consuming him from within. The room seemed to grow darker, the shadows merging with the growing storm brewing inside Steve's heart.

With every passing moment, the ancient trees outside swayed and whispered, their branches scratching against the windowpane as if seeking entry into the house. Their movements echoed Steve's internal turmoil, reflecting the wild beating of his heart and his growing obsession with the enigmatic puzzle that was Teresa. The wind howled through the trees, its ghostly voice carrying the unspoken questions that haunted him, intertwining with the mysterious forces of nature that governed their lives.

In the silence of the dimly lit living room, Steve could feel the weight of destiny hanging heavily in the air. The mysterious package and Teresa's evasive behavior seemed to be harbingers of a greater loss yet to come, entwined with the powerful forces of nature that governed their lives. His thoughts turned to the Indigenous beliefs and traditions he had once dismissed as mere superstition, wondering if they held the key to understanding the unsettling events unfolding before him.

As the wind continued its eerie symphony outside, Steve's eyes never left Teresa, his suspicion casting an ominous shadow over the room. The flickering candlelight cast strange shapes on her face, transforming her soft blue eyes into pools of darkness, hinting at the secrets she kept hidden deep within. In the dim glow, the boundaries between reality and imagination blurred, and Steve found himself caught in the grip of a foreboding presence that threatened to consume them both.

And so, they stood in the dimly lit living room, each locked in their own private turmoil, the tension between them palpable, like a silent storm brewing on the horizon. The shadows whispered their secrets, the trees swayed in the embrace of the wind, and the ancient forces of nature watched over them, waiting for the moment when destiny would reveal itself in all its raw and untamed power.

The tension in the living room thickened, the air heavy with unspoken accusations and fear. Steve's clenched fists trembled at his side while Teresa's gaze darted nervously around the room, her slender fingers fidgeting with the hem of her dress.

"Stop avoiding the question, Teresa," Steve growled, his voice low and menacing. "What's in that package I found in your room? Are you involved in something illegal?"

Teresa's eyes widened, and she took a step back, her shoulders tensing as if preparing for an attack. "I... I don't know what you're talking about, Steve," she stammered, her voice quivering with apprehension.

"Damn it, Teresa!" Steve barked, his voice louder and more aggressive now. "I've been watching you for days, and your behavior doesn't add up. Do you think I'm stupid? That I wouldn't notice?"

His words lashed at her like jagged lightning bolts, each one cutting deeper into her fragile facade. Her heart raced like a trapped bird beating its wings against the bars of its cage, desperate to escape the suffocating uncertainty that enveloped her.

"Steve, you're scaring me," Teresa whispered, her body

language becoming defensive as she crossed her arms over her chest, shielding herself from his verbal onslaught. "I swear I have no idea what you're talking about."

"Then explain yourself!" Steve demanded, taking a step closer, his face contorted with anger. The shadows of the room seemed to stretch, reaching for them both, eager to swallow them whole.

The dimly lit living room seemed to close in around Teresa, its walls pulsating with the tension that crackled between her and Steve like static electricity. The air was thick with a suffocating heaviness, as if the very atmosphere were an extension of the storm brewing within their souls.

"Tell me the truth!" Steve roared, his hand shooting out to grab Teresa's arm, fingers digging into flesh like talons of an angry predator.

"Let go of me!" Teresa cried out, her voice ragged with fear and desperation. She shoved him away with all the strength she could muster her heart pounding in her chest like an ancient drumbeat echoing through time.

In that moment, the room seemed to shudder, the shadows quivering on the walls as if disturbed by some unseen force. And then, there she was - Lucy's spirit, glowing softly and hovering in mid-air, her ethereal presence casting an otherworldly light upon the scene.

"Lucy..." Teresa whispered, her breath catching in her throat, her eyes wide with shock and wonder. The sight of her daughter filled her with a confusing blend of relief and terror - relief that Lucy was here, and terror at what this might mean for the world they inhabited.

Steve stumbled backward, his grip on Teresa's arm releasing as if burned by fire. His face contorted in confusion, unable to understand the apparition before him. "What...what is this?" he stammered, his voice trembling with uncertainty.

Teresa's mind raced, seeking understanding amid the chaos of emotions swirling within her. She felt the weight of generations bearing down upon her, the whispers of ancestors urging her to embrace her destiny and protect the ones she held dear from forces beyond their keen.

"Steve," she said, her voice quavering but resolute, "I don't know what you've been thinking, but I am not involved in anything. I swear on Lucy's memory."

"Then how do you explain this?" Steve demanded, gesturing wildly at the apparition of their daughter. His anger was momentarily overshadowed by his bewilderment, but it still simmered beneath the surface like a dormant volcano awaiting eruption.

"Maybe... maybe there's more to this world than we can see or understand," Teresa suggested hesitantly, her gaze never leaving Lucy's form. "Perhaps there are forces at work here that defy our comprehension."

As Lucy hovered between them, her spirit casting its ethereal glow upon the turmoil of emotions within the room, it seemed as if the very fabric of reality was unraveling before their eyes. And yet, for all the confusion and fear that gripped them, there was also an undeniable sense of awe and wonder - for in seeing the impossible, they had glimpsed the infinite tapestry of existence, of life and death intertwined in a dance as old as time itself.

The air in the living room seemed to thicken, charged with an energy that crackled like static electricity. Lucy's spirit, once a soft and gentle glow, began to intensify, her ethereal form pulsating with a fierce luminescence that bathed the room in otherworldly light. Her once tender gaze now blazed with determination, as if she had tapped into ancient wellspring of power that surged through her very essence.

"Mom," Lucy's voice echoed softly, yet carried a soothing resonance that seemed to reverberate through the very core of Teresa's being. A sudden warmth enveloped her heart, like the embrace of a long-lost loved one, and she felt an inexplicable sense of calm despite the storm brewing around her.

Steve, however, appeared unaffected by the serenity exuding from Lucy's spirit. His eyes still burned with rage; his fists clenched tightly at his sides as if trying to hold the fury within.

"Steve," Teresa whispered, her voice barely overheard above the hum of energy that filled the room, "let me go."

Steve hesitated, torn between his anger and the bewildering presence of Lucy's spirit. It was in this moment of indecision that Teresa seized her chance. With a sudden burst of speed, propelled by a newfound courage ignited by her daughter's spectral intervention, Teresa sprinted towards the door. Her footsteps were muffled by the thick carpet, and Steve's attention remained riveted on Lucy's radiant form.

As Teresa dashed out of the room, she couldn't help but steal a glance back at her daughter's spirit, her heart swelling with equal parts sorrow and gratitude. In that brief instant, their eyes met, and Teresa knew that Lucy would always be with her, guiding her through the darkness of life's challenges.

"Thank you," Teresa mouthed silently, the words forever etched in her heart. And just as she slipped away, unseen by Steve, Lucy's spirit began to fade, her light gradually diminishing until nothing remained but the faintest trace of an ethereal glow.

Only then did Steve notice Teresa's absence, his eyes darting around the room in frantic search for her. A bitter sense of defeat washed over him, mingling with the remnants of his anger and confusion like poison in his veins. But deep within him, a seed of curiosity took root, sprouting into an insatiable hunger to uncover the truth behind the mysterious package and the connection to Lucy's otherworldly intervention.

"Wait," he whispered into the void left by Teresa's departure, the word barely escaping his lips before it was swallowed by darkness. The room now felt hollow, devoid of warmth, leaving Steve with only the cold embrace of uncertainty to cling to as he embarked on a journey that would forever alter the course of their lives.

CHAPTER 4

Lucy's eyes fluttered open to a dimly lit room, her small body lying in her bed. She blinked several times, trying to make sense of her surroundings. As she looked around, confusion settled in. It was as if she was waking from a bad dream. She rubbed her eyes and sat up slowly, she could feel the warmth streaming through the window. The sun casting warmth throughout the room.

"Am I dreaming?" Lucy whispered to herself; her voice barely noticeable. She shivered, feeling a strange chill enveloping her as she slowly stood up. Lucy slowly crawled herself out of the warm bed, growing increasingly aware of her surroundings. Her body felt strangely heavy, as if pulled to the ground by an invisible force. She could make out strange shapes in the shadows - tall figures swathed in robes with hoods that hid their faces. One of them hissed something at her that she couldn't quite make out, then faded away like a wisp of smoke.

Walking out of her room, Lucy found herself standing in front of her mother's bedroom. She tried to open it but found that it wouldn't budge. Suddenly, a chill ran down her spine as she heard a voice from inside the room - Steve's voice. He was arguing with someone and seemed to be getting angrier by the second. Lucy recognized his voice and realized that he was talking to her mother. Lucy tried to knock on the door, but her hands would not move. She realized then that something was wrong, terribly wrong.

Lucy's heart raced as she listened to Steve and her mom discussing a funeral, it was her funeral. Now she understood why she had been brought back from the dead - to find justice for her death and ensure that Steve paid for his crime! With newfound clarity, Lucy was determined to bring justice for her mother and make sure that Steve faced the consequences of his actions.

Before she could take another step, she heard a soft, familiar voice calling her name.

"Lucy," it whispered, echoing through the empty space like a gentle breeze. Her heart skipped a beat as she recognized the voice, she had thought was gone forever.

"Da...Daddy?" Lucy stuttered, unable to believe what she was hearing. She turned to see Tom, her father, standing before her – a faint, transparent figure that somehow felt real.

"Lucy, my little girl..." Tom's voice was soothing and comforting, despite its ethereal quality. "There's something you need to understand. You're not dreaming, but you're also not quite... alive."

Lucy furrowed her brow, trying to process her father's words. "What do you mean, Daddy?"

"Sweetheart, you're a not here," Tom explained, his expression filled with love and concern.

Confusion and fear swirled within Lucy; she was still dreaming. She needed to wake up but the longer she stayed in the dream, the longer she could stay with her dad.

Tom, sensing her distress, took her hand and smiled reassuringly. "I know this is a lot to take in," he said, his voice gentle and reassuring. "But I'm here with you now and I won't leave your side."

Gathering up all her courage, Lucy held hands with Tom and allowed him to guide her through the process of becoming a part of the house. As they stood there in the dark hallway linking their minds together, she finally felt something shift within her, an invisible connection forming between herself and her dad as they shared thoughts and feelings beyond words.

For what seemed like hours they stayed like this until finally Lucy sensed a presence near them - she was not sure what it was, but it was dark! She backed away from her father. His figure had become dark, his face no longer recognizable.

The darkness enveloped Tom's figure, obscuring his features and transforming him into an unrecognizable form. Lucy's heart raced as she felt a sudden chill in the air, and a sense of dread filled her thoughts. It was time to wake up.

Suddenly, the darkness began to move, snaking towards Lucy with terrifying speed. She tried to back away but found herself rooted to the spot. A voice whispered in her ear, cold and menacing.

"Welcome to the afterlife, little ghost," it hissed, its breath icy against her skin. "You may think you're safe with your daddy, but there are things in this realm that he cannot protect you from."

Lucy's mind raced as she tried to wake herself from the dream. She closed her eyes and focused on her mother, summoning all her strength to reach out to her. Suddenly, a blinding light filled her vision, and the darkness retreated back to where it came from. And then a crash from the living room.

Lucy opened her eyes and ran down the stairs to the kitchen. She saw Steve bending down and picking up the photo frame from in front of the fireplace. She saw her father's warm and welcoming smile. Tom's presence was comforting and reassuring, and Lucy felt herself relaxed in her father's presence.

Lucy followed Steve's footsteps back to the living room as he walked ahead of her. Her eyes were at once drawn to her mother, seated at the table cradling a cup with both hands and looking drained. Tears filled her mother's eyes, yet Lucy couldn't understand why she was so upset. She looked from the doorway, but neither of them noticed her presence. There had to be something terribly wrong, though what could have happened if she hadn't heard anything?

Lucy placed her hand softly on her mother's shoulder. The soft touch brought no response to her mother. "Mom, what is wrong? I am here, please tell me?" Still no response. Lucy could not understand why her mother was so distant.

"Steve, I don't understand, why Lucy, why my baby girl?" The tears in her mother's eyes, the pain in her voice.

"I know, but she is gone. You have to move forward. We can try and have a child of our own. Or we can adapt, if you would like." Steve voice hurt Lucy's head. The sound echoed like a train racing toward her.

Lucy remained frozen in place. Was this what her father meant when he said she was no longer here? Had the darkness taken to calling her the little ghost?

But Lucy refused to accept that. She couldn't be gone. She was still here, standing in the doorway, hearing every word that her parents were saying. She stepped closer, her footsteps echoing through the quiet kitchen.

"Mom, Steve, I'm right here," she said, her voice shaking.

Tom was standing in the corner of the kitchen watching Lucy. Lucy looked above her father's head, and what she saw was breathtaking. Above him hung a bright golden light, its rays radiating warmth and comfort like her father's embrace. She felt a strange pull towards it, as if it were calling out to her soul.

Tom seemed to notice her gazing up at the light, and with a gentle smile he said, "It is time for you to go, Lucy." He gestured with his hand towards the light, as if inviting her to its warm embrace. The thought of leaving the kitchen made Lucy feel sick to her stomach; she didn't want to leave the only home she had ever known.

However, Lucy felt an inexplicable force drawing her closer and closer towards the light until finally standing before it and reaching out both hands in anticipation. Tom stepped forward and held out his own hands before hers in a gesture of protection. With one final look back at the kitchen behind her - filled with memories of laughter and love - Lucy stepped back into the kitchen.

"I can't go, not yet. I have to help mom."

CHAPTER 5

In the days that followed, Teresa mourned the loss of her daughter with a quiet, all-consuming grief. She retreated into herself, her once-vibrant spirit now dampened by the dark cloud that hung over their home. Steve watched her from a distance, his guilt gnawing at him like a relentless tide.

As the nights grew warmer and the trees outside began to grow their leaves, the once-familiar landscape surrounding their home became a haunting reminder of the terrible events that had transpired. Lucy was starting to see the truth about what happened to her. She had to find a way to tell her mom.

"Steve," Teresa whispered one evening as they sat in the dimly lit living room, her eyes brimming with tears. "I can't help but feel that something isn't right. That there's more to Lucy's death than we know." She searched his face for answers, her heart aching for the truth that seemed forever out of reach.

"Sweetheart," Steve replied, his voice trembling, "sometimes, terrible things happen for no reason at all. We just have to find a way to accept them and move on."

But even as the words left his lips, he knew that he could never move on from the horrifying reality of Lucy's death. The power of nature, which once served as a source of inspiration and solace, now stood as a constant, judgmental presence, its gaze unwavering as it bore witness to the darkness within his soul.

"Destiny," he whispered to himself, as the wind howled outside, and the shadows danced across the walls. "What a cruel game you play." His words echoing in Lucy's head, the thundering of the train again and again.

The sun had long since set, casting a darkness over the house as Steve and Teresa sat across from each other at the kitchen table. The only light came from a flickering candle, its flame casting shadows that seemed to dance in time with the tension that hung heavy in the air between them.

"Steve," Teresa began, her voice barely clear as she nervously twirled a strand of her wavy blonde hair. "I just... I can't shake this feeling that there's something you're not telling me about Lucy."

Steve clenched his jaw, his knuckles turning white as he gripped the edge of the table. He tried to maintain an air of calm, but the weight of his guilt was becoming too much to bear. "Teresa, we've been over this. It was a terrible accident, that's all."

Just as the words escaped his lips the candle flames bleeped out. A cold chill filled the room. Teresa shivered and looked around the dark room. In the corner, she thought she had seen a glimpse of Lucy. A small smile perched on her lips and sent Steve into a rage.

"Enough!" Steve snapped, slamming his fist down on the table, causing the candle to topple over. The sudden outburst startled both of them, and for a moment, they stared at one another in stunned silence.

In the shadows, Steve saw his own terror reflected back at him, more monstrous than any creature lurking in the depths of the forest. As the fear gripped him, he couldn't help but wonder if the spirits of nature were conspiring against him, punishing him for his heinous actions. He felt as though the very roots of the earth were tightening around him, choking him with their ancient wisdom and unyielding judgment.

"Steve..." Teresa whispered, her voice trembling with emotion. "Please, I need the truth. For Lucy."

"Sometimes, the truth is too painful, Teresa," he choked out, his voice barely a whisper. "Some secrets are best left buried."

As Steve stared into the darkness beyond the flickering candlelight, he couldn't shake the feeling that the walls of deception he'd so carefully constructed were beginning to crumble, and soon, the dam would break, unleashing a torrent of truth that would drown them all in its unforgiving depths.

"Destiny," he thought, his heart heavy with dread. "What a cruel game you play."

*****

The Thompson family home was an old, Victorian-style house with a layout that seemed to defy logic. A Victorian house with grand tall pillars stretching up towards the sky, windows adorned with curtains that sway lightly in the night breeze. Inside was a maze of rooms, each filled with gleaming antiques and old photos that seemed to be watching you as you passed them by. Its narrow hallways and creaking stairs led to labyrinthine rooms filled with antique furniture handed down through generations. The creaking of the stairs as one ascended into the labyrinth of rooms, the muffled echoes of laughter and conversations from years gone by that whispered through the walls. The faint ticking of an old grandfather clock that is only heard when all else is still, and the occasional squawk of a bird outside the window.

Its walls are stained with decades of wear and tear, and each step through its labyrinth-like corridors offers a different story. The velvet upholstery of the furniture is invitingly soft, each piece holding its own mysteries within its faded fabrics. The wooden floorboards that creaked with every step, a musty smell lingering in the air from old furniture and dust collecting in every nook and cranny. The thick carpet underneath feet with its intricate patterns and designs, inviting you to explore further but warning of what lies ahead.

Teresa had a special relationship with her home; it was a place she could go to remember Lucy's short life, her laughter, and the memories they shared together as mother and daughter. It was the home that she and Tom had bought to raise their family. She often found herself wandering aimlessly through its hallways, lost in thought while reflecting on the difficult road ahead of her.

But despite everything that had happened, Teresa still felt Lucy's presence in her home. She could hear the sound of her daughter's laugh echoing through the halls and smell the scent of her favorite perfume lingering in the air. It gave Teresa a sense of comfort and peace knowing that she could still feel close to Lucy even if she couldn't be there physically anymore.

Teresa stood in the dimly lit living room, her fingers idly tracing the intricate patterns on the velvet armchair. Long shadows cast by the gas lamps flickered across the Oriental rug underfoot, giving the impression of writhing serpents. The clock on the mantelpiece ticked away the seconds, each beat puncturing the heavy silence that cloaked the room like an oppressive fog.

Steve lay in bed, staring at the ceiling, unable to sleep. The quiet tick-tocking of the grandfather clock in the hallway was keeping time with his racing heart. Shadows stretched across the room like gnarled fingers, grasping at something unseen.

"Steve," whispered a voice inside his head, so faint it could have been the wind rustling through the trees outside. Steve's blood ran cold. It was Lucy's voice, as sweet and gentle as he remembered it from when she was alive. His body tensed, and he squeezed his eyes shut, praying that it would stop.

"Steve," the voice repeated, more insistent this time. Driven by the supernatural events happening in the house, the voice grew louder, almost as if Lucy herself was standing beside him. Caught between the realms of wakefulness and sleep, Steve was a prisoner in his own mind, forced to confront the ghostly echoes of his deepest regrets.

"Leave me alone," he begged under his breath, desperation seeping into his voice. But the voice continued to haunt him, relentless in its pursuit. With each repetition, Steve felt his grip on reality slipping further away. Steve paced back and forth; his anxiety palpable in every strained footstep. With furrowed brow, he glanced nervously at the door as if expecting someone to burst through at any moment. He finally got up and walked downstairs to find Teresa, who had retreated within herself, her gaze lost among the dancing shadows.

Steve's agitation increased; his restlessness palpable. He struggled to focus on anything else but the voice in his head, and it began to take a toll on his work and relationships. He caught himself snapping at Teresa over trivial matters, his temper flaring like a match in a dark room. It was time to confront her, he needed to get out of the house.

"Steve, you're a million miles away," her voice barely above a whisper. "What's going on with you? Is it about Lucy?"

"Terri, I don't think... maybe I should leave you alone," Steve stammered, his voice cracking under the weight of unspoken fears. "I just... I can't help but feel like something's not right here."
Steve could not handle the fear he felt in house. He knew if he were to stay his secret would come out, that he would not be able to hold it in. After all, what he wanted was a family and now with Lucy dead, Teresa could not give him the children he wanted.

"Go, then," Teresa whispered, her voice barely noticeable above the ticking clock. As Steve hesitated, she looked up at him with tear-filled eyes. "Please, just go."

With a heavy sigh, he conceded and reluctantly left the house, leaving Teresa to confront the horrors that haunted her heart and home. Teresa understands that Steve could not manage the strange happenings in the home but to her it was signs that Lucy was still with them. This gave her comfort, where it was driving Steve insane.

Teresa stood in the house all by herself for the first time since Lucy had passed away. In that moment, she became aware of all the unusual things happening around her. At first, it was subtle: doors moving with no one near them and faint murmurs emanating from vacant rooms. Then they got bolder: objects moving on their own, ghostly footsteps heard throughout the halls, and an unnatural coldness in the air.

Tears streamed down Teresa's face as she remembered all the good times that they had shared together as a family before Lucy passed away. Teresa finally understood why so many strange things were happening—it was because Lucy wanted them all to know that she was still with them, even after death.

One evening, while Teresa was in the kitchen preparing dinner, a gust of icy wind swept through the room. She shivered and turned towards the window, only to find it securely closed. Confused, she began to question her own sanity – until she noticed that the knives on the magnetic strip had rearranged themselves into an unsettling pattern that seemed to spell out a name: Lucy.

"Lucy?" Teresa breathed, her heart pounding wildly in her chest. Could it be possible that the spirit of her deceased daughter was trying to communicate with her? Was she trapped in this house, unable to move on or find peace?

Teresa stood in the dimly lit hallway, her heart hammering against her chest as she stared at the framed family pictures that now hung askew, their once perfect alignment disrupted. An uneasy feeling settled over her like a shroud, suffocating her with its weight.

"Lucy, are you here?" she whispered into the silence, her voice trembling with a mixture of fear and desperate hope. The air seemed to thicken around her as she waited for a response, her breaths coming in shallow gasps. A cold breeze brushed past her, sending goosebumps racing down her spine.

"Mom?" Teresa flinched at her own thoughts, imagining Lucy's sweet voice filled with confusion and longing. It couldn't be real, could it? Was it merely the product of her grief-stricken mind, or was there something more sinister at work within the walls of their home?

She clenched her fists, determined to find answers. "I don't know what's happening, but I need to understand," she murmured, mostly to herself. "If it truly, is you, Lucy, I will do everything in my power to help you." Her resolve, fueled by love and an overwhelming desire for closure, began to crystallize into action.

Teresa ventured deeper into the house, each cautious step echoing through the oppressive silence. Shadows clung to the corners, their darkness a stark contrast to the faint moonlight filtering through the windows. The wallpaper, which she had painstakingly chosen years ago with Lucy's favorite flowers woven into the design, seemed to blur and shift before her eyes, creating a sense of disorientation.

"Help me understand, Lucy," she pleaded, her voice barely a whisper. "What happened to you?" In the stillness, she strained to hear any response, any sign that her beloved daughter was trying to communicate with her from beyond.

*****

Lucy stood near her mom, her small ghostly figure lingering in the shadows. She was pleased that Steve had moved out of the house. She could not stand his voice in her head. The sounds were intensified to a point she could not bear it. Her task now was to help her mom find peace and closure. Lucy wondered what had happened to her mom, why was she so distant and detached from the world around her?

As Lucy pondered these questions, she noticed a faint whisper in the air. It sounded like her mom's voice, but it was too faint to make out any words. She concentrated, focusing all of her will on trying to hear what her mom was saying. Suddenly, the whisper grew louder and clearer, and Lucy could hear her mom's voice calling out her name.

"Lucy, where are you?" her mom's voice begged.

"I'm right here, Mom," Lucy said, stepping out of the shadows.

Her mom stopped in her tracks, looking around the empty room as if searching for something. "Is that you, Lucy? Are you here with me?"

"Yes, it's me, Mom," Lucy said, hoping her mom could hear

her voice.

Her mom looked up at the ceiling, tears streaming down her face. "I miss you so much, Lucy. I wish you were here with me."

Lucy felt a pang of sadness in her chest, but she knew she couldn't give in to her emotions. She had to be strong for her mom. "Mom, I am here with you, always. I want to help you find peace. Can you tell me what's wrong? Why are you so sad?"

Her mom let out a shaky breath and wiped away her tears. "It's just hard, you know? After you died, everything fell apart. Steve became distant and cold, and I... I just couldn't deal with the pain. It was too much for me to." Teresa thought she was going mad, talking to her daughter like she could hear, like she was in the room.

Teresa gathered her thoughts and walked toward the living room. She stood in the center of the room, a place once filled with laughter and warmth, an eerie silence enveloped her. The absence of sound was deafening, pressing down on her with the weight of her own despair. In that moment, she vowed to uncover the truth hidden within the shadows, to find answers that would bring peace to both her and Lucy's restless spirit.

"Whatever it takes," she whispered fiercely, her blue eyes reflecting the determination that burned within her soul. "I will find out what happened to you, my sweet girl. I promise."

Each morning, Teressa sat on Lucy's bed, it had become a ritual. She sat with her coffee in hand and talked to Lucy about the day ahead. One morning during her normal routine of telling Lucy about her day, the investigation into her death and her need to make sure Lucy was at rest, she watched, a flicker of movement caught her eye - an ethereal figure gliding through the hallway. It vanished just as quickly as it appeared.

"Lucy?" Teresa's heart raced as she replayed the clip in her mind, desperate to find some semblance of a pattern or clue in the ghostly image. Her thoughts swirled like autumn leaves caught in a gust of wind, each one another piece of the puzzle.

Teresa sighed, her eyes drifting back to the room Lucy once occupied. She knew that pursuing these thoughts was not healthy and would only create a lonely path, fraught with obstacles both seen and unseen. But she was sure something was out there, lurking just beyond her grasp, and she couldn't give up now. Not when Lucy needed her.

A TANGLED WEAVE: Death of a Child

CHAPTER 6

For two decades, Detective Samuel "Sam" Davis had been on the police force, after living for 15 years in the city, where he felt like he could never reach a satisfying conclusion. He devoted himself to bringing justice to this small country town. Sam was ready for a slower pace of life. He'd never imagined he would be involved in a murder investigation in such a quaint and peaceful village. How could a child's death occur here, among the old homes and tight-knit community?

Sam drove to the town square in search of answers. He walked around, looking in shop windows and listening in on conversations between locals. Everyone seemed to know of Lucy, but no one could tell him anything new about her death.

Suddenly, he heard a voice calling out from an alleyway. Sam followed the voice to find an old man sitting with his back against a wall. The man introduced himself as George and he said he had something important for Sam: a drawing that Lucy had made for him. George explained that Lucy believed she was being watched by someone.

George was an elderly gentleman who was well-known in the neighborhood for being friendly and kind. He attended the same church as Lucy's biological father before he passed away - so, when George heard about her death, he decided to give Sam a drawing that might help him investigate further.

Sam thanked George and took the artwork back to the police station with him. He hung it up on his wall and stared at it for a while, entranced by all its intricate details. He thought that if he looked at it carefully enough, maybe he'd be able to peel away the layers of this conundrum and get closer to solving what happened to Lucy.

As Sam studied the drawing, he noticed the man in the artwork looked a lot like Steve. Sam packed up his things and decided it was time to talk with him again. He was just sitting in the office waiting for the autopsy report, this was not getting any closer to finding the person that took the life of this little girl.

A TANGLED WEAVE: Death of a Child

Sam was standing outside the motel room that Steve Bird had rented after the separation from Teresa. He was not surprised that the two were split up. During the first investigation into the death of Lucy, he felt that Teresa deserved better. Teresa seemed to be a kind and loving woman, not like her husband Steve. This man gave off the impression he was better than others, that he could do no wrong.

It was hardly an unusual decision on Teresa's part, but he was grateful that she had decided to keep her first husband's name when they married. She had mentioned that it was so Lucy could hold onto the family name. He thought it was a nice gesture for the young girl who was now being raised by a stepfather.

He shook his head and focused back on the task at hand. He reached into his pocket and pulled out a small notebook, flipping through the pages until he found what he was looking for. The room number of Steve Bird, notes for the initial interview, his stories are always changing. He checks on Lucy during the night and then he doesn't. He reads her a bedtime story and then she goes to bed by herself. Why are his stories changing?

Sam cleared his throat and knocked on the door. "Mr. Bird, I need to speak with you." Steve slowly opens the door. He looks as though he has not slept in days. "Can I come in?"

"I need to know if you remember anything else from that night." Sam notices Tom's grip on the door handle to the room tightened for a moment before he released it and opened the door for the detective. "I remember her going to bed as soon as her mom left for work. It was a school night, and she had an exam the next day. I checked on her a few times, but everything seemed normal. So, I went to the bar for a drink, you can ask them. I was there."

Stepping into the room, Sam is met with a scene of disarray. Beer bottles, pizza boxes and newspapers are strewn around the room - it was obvious that the housekeeper service had been avoiding this space for days.

Sam nodded and made notes in his notebook as Tom spoke. "And did you notice anything unusual that night? Any strange noises or people around the house?"

Tom thought for a moment before shaking his head. "No, nothing out of the ordinary. It was a quiet night, just like any other."

Sam thanked Tom for his time and promised to keep him updated on the case. As he walked out of the motel, Sam couldn't shake off the feeling that there was more to this case than meets the eye. He decided to do some more digging, maybe talk to Lucy's friends at school and see if they knew anything that could help.

As Sam got into his car, he heard a faint voice whispering in his ear. "Don't give up, Detective Davis. There's more to this than you think." He turned around, but there was no one there. Sam shuddered and started the engine. He was determined to solve this case, not just for justice, but for Lucy's restless spirit as well.

The drive to the Thompson family home was short, he would stop by on his way back to the station. He wished the autopsy would get back, he needed to know if they found anything on body that would give a clear direction to his investigation. It had been six months and no answers for Teresa, she deserved to know what happened to her daughter.

Sam took a deep breath and stepped out of the car in front of Teresa's home. He was determined to find the underlying cause of this case, no matter what he had to do. He walked up to Teresa's house and knocked on the door.

After a few moments, it opened, revealing Teresa standing in the doorway. She looked weary and her eyes were red from crying. Sam could hear a faint whisper in his ear, "Help her".

"Teresa," Sam began, "I'm so sorry for your loss. I wanted to come by and make sure you're okay."

Teresa nodded but remained silent, her gaze fixated on the floor. After what felt like an eternity of silence, she finally spoke up. "Have you heard anything? Do you have any leads? Please come in," she said softly. "I need to know what happened to my daughter." She paused for a moment before continuing, her voice becoming more reserved as she spoke. "I believe something happened that night that nobody wants to talk about. But I can't put my finger on it."

Sam listened intently as Teresa spoke and nodded his head in understanding. He thanked her for her time and promised he would look into every possible lead until they found out what happened to Lucy that night. As he began to leave the house, Sam felt a chill run down his spine as if someone were watching him from within the dark shadows of the house - perhaps Lucy's spirit was still there with them all this time watching over them? The voice in his head kept repeating, "Help her, don't leave.'

"I would like to take in Lucy's bedroom, if this would be

okay." Sam voice was sincere as he spoke softly no to upset Teresa any further.

"Okay, I have not changed anything since that night. I have not even been able to clean it. I tried several times, but there just seems to be a chill around it. Too much for me to do right now." Sam could see the trauma that Teresa felt, his heart went out to her like no other case had given him.

Detective Sam Davis nodded, his piercing blue eyes reflecting the determination that drove him forward. "If there's something here that can help us uncover the truth, we'll find it." His gravelly voice carried the weight of experience, but also the desire to serve justice.

The two made their way to Lucy's bedroom. As they got closer, Sam felt a chill run down his spine and an uneasy feeling in the pit of his stomach. The door handle was even colder than the rest of the house, and he could feel something warning him not to enter. Despite this, he took a deep breath and opened the door. The room was spotlessly clean, which seemed odd given that Lucy had been gone for six months now. He searched around the room for any clues that could help them find out what happened to her.

The bedroom was much like any other 12-year-old girl would have. There were piles of stuffed animals, a small bookshelf, and pictures of her with her family. Sam picked up a photo of Lucy and her father, Tom, both beaming with happiness. As Sam looked closer, he noticed something odd in the photo - a strange figure lurking in the background. It was almost transparent, but its eyes seemed to glow with an otherworldly light.

Sam shook his head, reminded himself that he was looking for rational answers, and placed the photo back on the shelf. Something caught his eye in the corner of the room - a small wooden box hidden behind a stack of books. He approached it cautiously, and as he opened the lid, he found a small piece of paper with the words "Help her" written in a shaky hand.

Suddenly, Sam felt a chill rush through him, and he heard the door shut behind him. He spun around to see the figure from the photo staring at him in silence. Sam was paralyzed with fear, unable to move or even yell out. The figure slowly moved closer, its gaze never leaving his own.

"Here," Teresa said softly as she handed Sam a drawing, her eyes starting to fill with tears. "This is one of Lucy's last drawings."

A TANGLED WEAVE: Death of a Child

Teresa's words brought the detective back to his senses. Sam took the drawing from Teresa's hands and examined it closely, a chill running down his spine as he noticed that the subject in the sketch was Tom, the very man that a moment ago was walking towards him. He felt a wave of dread wash over him as he stared into the eyes of the late husband, and he knew that whatever force was at play was making this investigation more difficult.

"Can I take this with me?"

"Yes, of course, will it help?"

"I am not sure yet, but anything we find might be a clue. I would like to dig a bit more into your daughter's life." Sam was not sure what it all meant, but he needed to find answers for this family, for Teresa.

When Sam walked out the door that evening, it left a strong impression on him. Had he seen something in the bedroom? Or was his head playing tricks on him? This investigation was more intense than most cases he had worked on before. Maybe it was Teresa who was making him feel this way; she was quite fascinating. She had gone through a great deal of hardship, losing her husband and daughter. He remembered she had a sister, but they lived far away from one another. It made him glad to see that Teresa still had a sense of community with the church and her neighbors, providing her with the support she needed.

CHAPTER 7

"Lucy?" she called out tentatively, but her voice was swallowed by the relentless tempest. The old wooden door at the end of the hallway began to swing open, its hinges groaning in protest. Teresa's heart thudded in her chest as she approached with cautious steps, her eyes darting around for any sign of what could be causing these strange occurrences.

"Who's there?" she demanded, her breath catching in her throat. The room beyond the door lay shrouded in darkness, its secrets hidden from view. As she reached for the light switch, a cold breeze swept past her, carrying with it the faintest scent of wildflowers – Lucy's favorite.

"Lucy?" Teresa whispered, her voice trembling with a mixture of fear and hope. She flicked the switch, and the room was bathed in a harsh, artificial glow. At first glance, everything seemed normal, but as her eyes adjusted to the light, she noticed that a small picture frame on the dresser had been knocked over, the glass shattered into a thousand glittering shards.

"Is this your way of telling me you're here, sweetie?" Teresa asked the empty room, her hands shaking as she picked up the broken frame. It was a photograph of Lucy, her green eyes alight with laughter and her long, curly hair fanned out around her like a halo. Teresa's own blue eyes welled up with tears as she clutched the picture to her chest, feeling a desperate need to connect with her daughter and find out what had happened to her.

"Show me more, Lucy. Give me a sign," she implored, half afraid of what she might discover but driven by a mother's love and an unyielding desire for the truth.

As if in response to her plea, a series of thuds reverberated through the house, like footsteps ascending the stairs. Teresa's pulse quickened, her breaths coming in shallow gasps as she followed the phantom procession up the staircase. Each creak of the wooden steps seemed to mock her, taunting her with the knowledge that something was amiss – something beyond her understanding.

A TANGLED WEAVE: Death of a Child

*****

Teresa tossed and turned in her sleep, the thin bed sheets tangling around her legs like ivy vines. Her body ached with exhaustion, but her mind refused to surrender to the darkness that enveloped her small bedroom. In the quiet corners of her dreams, a world unfolded, both vivid and immersive.

She found herself standing at the edge of a dense forest, the branches above her intertwining and forming an eerie canopy. The air was thick with the scent of damp earth and ancient secrets, as if the very trees themselves whispered the stories of those who had come before. Teresa hesitated for a moment, feeling the weight of nature's gaze upon her shoulders. But then, with a deep breath, she stepped forward into the unknown.

"Mommy," called a familiar voice, echoing through the twisted trunks and gnarled roots. Teresa's heart leaped in her chest, recognizing the gentle lilt of her daughter Lucy's voice. She looked around frantically, desperate to find the source of the sound.

"Lucy?" she cried out, her voice cracking with emotion. "Where are you, sweetheart?"

"Here, Mommy," the voice responded, leading Teresa deeper into the heart of the forest. The shadows grew darker and more forbidding, but there was no fear in Teresa's heart – only a fierce determination to follow the path laid out before her by fate.

As she came upon a clearing bathed in moonlight, she saw Lucy standing there, her long, curly brown hair framing her pale face, and her bright green eyes glimmering with tears. Teresa's heart swelled with love and grief, but as she reached out to touch her daughter, her fingers passed through the ghostly apparition like wisps of smoke.

"Lucy…" Teresa whispered, her voice choked with emotion.

"Mommy, I drew something for you," Lucy said, her voice trembling as she held up a piece of paper. Teresa recognized her daughter's distinctive style, the gentle strokes and vibrant colors that danced across the page.

"Show me, my love," Teresa urged, her eyes filling with tears as she gazed upon the drawings. She focused on the details, trying to decipher the message her daughter was trying to convey. There were colors, shapes, and symbols that seemed to hint at something sinister

— something that caused a chill to race down her spine.

The drawing showed a man with short, dark hair and a strong build. His face was twisted in anger, and his hands were stained red, like blood. Teresa's breath caught in her throat as she realized that the man bore a striking resemblance to Steve, their seemingly kind-hearted neighbor who became her husband. He had been so eager to help her with Lucy after Tom died.

"Lucy, what are you trying to tell me?" Teresa asked, her voice stifled as she stared at the haunting image. The ghostly apparition of Lucy looked into her mother's eyes, sadness and fear clouding her emerald gaze.

"Be careful, Mommy," Lucy whispered, her voice fading like a soft breeze through the trees. "He's not what he seems."

As the dream began to dissolve around her, Teresa clung to the image of her daughter, desperate to keep her close. But like sand slipping through her fingers, Lucy vanished into the night, leaving her mother to face the cold reality of her loss and the unsettling truth hidden within her dreams.

"Was it just a dream?" she wondered, her mind racing with unanswered questions. "Or was it something more?"

"Lucy, what are you trying to tell me?" Teresa murmured into the oppressive silence; her words swallowed by the shadows that seemed to press in around her. She tried to make sense of the drawings her daughter had shown her, the colors and shapes swirling together like a storm brewing on the horizon. The looming figure of Steve, his hands smeared with blood-red paint, loomed large in her memory, igniting fear and doubt within her heart.

The wind whispered through the trees outside her window, echoing the soft, fading voice of her precious daughter. Though she strained to catch the ghostly words, they eluded her grasp, leaving her feeling more lost and alone than ever before.

"Be careful, Mommy. He's not what he seems." Lucy's warning echoed in Teresa's ears, the weight of its implications settling heavily on her chest, making it difficult to breathe.

Teresa grappled with the possibility that Steve, the man who had appeared so kind and supportive in their time of need, the man who shared her life for years, might have had a hand in her daughter's death. The thought twisted like a knife in her gut, leaving her feeling sick and disoriented. Conflicting emotions roiled within her, uncertainty warring with dread as she struggled to reconcile the image of the man, she married she had come to know with the sinister figure from her dream.

"Is it possible?" she wondered aloud; her voice muffled above the sound of her own ragged breathing. "Could Steve really have hurt Lucy?"

As the night wore on, Teresa found herself unable to sleep, her thoughts consumed by the terrifying implications of her daughter's message. The once-peaceful sounds of the night, the rustling leaves, and the distant hooting of an owl, now seemed to carry a sinister undertone, as if nature itself was warning her of the danger that lurked in the shadows.

"Destiny has brought you this message," she remembered her grandmother saying when Teresa was just a child, speaking of the Indigenous beliefs their family held dear. "The spirits speak through dreams, guiding us toward our true path."

"Is this my destiny?" Teresa questioned, her hands clutching at the damp sheets. "To uncover the truth behind Lucy's death and bring justice to her spirit?"

She stared into the darkness, the ghostly image of her daughter's face still etched in her mind, her final words echoing like a haunting refrain: "Be careful, Mommy."

As dawn approached, the first pale light of morning crept through the window, casting eerie shadows across Teresa's face. She knew that she could not ignore the warning of her dream any longer. The time had come for her to face the storm that raged within her heart and confront the chilling truth hidden deep within the shadows.

"Lucy, I will find the answers," Teresa whispered, her voice steeling with resolve. "I promise you."

As Teresa lay there, the fragile tendrils of dawn crept into the room, casting eerie shadows across the walls. Her thoughts returned to Lucy's drawings and the haunting images that seemed to hold the key to untangling the web of deceit that surrounded Steve.

"Time is running out," she whispered to herself, her eyes clouded with worry. "I must decipher the truth before it's too late."

And in that moment, as the sun rose and the world around her began to stir, Teresa vowed to uncover the secrets hidden within Lucy's drawings - to reclaim her destiny and avenge her daughter's death, no matter the cost.

But as she stared at the bleak horizon, a shiver ran down her spine. An uncanny sense of foreboding settled over her like a shroud, leaving her filled with trepidation. Unbeknownst to Teresa, her decision to delve deeper into the mystery would lead her on a perilous journey - one fraught with danger, deception, and betrayal.

For now, however, the path forward remains shrouded in darkness, obscured by the flickering shadows cast by the past. And as Teresa stepped into the unknown, guided only by her love for her daughter and her determination to unveil the truth, the winds of fate gathered strength, heralding the approach of a storm unlike any she had ever faced before.

A gust of wind rattled the windows, stirring Teresa from her contemplation. The room felt colder, more sinister than before, and she knew she couldn't face this journey alone. She needed someone she could trust, someone who would understand the weight of the dreams that haunted her.

"Rose," she murmured, thinking of her older sister, a woman whose wisdom and strength had always been a guiding light in her life. With trembling fingers, she picked up her phone and dialed Rose's number, praying that she would answer.

"Hello?" Rose's warm voice came through the line, instantly soothing Teresa's frayed nerves.

"Rose, it's me, Teresa," she said, struggling to keep her voice steady. "I need your help."

"Of course, sis," Rose replied without hesitation. "What's going on?"

Teresa hesitated for a moment, unsure of how to articulate the terror that gripped her heart. "It's about Lucy," she finally whispered, feeling tears prick at the corners of her eyes. "I've been having these dreams...and I think she's trying to tell me something."

As she recounted the details of her dream, the vivid images of Lucy's ghostly presence, the strange happenings in the house, and the cryptic drawings that hinted at Steve's involvement in her death, Teresa could sense Rose's growing concern.

"Those Indigenous beliefs we were raised with, about the spirits guiding us through dreams..." Teresa said in a hushed tone, her throat tight with emotion. "Do you really think that's what's happening here? That Lucy is reaching out from beyond the grave?"

"Listen to your heart, Teresa," Rose advised gently. "If you truly believe our ancestors are speaking through Lucy's spirit, then you must follow their guidance. But tread carefully – there's darkness lurking in the shadows, and you must be prepared for whatever truths you may uncover."

Determined to make sense of the cryptic messages hidden within her dreams, Teresa found herself growing more suspicious of Steve. She could no longer ignore the gnawing feeling in her gut that told her something was amiss. With Rose's support, she began to delve into Steve's past, searching for clues that might reveal his true nature.

"Did you know he wanted to be a father?" she asked Rose one evening as they pored over articles and records related to Steve's life. "He's always been so caring and protective...but I can't help but feel there's more to him than meets the eye."

"Sometimes, the people we think we know best are the ones capable of hiding their darkest secrets," Rose replied somberly, her eyes dark with concern. "Just promise me you'll be careful, Teresa. You're walking a dangerous path, and I don't want anything to happen to you."

Teresa nodded solemnly; her heart heavy with the burden of her newfound purpose. As the sisters delved deeper into the shadows surrounding Steve's past, a chilling darkness seemed to descend upon their lives, threatening to engulf them at every turn.

But Teresa refused to be deterred, her determination fueled by the promise she had made to her daughter's restless spirit. No matter what dangers lay ahead, she would not rest until the truth was revealed, and justice was finally brought to light.

A distant rumble of thunder echoed through the sky, casting strange shadows across the dimly lit room. Teresa sat in her favorite armchair by the window, a steaming cup of coffee cradled between her hands. The wind whispered through the trees outside, seeming to murmur dark secrets that only she could hear.

"Steve always seemed so good with Lucy," Teresa mused, her thoughts drifting back to happier times. "When we first meet, he'd spend hours teaching her how to draw, showing her tricks and techniques that I never could have imagined."

"Mom, look what Steve taught me!" Lucy's excited voice rang through Teresa's memory, her eyes shining with pride as she held up a beautifully drawn image of a raven.

"Remember how he took her out for ice cream every weekend?" Teresa continued, her heart aching with nostalgia. "How he'd help her with her homework and tell her stories about his own childhood adventures?"

"Lucy adored him at first," she whispered, her voice trembling with emotion. "So why do I feel like there was something sinister lurking beneath the surface?"

"Lucy didn't just draw random pictures, she was trying to tell me something," Teresa realized, her mind racing with possibilities. She recalled Steve's fascination with Indigenous beliefs, and how he would share stories of ancient rituals and legends with Lucy. Could the drawings be connected to those tales somehow?

As if in response to her thoughts, the wind picked up, its mournful howl echoing through the house like a spectral cry. Teresa shivered, feeling as though unseen forces were aligning against her.

Rose cautioned her sister, "Be wary of the path you take, it may bring with it terrors far greater than what you envision." Rose had met many unsavory people in her life, living in the city running a small tarot card reading business. This didn't make much sense to Teresa who preferred tangible things. But Rose was like their grandmother, closely tied to the old way of life. Despite this, their bond as sisters was always the strongest connection.

"Mom, don't be scared," Lucy's voice seemed to whisper in the wind, a faint but reassuring presence. "I'll guide you through the darkness, and together we'll uncover the secrets that have been hidden for far too long."

"Steve may have deceived me before," she thought grimly, her resolve hardening like steel. "But I won't let him deceive me again. The truth will come to light, and when it does, he'll finally face the consequences of his actions."

"Contact Maggie and Elizabeth, from the church, they can help you." Rose had always been her reassuring voice even after Tom died. "They will know if there is something there."

Teresa hung up the phone. She was not certain contacting Elizabeth and Maggie was the right thing to do. Teresa and Elizabeth had been friends for many years. But when Elizabeth started spending more time with Maggie and after her husband's death, they grew apart. The rumors around the church were that they were a bit strange in their beliefs in the afterlife. But she trusted Rose, Rose would not have suggested it if she thought there was anything inappropriate.

As the storm continued to rage outside, Teresa felt a strange sense of calm envelop her, as though nature itself had acknowledged her unwavering determination. Little did she know, however, that her journey into the heart of darkness would lead her down a path from which there could be no return.

CHAPTER 8

The sun was an orange stain in the otherwise dark sky, its light piercing through the fog and illuminating every corner of the sleepy country neighborhood. It was a reminder of the happy memories that once lingered there, yet now weighed heavy with grief and worry. The silence was deafening in the sleepy country town, only broken by the occasional chirping of birds that echoed off the walls. It was a quietness full of sorrow and pain, as if all were mourning a loss they couldn't put into words.

Teresa Anne Thompson sat in her small, dimly lit kitchen, her wavy blonde hair falling softly around her face as she absentmindedly stirred her coffee. The soft blue of her eyes seemed clouded by the events that had forever altered her life. She was a resilient woman, with a loving heart that had been stretched to its limits in recent months. Her world had crumbled around her, making it difficult to trust anyone.

Elizabeth Jane Miller, Teresa's lost best friend and confidante, sat at the table across from her. Elizabeth's shoulder-length red hair framed a face set with determination; her fiery spirit clear even in her stillness. She was fiercely loyal and protective, a pillar of support during Teresa's darkest times.

"Coffee?" Teresa offered quietly; listening to the raindrops hitting the windowpane.

"Thanks," Elizabeth replied, gratefully accepting the warm cup. "So, you wanted to talk about Lucy?"

With a heavy sigh, Teresa nodded. Months had passed since Lucy's death, but the pain still felt fresh. The 12-year-old girl, with her curly brown hair and bright green eyes, had been her entire world. And now, she was gone.

"Something has been bothering me, Liz," Teresa began hesitantly. "I can't shake this feeling that there's more to Lucy's death than what we've been told."

"More?" Elizabeth asked, concern etched on her face.

"Something just doesn't add up," Teresa explained, her voice shaking slightly as she recounted the inconsistencies in the official report. The position of Lucy's body, the lack of any clear motive, and the strange markings found near the scene — they all pointed to something more sinister.

As the two friends discussed their suspicions, a knock on the door interrupted their conversation. Opening the door revealed Maggie Lynn Walters, their kind-hearted neighbor who lived just a few houses away. Maggie's silver hair was tied up in a bun, her warm eyes reflecting the comforting presence that endeared her to everyone.

"Hello, dear," Maggie greeted Teresa with a smile. "I heard the two of you talking and wondered if I might join."

"Of course, Maggie," Teresa replied, welcoming her inside. Maggie Lynn Walters was in her sixties, her silver hair tied up in a bun, her face etched with wisdom and warmth. She had lived in the neighborhood for years and had always offered a listening ear and sage advice when needed.

As the three women sat around the kitchen table, Teresa, appeared vulnerable as she clutched a steaming mug of tea in her trembling hands. She hesitated before speaking, her voice barely audible as she shared her fears and concerns. "I don't know what's happening anymore, but I can't ignore it any longer."

Maggie reached out to gently pat Teresa's hand, offering her support. Elizabeth, her red hair like a fiery halo, leaned forward, concern etched on her face. "Teresa, we're here for you. Whatever it is, we'll figure it out together."

As the wind howled outside, rattling the windows of Teresa's living room, she took a deep breath and began to recount the strange events that had been unfolding in her home. "It started with little things," she explained, her voice shaking. "Cupboard doors left open when I was sure I'd closed them, objects moving on their own... And then there were the sounds."

"Sounds?" Elizabeth asked, her green eyes wide with concern.

"Footsteps in the hallway at night, whispers that seemed to come from nowhere..." Teresa shuddered, remembering the chill that had coursed through her as she lay in bed, straining to hear the ghostly noises.

"Did Lucy believe she could talk with Tom?" Maggie inquired gently, her silver hair glinting in the flickering lamplight.

Teresa shook her head, tears welling up in her blue eyes. "She talked to him every day; it was like they would continue complete conversations."

"Have you considered speaking with a medium? Someone who might be able to communicate with Tom?" Elizabeth suggested, her fiery red hair framing her determined face.

"I'm not sure," Teresa admitted, uncertainty weighing heavy on her shoulders. "I've never believed in that sort of thing before, but now..." Teresa was afraid to admit that she felt this was her last hope. "Rose asked me to call you, maybe there is something here. I am not sure."

"Sometimes, we have to be open to possibilities we never considered, especially when it comes to our loved ones," Maggie reassured her, her warm smile offering solace amidst the encroaching darkness.

"Thank you, both of you," Teresa whispered, feeling slightly more grounded with her friends at her side. "I just want to understand what's happening and find a way to help Lucy. I can't bear the thought of her not being at rest."

"Whatever happens, we'll be here for you," Elizabeth vowed, her protective nature shining through. "We'll get through this together."

As the women sat together in the dimly lit kitchen, the wind outside seemed to carry whispers of secrets yet untold, and the shadows cast by the flickering light danced like phantom figures across the walls. Unbeknownst to them, Lucy hovered nearby, unseen but ever-present, as she tried to bridge the divide between her world and theirs, guided by her late father's wisdom.

"Years ago," Maggie began, her voice low and measured, "I had my own encounters with the supernatural. I would see apparitions in the corners of my home, hear voices carried upon the wind. I learned quickly that sometimes, there are forces beyond our grasp that seek to make themselves known."

Teresa listened intently, her eyes wide with a mixture of fear and fascination. She needed answers, needed to understand the strange events occurring around her, and Maggie seemed well-versed in this otherworldly realm. "How did you deal with these experiences? What can I do to protect myself from negative energies?"

Maggie leaned forward, her eyes softening with compassion.

A TANGLED WEAVE: Death of a Child

"The first thing I did was learn about my ancestors' beliefs. They believed that spirits were everywhere – in the trees, the rocks, the rivers. Some were benevolent, offering guidance and protection, while others harbored darker intentions."

"Is there a way to tell them apart?" Teresa asked, her fingers nervously twisting a stray thread from the frayed hem of her skirt.

"Sometimes, it's simply a matter of intuition," Maggie replied. "But there are also signs – cold spots, unexplained noises, objects moving on their own. These could indicate a presence trying to gain your attention."

"Like what's happening in my house," Teresa murmured, her voice barely heard above the wailing of the wind.

"Perhaps," Maggie agreed. "But not all spirits are malevolent. Some may be seeking closure or trying to pass along a message."

"Like Lucy," Teresa whispered, her eyes filling with tears as she thought of her daughter, lost to her in life but perhaps still present in spirit.

"Perhaps," Maggie repeated, her voice gentle. "I can help you learn more about this realm, guide you in your understanding. But I must warn you – the path is not for the faint of heart."

Teresa took a deep breath, determination stealing her resolve. "I'll do whatever it takes to understand what's happening and find a way to communicate with my daughter."

As the storm continued to weep outside, Teresa felt a newfound sense of purpose welling up inside her. She would brave the darkness, walk the path laid out before her by destiny, and discover the truth that lay shrouded in mystery. For her daughter, for herself, and for the undeniable power of nature that echoed through every heartbeat, every breath, and every whispered word carried upon the wind.

"Elizabeth, thank you for being here," Teresa said quietly, her voice wavering as she clung to her friend's hand. "I just don't know what to do anymore."

"Hey, we'll get through this together," Elizabeth replied, squeezing Teresa's hand gently. "I can help research the history of the house, or we could contact a medium – someone who can offer more guidance."

"Thank you," Teresa whispered, grateful for her friend's unwavering support. The room seemed to close in around her, the air thickening with unseen energy that hung heavy and oppressive. A cold breeze crept beneath the door, sending shivers down her spine.

"There are rituals we can perform using sacred herbs and crystals," Elizabeth explained, her mind racing as she tried to recall everything her enigmatic mentor had shared. "But I'm not certain... I still have so many questions."

"We will find the answers together," Maggie declared, her fiery spirit igniting a spark of hope within Teresa. "We'll face whatever comes our way, side by side. I promise."

As they spoke, the windows began to rattle and cause the lights to flicker once more. Teresa couldn't help but wonder if Lucy's presence lingered nearby, watching over them as they grappled with the mysteries of the unknown.

The three women looked around, all feeling the eerie atmosphere of the house. The lights flickered erratically before an unexpected silence descended. As they stayed rooted to their seats at the table, the back door creaked open slowly and a chill spread through the room making it difficult for them to breathe. Teresa stood up and shut the door without any sign of distress; she had done this multiple times in recent months. The other two just glanced at each other cautiously, aware that something was in there with them.

"Let's start with the research then," Teresa decided, determination flaring within her. "Lucy deserves to be heard, and I won't let fear stand in my way."

"Agreed," Elizabeth nodded, her eyes shining with resolve. "We'll uncover the truth together, no matter what it takes."

As they prepared to delve deeper into the supernatural world that had invaded their lives, Teresa couldn't shake the feeling of being watched, as if unseen eyes followed her every move. The wind seemed to whisper secrets known only to the spirits themselves, hinting at a hidden destiny that awaited her just beyond the shadows.

For now, however, she took solace in the knowledge that her friends would stand by her side, guiding and supporting her through this dark, uncertain journey into the unknown. And perhaps, she thought, that was enough to face whatever truths lay hidden in the shadows of her once-familiar home.

Teresa looked at her friends, her eyes filled with gratitude and a newfound sense of hope. "Thank you both for being here," she said softly, her voice quivering with emotion. "I don't know what I would do without your support."

Elizabeth reached over and squeezed Teresa's hand reassuringly, while Maggie offered a gentle smile.

"Let's confront this together," Teresa voice growing stronger as she drew upon her inner reserves of strength. "Whatever is causing these disturbances, whether it be Lucy or something else entirely...we'll face it head-on."

Maggie nodded solemnly. "You're right, Teresa. We can't let fear hold us back. Together, we'll find a way to communicate with the spirits and bring peace to your home."

"Alright then," Teresa declared, her blue eyes blazing with resolve. "It's time to take a stand. We'll start by researching the history of this house, and if necessary, we'll contact a medium to help guide us further."

"Count me in," Elizabeth said firmly, her own determination reflected in her gaze. "I'll do whatever it takes to help you and Lucy find peace."

"Me too," added Maggie, her voice steady and unwavering. "We're in this together, Teresa. You're not alone."

With each word of encouragement, Teresa could feel the weight of isolation lifting from her shoulders. The knowledge that her friends stood beside her, ready to face the unknown together, filled her with a newfound sense of strength and courage.

Maggie and Elizabeth began to say their good-byes and walked toward the door. They were going to begin their research, Teresa's mind buzzed with questions and possibilities. Yet through it all, one thought remained clear: she would do whatever it took to unlock the secrets that lay hidden within her home, and to free her daughter's spirit from its ethereal prison.

She appreciated their support, but something gnawed at the edges of her confidence, leaving her feeling vulnerable and exposed. Despite the newfound knowledge shared by her friends, she couldn't shake the nagging feeling that they were unprepared for the supernatural forces that haunted her home.

"Maybe we should contact the police," Teresa suggested hesitantly, her blue eyes clouded with unease.

"Will they be able to help?" Elizabeth questioned softly; her brow furrowed in concern. "I'm not sure they'll understand what we're dealing with."

"Perhaps not," Teresa admitted, her fingers twisting nervously in her lap. "But I just...I need to do something. I can't bear the thought of my Lucy trapped here, suffering. And then again, what if it is not Lucy? What if someone is trying to play tricks on me? Maybe, someone is trying to take advantage of my grief."

"Whatever you decide, we'll be there for you," Maggie assured her, placing a comforting hand on Teresa's shoulder. "You don't have to face this alone."

As the wind cried outside, a mournful symphony that seemed to echo the turmoil within her soul, Teresa found herself questioning her own destiny. Would she ever be able to free her daughter from the clutches of the supernatural realm? Or was she doomed to watch helplessly as Lucy's spirit remained forever tethered to their haunted home? Or was it Steve just playing mean tricks to make her lose her mind?

"Thank you," Teresa whispered, her voice choked with emotion. "I couldn't do this without you."

CHAPTER 9

Teresa hesitated; her gaze fixed on the fading light outside. "I've been going through Lucy's things, trying to find some answers." She paused, swallowing the lump in her throat. "There were... inconsistencies."

Sam was becoming accustomed to answering his cell phone when Teresa called. "Such as?"

"Her diary of drawings, for one thing. There are pages missing, torn out. And I found one hidden beneath her bed, but it seems important." Teresa tells Sam it is about Steve and Lucy. Steve is angry and shaking his fist at Lucy, who is curdled up in the corner of her room.

"Have you shown it to anyone?"

"Only Elizabeth and Maggie," Teresa replied, thinking of the kind-hearted neighbors who sat in her kitchen earlier in the day.

The room was heavy with the weight of their shared concern, each of them bound by a desire to uncover the truth about Lucy's untimely demise. The sun dipped lower, casting long shadows that seemed to echo the darkness that had befallen their lives. As the last light vanished beyond the horizon, they knew their investigation was just beginning, and that the answers they sought were hidden somewhere in the murky depths of secrets and lies.

"I will stop by tomorrow and take a look. Try and get some sleep now." Sam's heart went out to her. She was becoming desperate to find anything to help with the investigation. Sam understood this, he was more than willing to give her the time she needed for grief. Besides, he enjoyed speaking with her.

*****

Detective Samuel "Sam" Davis stood in front of his office desk, the evening sun casting long shadows on the walls. His piercing blue eyes were fixated on a dusty file he had just retrieved from the depths of the cold case archives. The worn-out folder seemed to be gasping for air as it laid open in front of him, revealing its secrets after years of neglect.

"Tom William Thompson," Sam muttered under his breath. The name weighed heavily on his mind, like loose earth piled upon a grave. He remembered Lucy's bright green eyes, full of heartbreak, and knew that he couldn't let this case go unsolved any longer.

"Car crash, huh?" Sam said aloud as he examined the report. The details of the accident sent shivers down his spine, but something gnawed at the back of his brain, urging him to question the circumstances surrounding Tom's death. Could it have been more than just an unfortunate twist of fate?

As he delved further into the report, Sam couldn't shake the feeling that there was more to this tragedy than met the eye. Steve Michael Bird's name appeared within the report, stirring the detective's gut instincts. It was time to dive deeper into the dark abyss.

"Maybe it wasn't an accident after all," Sam mused, his voice echoing through the empty room. A storm began to brew within him, fueled by determination and a sense of duty. He grabbed his coat and made his way to the scene of Tom's car crash, knowing that he must uncover the truth about his death, not only for Lucy's sake but also to potentially bring Steve to justice for his crimes.

The sky had turned a deep shade of gray as Sam arrived at the desolate stretch of road where Tom's life had come to an abrupt end. The wind whispered through the trees, carrying with it the chants of ancient spirits and the secrets of a long-forgotten past.

"Tell me what happened here," Sam beseeched the wind, as if it could reveal the truth. His heart was heavy with sorrow and the burden of duty. He knew he had to unmask the true face of this tragedy and bring closure to the Thompson family.

As Sam walked along the lonely road, he couldn't help but be reminded of his years of training. The courses that were supposed to teach him to see the signs that would uncover the truth. He wondered where the signs were now.

The power of nature roared in the distance, a thunderous lament for all who had been taken too soon by the hands of fate. It was a force that could not be ignored or underestimated: an unstoppable current that continued to shape the lives of those left behind.

"Tom," Sam whispered, his breath visible in the frigid air. "I will find the truth about you and Lucy." And with that solemn vow, the detective set forth on his quest, determined to uncover the secrets that lay hidden beneath the surface of Tom's tragic demise. Though the path before him was filled with darkness and uncertainty, Samuel Davis would follow it to its inevitable conclusion, guided by the indomitable spirit of justice.

The sun hung low in the sky, the road was slick from the rain that had been falling earlier that day, making the air heavy with the scent of damp earth and decaying leaves. A dense fog had settled over the area, obscuring the once familiar landscape, and transforming it into a twisted labyrinth of shadows and uncertainty.

"Tom," Sam muttered to himself as he surveyed the mangled guardrail that had never been repaired. The place where Lucy's father had lost his life. He could almost hear the screeching tires and the deafening crunch of metal against metal as the car plunged off the road and into the ravine below. The trees surrounding the accident scene seemed to whisper their own mournful tale of sorrow and loss, their branches swaying gently in the cool evening breeze.

"Did you really think you could hide your secrets here?" Sam asked the empty air, as if the spirits that lingered in the shadows might answer him. He was determined to uncover the truth, to reveal the sinister forces that had claimed Tom's life and left a family shattered in its wake.

"Detective Davis?" A voice called out behind him, pulling Sam from his introspection. It was Officer Jenkins, a fellow officer who had been assigned to help in the investigation. "I found something you might want to take a look at."

"Show me," Sam said, his eyes narrowing with determination as he followed Jenkins back to his squad car.

"According to the records I pulled up, Steve Bird missed work the day of the accident," Jenkins revealed, handing Sam a printout of Steve's attendance log. "And get this – he purchased gas just a few miles away from the crash site that same day."

Sam's heart raced, his mind racing with possibilities. Could it be? Was Steve involved in Tom's death? As the weight of this latest information settled upon him, the detective felt a deep, chilling dread claw at his soul. Steve had been there, lurking in the shadows like a vengeful specter, waiting to strike.

"Jenkins," Sam said, his voice barely above a whisper as he

clutched the printout tight in his hands. "Keep digging. There has to be more to this."

As Sam stood there, staring into the abyss of the darkening sky, he knew that he could no longer ignore the signs that had led him here. The spirits of the land beckoned to him, urging him to uncover the truth that lay hidden beneath the surface. He owed it to Lucy and her father to bring their tormentor to justice. And so, with renewed purpose, Detective Samuel Davis vowed to press onward, following the twisted path of destiny wherever it might lead.

*****

Detective Sam Davis sat in his office, the dim light from the desk lamp casting shadows on the cluttered surface. Folders filled with reports and photographs sprawled out before him, each one a piece of the puzzle he was desperately trying to solve. He opened another file, his eyes scanning the contents. He finally received a warrant to check bank statements for Steve Bird and the family along with their internet history.

"Steve Bird," he muttered under his breath. "What secrets are you hiding?"

Sam's eyes widened as he read further. Steve had moved into the house next to the Thompson's just a few months before Tom's fateful car crash. His fingers traced the words on the page, heart pounding at the implications. But it was the next piece of information that truly caught his breath and sent a shiver of cold realization down his spine: Steve had been searching the internet for brake lines on a vehicle. Sam pulled the MVD report for Steve, Steve owned a Chevy Impala but the search for brakes was for a Ford.

"Dear God," Sam whispered, feeling the weight of this discovery like a stone in his chest.

"Detective Davis?" called Officer Jenkins from across the room. "You look like you've seen a ghost."

Sam looked up, his face pale and contorted with shock and disbelief. "Jenkins, I think we may have found a connection between Steve Bird and Tom Thompson's accident."

"Are you serious? What did you find?" Office Bill Jenkins had been assisting Sam on this case for the last three months. He was young and enthusiastic man. He didn't have a family but a pretty girl that he had been seeing since high school. One day, Sam thought, the two would make a perfect couple.

"Steve moved in next door to the Thompson's just a few months before the crash. And..." Sam hesitated, struggling to find the words. "He was researching brake lines on a vehicle that was not his."

"Jesus Christ," Jenkins breathed, immediately understanding the gravity of the situation. "It all makes sense now."

"Doesn't it?" Sam replied, anger simmering beneath the surface. All the pain and suffering Lucy and Teresa had gone through – losing Tom, then Lucy herself – and now this twisted revelation threatened to tear apart whatever semblance of normalcy they had left.

Sam clenched his fists, the papers crinkling beneath his grip. The quiet, haunting whispers of the wind outside seemed to echo the voices of those who had been wronged, urging him to bring justice to their shattered lives.

"Jenkins," Sam said through gritted teeth, "we need to find more evidence. A simple gas receipt and him taking the day off, does not show anything."

"Understood," Jenkins replied, determination in his eyes. "I'll start looking into Steve's background right away."

Sam nodded and returned his gaze to the documents spread before him. He could feel the power of destiny weaving its tangled web around him, drawing him ever closer to the truth that lay hidden behind closed doors and whispered secrets.

And as the storm clouds gathered on the horizon, Detective Samuel Davis knew that it was his duty – no, his destiny – to follow the trail wherever it led, no matter how dark the path or twisted the journey.

For Lucy. For Tom. And for all those whose stories had yet to be told.

"Jenkins," his voice barely audible above the howl of the wind, "consider this – Steve moves in next door just months before Tom's accident, then suddenly searches for brake lines on a vehicle. It can't be a coincidence."

"Perhaps," Jenkins conceded, his eyes narrowing as he pondered the connection. "But we need solid evidence to prove it."

"Right," Sam agreed, stroking his chin thoughtfully. "We know Steve was off work the day of Tom's crash, and that he bought gas nearby. But did anyone see him at the scene?"

"None of the witnesses mentioned him," replied Jenkins, shaking his head. "But maybe there's something else, something we've overlooked."

Sam's piercing blue eyes scanned the documents scattered across the table, searching for the elusive clue that would seal Steve's fate. He could feel the weight of destiny pressing down upon his shoulders – a force as relentless as the storm brewing outside, stirring up the restless spirits that dwelt within the shadows.

"Wait," Sam muttered, his gaze falling upon a small, seemingly inconsequential detail. "This receipt from the gas station – it shows Steve bought a pair of gloves along with the fuel. What if he wore them to avoid leaving fingerprints on the car?"

"Could be," Jenkins nodded, leaning in to examine the receipt more closely. "It's not definitive proof, but it's a start. We should test the theory by checking for any missing gloves in Steve's house."

"Agreed, but it has been too many years to find a set of gloves. We need something else." Sam said, determination lighting his eyes. As they worked to gather the evidence, the wind outside seemed to echo their resolve.

"You should ask Mrs. Thompson about the relationship between them before Tom's death." Jenkins knew that Sam would be ready for any excuse to see Teresa. "I will try and find out more about Steve Thompson before he relocated to town. And you have already told Mrs. Thompson you would see her this morning."

CHAPTER 10

The wind whispered softly through the curtains of Teresa's home, casting flickering shadows across the living room like phantom dancers. The house had been her sanctuary for years, but recently, its walls seemed to hold secrets and unexplained phenomena that left her feeling uneasy. It was here, where her daughter Lucy's presence lingered in every corner, like an ethereal perfume, tinging the air with a blend of sadness and longing.

Teresa sat on the sofa, clutching a cup of coffee between her trembling hands. The steam rose and curled into the air, merging with the tendrils of memories that filled her thoughts. Her heart ached for her lost family, and she longed to protect what remained. As she gazed out the window at the darkening skies, her mind drifted to Steve, who claimed to have only good intentions but whose actions belied something far more sinister.

A sudden chill swept through the room, causing Teresa to shiver involuntarily. She looked around, sensing that she was not alone. And then, before her disbelieving eyes, a vision of Lucy materialized. The young girl stood there, her long, curly brown hair framing her pale face, and bright green eyes filled with a mixture of sorrow and determination. Her small form seemed to shimmer in the dim light, as if she were made of nothing more substantial than moonbeams and cobwebs.

"Mom," Lucy whispered, her voice hushed above the rustle of the wind outside. "I need you to listen. It's about Steve."

Teresa stared at her daughter's visage, her heart pounding in her chest. She couldn't deny the reality of what she was seeing; this was no mere trick of the mind or figment of her imagination. There, in her own home, stood her beloved child, reaching out from beyond the veil, urging her to confront the man who had insidiously infiltrated their lives.

Questions and doubts swirled in Teresa's mind like a dark storm, but she knew that her daughter would never deceive her. With her heart heavy but her resolve steeling, she held onto Lucy's vision. As the visual sense of her daughter faded away, Teresa was left with a numbing sense of both fear and determination. As the wind continued to whisper through the house, she knew that it was only a matter of time before destiny would lead her down a path from which there could be no turning back.

The air in Teresa's home had become thick with an eerie, oppressive energy that clung to her skin like a damp shroud. Shadows seemed to dance on the walls, taunting her as she tried to make sense of the strange occurrences that had beset her once-peaceful sanctuary. The wallpapered living room where she had spent countless hours cradling Lucy in her arms now felt foreign, tainted by an unseen force that whispered of injustice and retribution. The scent of wildflowers that used to permeate the house had been replaced by a faint, acrid odor that made Teresa's stomach churn.

As Teresa walked toward the kitchen for another cup of coffee, the supernatural occurrences became increasingly intense. A door creaked open, revealing a room shrouded in darkness where the ghostly silhouette of a rocking chair swayed back and forth, propelled by an unseen force. The sound of footsteps echoed behind her, but when she turned, there was no one there – just the soft laughter of a child carried away in the breeze.

A knock sounded from the door, jolting Teresa back to the present moment. She opened it to find Sam standing on the other side.

"Thank God!" Teresa was relieved to have the interruption. She was beginning to think she was losing her mind. All the things happening in the house. She was beginning to think they were in her mind. "Would you like a cup of coffee?" she offered as she ushered him inside.

"Yes, that would be nice," he replied. They settled down at the kitchen table which had been covered in papers awaiting his arrival.

Sam listened intently as Teresa recounted the strange occurrences in her house. He was struck with a feeling of dread as she described the missing diary pages and the hidden drawing, but he tried to remain composed.

"Her diary of drawings, for one thing," Teresa continued. "There are pages missing, torn out. And I found one hidden beneath her bed, but it seems important."

She pulled out a piece of paper from her pocket and carefully

A TANGLED WEAVE: Death of a Child

unfolded it, revealing a drawing of a man with his fist raised in anger at a little girl cowering in the corner of her room. Sam recognized it immediately as Steve and Lucy.

The sight was unsettling, and Sam felt an overwhelming sense of dread wash over him. He knew he had to get to the bottom of this case quickly before something worse happened.

Teresa nodded as if she could read his thoughts. "I'm so worried… I think we should investigate further." She sighed deeply before standing up for another cup of coffee.

Sam sat in silence, staring at the drawing in front of him. The way the man's muscles bulged as he shook his fist and the fear etched on the girl's face made his stomach twist with unease.

"I agree," Sam finally said as Teresa placed a fresh cup of coffee in front of him. "We need to find out what really happened between Steve and Lucy."

Teresa nodded; her eyes wide with worry. "But how?"

Sam paused, thinking carefully. "I start by talking to anyone who knew them, friends, family, anyone. We need to find out if there were any signs of abuse or if something triggered Steve's anger."

Steve was uneasy about bring up the relationship between Steve and Tom, but he needed to ask the questions. "I know things are hard for you right now, but I need to ask you some questions about Steve. And also, Tom."

"Okay, what is it?"

Tell me about when Steve moved in next to you. What do you know about his past? And how was the relationship between the two before Tom's accident.

The sun glowed through the kitchen window, its soft light filtering into the room where Teresa and sat in the kitchen. Her heart weighed heavy in her chest as she recounted memories of her late husband, Tom, to Detective Davis.

"Tom," Teresa began, her voice trembling with emotion, "he was always so loving and kind. He never hesitated to help anyone in need, especially our neighbors." She glanced out the window at the house next door, shrouded in shadows. "Even Steve, when he had just moved in."

Sam's piercing blue eyes studied Teresa's face intently, his brow furrowed with concern. "Tell me more about their relationship," he urged, sensing there was more to this story than what met the eye.

Teresa sighed, wringing her hands together nervously. "They became fast friends, almost inseparable from the moment they first met. Tom always had a knack for making people feel welcome, and he took Steve under his wing without a second thought." A sad smile tugged at the corners of her mouth as she recalled happier days. "Tom even made it his mission to find a woman for Steve to marry, knowing how much he longed for a family of his own."

The detective leaned forward, elbows resting on his knees, his expression grave. "And did Tom ever suspect anything... off about Steve?"

Lost in thought, Teresa stared at the patterns on the wooden floor, her mind drifting back to the times she'd watched Tom and Steve laughing together over beers in their backyard. At the time, she hadn't questioned their friendship; it was only now that a sense of unease began to creep in, like ivy slowly choking the life out of a once-thriving tree.

"No," she whispered, shaking her head. "At least, not that he ever mentioned to me. But sometimes... sometimes I wonder if there was more to it than either of us could see."

As Teresa spoke, the wind outside picked up, rattling the windowpanes, and causing shadows to dance across the walls. The detective glanced around the room, unsettled by the atmosphere that had settled over them like a heavy cloud.

"Tom's love for his friends and neighbors was both his greatest strength and his most significant weakness," Sam murmured, as if speaking aloud a thought that had been haunting him. "And perhaps, in some way, it led to his tragic fate."

Teresa felt a shiver run down her spine, though the room was warm. She knew that whatever lay hidden beneath the surface of her husband's friendship with Steve, it was somehow connected to the darkness that now threatened to consume her entire world.

"Destiny is a cruel mistress," she whispered softly, looking out into the night. "We cannot escape her grasp, no matter how hard we try."

The wind began to howl outside, its fingers clawing at the windowpanes as Teresa wrung her hands together, her thoughts churning like the storm that raged beyond the walls of her home. The flickering light of a single candle cast eerie shadows across Sam's face, his eyes narrowed in concentration as he listened to Teresa recount her memories of Tom and Steve.

"Tom was so proud of his skills with cars," she said, her voice subdued above the roar of the wind. "He would always insist on fixing things himself, never wanting to ask for help."

"Did he ever work on Steve's car?" Sam asked, his voice steady despite the unsettling atmosphere.

"No, not that I remember," Teresa replied, her brow furrowing in thought. "But there was one time, just before... before everything happened..." She trailed off, her eyes suddenly filled with a strange, distant light.

"Tell me," Sam urged gently, his hand resting on her shoulder in a gesture of support.

"Steve would come over to help Tom," she whispered. "But that was not unusual."

Teresa searched his eyes, seeing the sincerity in their blue depths. She managed a small nod before dissolving into tears once more. Sam guided her gently into a chair, murmuring words of reassurance. But Teresa heard only the screaming of her broken heart, crying out for the child who would never return. There would be no peace until Lucy's spirit was avenged.

Teresa wiped her eyes, trying to compose herself. "I'm sorry, I just...I can't stop thinking about her. My sweet Lucy."

Sam sees that he has stayed his welcome and excuses himself. He knows that he has brought a lot of pain to her. Bringing up the past is always hard but doing it during this kind of investigation. He needed to give her some time alone.

CHAPTER 11

As they drove up to Tom's crash site, Elizabeth and Maggie exchanged uneasy glances. Teresa sat in silence, her hands nervously gripping the edges of her seat. The car came to a stop as they arrived, and Elizabeth turned off the engine.

The landscape was desolate and quiet, save for the occasional bird call from the nearby trees. Teresa got out of the car, moving slowly towards the guard rail. She placed a fresh bouquet of roses on top of it before turning back to face Elizabeth and Maggie.

She looked away as if she were trying to keep her emotions in check before continuing. "He was so enthusiastic about cars, always tinkering with them until they were perfect." Tears welled up in her eyes as she spoke about Steve. "Why would Sam ask about that? I do not understand where things are going with the investigation."

Maggie stepped forward and hugged Teresa tightly, offering her words of comfort as tears streamed down her cheeks. Elizabeth stayed back, feeling almost too awkward to offer her own hug or condolences but still conveying empathy through her expression alone.

Teresa had gone to that spot every year on the same day; this time, she had decided not to go alone. Her friends offered to go with her there before going to church. Even though the time was earlier than usual, Teresa was still able to share a few moments with Tom. The weeds had grown up quite tall since last year, due in no small part to all of the rain and storms. Teresa knelt down to clear away the weeds so she could see the marker that had been placed by the church. Elizabeth and Maggie stood close together for comfort as they watched Teresa work. A ray of sunshine cast an orange glow over them, causing something buried under the dirt to glint in the light.

Elizabeth noticed the glint and walked over to the spot where Teresa had been clearing away the weeds. She bent down and brushed away the dirt with her hands until she uncovered a small, silver chain and necklace. Elizabeth looked at it quizzically before turning to Teresa, who was still kneeling by Tom's wreckage.

A TANGLED WEAVE: Death of a Child

"Teresa, do you recognize this necklace?" Elizabeth asked, holding it up for Teresa to see.

Teresa gasped as she looked at the necklace. "That's Steve's necklace! It was a family heirloom. Look at the symbol, he said it was his family crest."

Teresa's mind raced as she tried to piece together the puzzle of Steve's past. She remembered hearing rumors that he had moved to town after a messy divorce, but she didn't know much else about him. Could he be involved in Tom's accident? She needed to get this to Sam, maybe it would help.

After a few moments of silence, Teresa thanked both of them before turning back to face the area one last time before getting into the car. As they drove away, no one spoke but everyone felt an unspoken understanding that this moment would be remembered forever.

The three women pulled into the church parking lot in a solemn silence, each one lost in their own thoughts. Teresa had missed so many Sundays in the six months since Lucy's passing, and it was a comfort to know that she was still welcomed here as if nothing had changed.

As they walked inside, the familiar smells of incense and freshly polished wood brought an unexpected wave of peace over them. Several people acknowledged them with nods but most remained focused on their own conversations. Teresa took a deep breath before making her way to Father Michael's office for her visit.

Father Michael had been a blessing during these past few months; never once did he try to diminish Teresa's feelings by telling her that Lucy was in a better place or with God now. These platitudes were somehow comforting for people, but for Teresa it only felt like an insult; after all, no one knew better than her what life with Lucy was like and to suggest that God would have taken her away from her seemed preposterous.

His office was filled with books on theology and philosophy, but amidst those he also held two pictures close - one of his late wife and the other of himself and Tom standing together at a charity event many years ago. Seeing both pictures side by side was like seeing two distinct parts of Father Michael: the man who believed fervently in faith and hope, despite all the darkness around us; yet also the man who valued moments of joy with his friends and family more than anything else.

Teresa took her seat in front of Father Michael's desk, while he settled into a chair next to her. She wasn't planning on delving right into the topic, but before she knew it, the words had already spilled out of her mouth. "Father Michael, do you think that Lucy might still be with me? I mean, not just in spirit, but as ... a ghost?"

Father Michael was taken aback by Teresa's sudden inquiry. He had always assumed her to be more rooted in the material realm. Yet he had also heard from the congregation that Teresa had been conversing with Maggie and Elizabeth, so this talk was likely what she yearned to bring up.

He studied Teresa carefully. He had known her for years, but this line of questioning was a surprise. He had always assumed she was one who firmly rooted herself in the material realm. Yet here she was, ready to confront the possibility of a spiritual one.

"My dear," Father Michael began slowly. "I'm not sure what to say. I've heard from the congregation that you have been conversing with Maggie and Elizabeth." He paused for a moment before continuing. "Is it something they have said? Something that has led you to question?"

Teresa hesitated before responding, unsure how much she should reveal about her conversations with Maggie and Elizabeth. Finally, she nodded her head and took a deep breath before she began to explain her suspicions about Steve's involvement in Tom's accident, including the necklace they found at the crash site and its presumed connection with Steve's family crest.

Father Michael listened intently as Teresa recounted her story. When she was finished, he reached across his desk and took her hand in his own large ones, offering whatever comfort he could in the moment.

"I can't disprove or prove your suspicion, my child," Father Michael said kindly after a few moments of contemplation. "But I urge you to remember that while there may be great pain and sorrow associated with ghosts in this world, we must also remember that there can be love too."

His words sent an unexpected wave of warmth through Teresa as memories of Lucy flooded back into her mind; from their long conversations on the front porch swing to their laughter echoing through other rooms in the house as they made dinner together every night. With sudden clarity Teresa knew that despite any fear or apprehension she felt around contacting Lucy's ghost, it would all be worth it if it meant being able to keep part of Lucy alive within them both forevermore.

With newfound determination Teresa thanked Father Michael before getting up from his office chair. As she reached for the door handle to his office, she turned to Father Michael, "Would you mind stopping by to see me this evening?" I have something I want to show you at the house.

Elizabeth and Maggie were deep in conversation with a number of the congregation when Teresa came out of the office. Ellen, a sweet woman in her eighty's was speaking about how the neighborhood was being torn down by the youths in the community. She believed that the children of today had no morals. Typical conversations for a before services for the elderly woman.

Elizabeth and Maggie excused themselves and joined Teresa in sitting towards the front of the hall. Teresa, Elizabeth, and Maggie sat in the front row of the hall, quietly listening to the congregation as they discussed the changing dynamics of the town. In particular, several of the members were expressing their worries about the increasing amount of young people in the area who seemed to be engaging in behavior that was not only disrespectful but downright dangerous.

The discussion eventually shifted to the best approach for managing these cases. A few suggested speaking directly with the parents of the children and getting them involved in order to resolve some of the issues. Others were adamant on having stricter laws and tougher consequences for those committing even minor violations.

Just then, Father Michael appeared from his office and addressed those gathered. He greeted them warmly. Everyone at once quieted down to listen to his sermon. Father Michael spoke about faith and community. Teresa had always enjoyed listening to him speak. It brought about a calm to her that she needed at this time.

Father Michael ended with a brief but heartfelt prayer asking for guidance from above; before inviting everyone, who wanted to join him in the courtyard for tea and cookies. With that said, services were concluded for the day, and everyone began filing out in small clusters of conversation while others made their way towards to the courtyard after saying goodbye to each other.

A TANGLED WEAVE: Death of a Child

With a sense of excitement tingling through her veins, Teresa followed behind Elizabeth and Maggie as they made their way out into the bright afternoon sunlight. They joined the members of the congregation in the courtyard.

Ellen was speaking with George, they knew what that conversation was about, so they all decided to try and rescue him for her spiteful comments about the kids in the community.

Teresa stepped forward, smiling. "George, hi! I have something for you that I found in Lucy's room." George looked up to the three women coming his way. One could see the relief on his face; he was glad to be away from Ellen. She might have been nice but her never-ending blabbering about things she didn't understand could get tiresome.

The four of them walked away from Ellen to find a quite spot near one of the benches. They slowly started discussing the changes in the community and how best to respond. George shared his experiences with Lucy at the library. He told them how Lucy was the grandchild he never had and how he missed her terribly. He spoke tenderly of how they would spend hours together in afternoons when Teresa was working a day shift. George would read stories to her and even share some of his own tales, and then she would draw pictures of what he told or made up on the spot.

The four of them laughed fondly at this memory. Maggie eventually asked why George and Lucy enjoyed spending time together so much, to which he simply replied that it was because they both appreciated literature, particularly stories that could carry a strong message. Maggie pointed out that storytelling was an essential part of life since it provided an avenue for teaching morals; something which all people need in order to live with one another peacefully.

George nodded in agreement before adding that maybe this is exactly why so many young people were misbehaving in town— because they weren't being taught any sort of moral code or values system upon which to base their actions. He suggested that maybe if there were more outlets for education and positive reinforcement, then perhaps these kids wouldn't be willful deviants. Everyone agreed with him, and soon enough their conversation began to fade.

Teresa told George he was always welcome to visit her; she would show him more of Lucy's drawings. George agreed and slowly walked toward Father Michael who was into a conversation with Ellen.

As the sun began to set, Teresa, Maggie and Elizabeth decided it was time to call it a night. Maggie pulled out her keys as they walked towards her car, while Teresa and Elizabeth discussed their plan of action for the next day.

The drive back to Teresa's place was quiet with only the sound of soft music playing in the background. As they drove past the old town hall, Elizabeth suggested that perhaps Teresa should contact her friend Sam, the detective about the necklace they found at the crash site. Maggie and Teresa both agreed that this was a promising idea.

When they arrived at Teresa's house, they got out of the car in silence and said their goodbyes. Maggie hugged them both tightly before getting into her car and driving off. As Teresa watched Maggie drive away, she thought about how strange it felt coming back home after such an emotional day. She hadn't expected to find out so much about George or Lucy's family situation.

Nevertheless, Maggie felt relieved knowing that George was doing okay now that he had been taken away from Ellen's mistreatment. She thought back to their conversation earlier in the afternoon when George spoke tenderly about his relationship with Lucy at the library—a relationship which seemed far too sweet for such a troubled young girl like Lucy.

As Maggie unlocked her door, she made up her mind—tomorrow she would start searching for answers regarding Lucy's family and perhaps even see if she could contact them herself on behalf of Teresa and Lucy's memory. With this newfound determination burning inside her chest, she stepped into her warm home and prepared herself for sleep.

*****

Elizabeth was lost in thought, her eyes fixated on the computer screen as she pondered whether or not to learn more about Teresa's house, a remarkable structure built in the 1700s and one of the oldest homes in their small town. Elizabeth gathered her courage and clicked on some keys, entering the home's address. She soon found out that the original owner was Frank Simms.

A TANGLED WEAVE: Death of a Child

Frank moved to America to make his fortune as a tailor while also investing on the side. He gained recognition for his knowledge among businessmen of the city; however, he spent a lot of time away due to his travels. This left his wife Lucy and their three children alone in the big house. Lucy had grown up with great wealth in England, which displeased her family when they found out Frank was taking them to America. As time passed by, Frank slowly ran out of money and resorted to various strategies to try and save what was left of his income. But nothing worked. His last attempt was to sell the home, yet Lucy refused to leave. On a stormy night he disappeared never to be seen again. People started saying Lucy and the children never set foot outside ever since and died a few months later without any record of what killed them.

The house had been passed around several times prior to a raging fire in the late 1800's which destroyed its major rooms. Consequently, the town had it condemned in 1875 until a wealthy Englishman purchased it to have it restored again. It was rumored that he was related to Lucy Simms, with whom the home was turned into a museum in her family name. However, another fire in the 1950's destroyed its main lobby and killed five people.

Elizabeth looked back on all this as she sat in her chair, wondering why she hadn't known any of this before. She had moved to the small town when she was just a little kid and still lives there; their family bought the same house in 1957. Then, it had just been an old, abandoned place; no one paid much attention to it. Usually, it stood empty for extended periods of time. There were families who tried living there but they didn't last long because of the extensive repairs that needed to be done due to its age. Eventually, they'd give up on the house and leave.

Elizbeth began a search for strange phenomenon in the house, reports that were given to newspapers in the past. As she looked through old articles, she noticed that the reports were consistent - people who stayed in the house reported hearing strange noises at night, like footsteps and doors creaking. Others claimed to have seen apparitions in the hallways or felt an unexplainable chill in the air. The more Elizabeth read, the more she realized Teresa's experiences were the same. Maybe this was not her Lucy, maybe it was the Lucy from the 1800's or even further back.

A TANGLED WEAVE: Death of a Child

She couldn't shake the eerie feeling that overcame her as she poured through the articles. The stories of death and despair that seemed to be woven into the very fabric of the house were too much to ignore. She knew that if she wanted to solve the mystery of the house, she would have to go on a mission to find out more about Lucy Simms and her family.

As she dug deeper into Lucy Simms' life, Elizabeth discovered that there was more to her story than just her tragic end. Lucy was known to be a skilled herbalist and had a vast knowledge of the natural world. Some claimed that she could even communicate with the spirits of the forest and the elements themselves.

Elizabeth couldn't help but wonder if this was what drew something supernatural to the house. Maybe Lucy's connection to the natural world was so strong that it somehow made the house a conduit for otherworldly beings. Elizabeth decided to take her discoveries to Maggie before telling Teresa. She has enough to worry about, maybe the house was just cursed. Maggie might know a way to cleanse the house, after all it was now Teresa's home. She had never mentioned anything before now.

CHAPTER 12

The next morning Teresa felt a sense of calmness settle over her after her conversation with Father Michael. She decided that she would spend more time at the church, and the sun was shining brightly, confirming it would be a momentous day. She got ready quickly and went downstairs for a cup of coffee before calling Detective Davis.

Sitting in the kitchen with her hot coffee in hand, she looked around the room for any sign that Lucy was with her. The air was warm, the sun shone bright through the windows. She almost missed the eerie feeling of Lucy's presence. Nevertheless, Teresa shook off the feeling and picked up her phone to call Detective Davis. As she dialed the number, her thoughts went back to the necklace. She placed the phone back on the table, she would just make a trip to the police station. She didn't want to wait any long to have this conversation with him.

As she finished her coffee, Teresa's thoughts turned back to George. She wondered how he was doing and decided to visit him later that day. She knew he must be feeling lonely and afraid after everything he'd been through. Perhaps she could offer him comfort and support.

With a sense of purpose, Teresa got up from the table and headed out the door, ready to face whatever challenges lay ahead. Teresa was becoming a normal visitor at the station; everyone knew who she was and why she was there without any introductions. They would at once walk her back to Detective Davis's office. He was on the phone when she arrived, so she sat outside waiting for him to motion her to come inside.

Sam greeted her with a warm smile and said, "Good morning, Teresa! It's good to see you again." Teresa smiled back and handed Sam the necklace she had found at Tom's crash site. "I thought you might want to take a look at this," she said. It...it belonged to Steve's mother." Teresa explained where she found it. She explained her normal trips to the crash site and how Maggie and Elizabeth had taken her there yesterday.

Sam took the necklace into his hands and examined it carefully. His expression was unreadable as he looked up at her. Sam's eyebrows shot up. "Are you certain this belongs to Steve mother?"

Teresa nodded. "Steve said it was a family heirloom. If it was there in the woods, then he had to have been there too." Her eyes pleaded with Sam to understand.

"This is interesting," he said slowly. This piece of jewelry seemed to link him to the case even further. "I will check into this immediately." The detective rubbed his chin thoughtfully. "It's compelling, but circumstantial. We would need more to tie him directly to an accident. Everything we have about Tom shows it was an accident."

"Thanks for your help, Teresa," Sam expressed with heartfelt appreciation as he put the necklace back on his desk. "I was wondering if Steve has any relatives?"

Teresa informed him that she did not think he had any family close by, mentioning that she thought he was an only child and both of his parents had passed away before they met.

Teresa's shoulders slumped. But then her eyes hardened with determination. "I'll find more proof. Whatever it takes. I owe it to Tom and Lucy to keep fighting."

Sam studied her for a moment, then put a hand over hers. "I know this is hard but promise me you'll be careful. Don't take any risks - let us manage the investigating." His voice was kind but firm.

Teresa managed a small smile. "I'll try. But I can't make any promises when it comes to getting justice for my daughter." Her blue eyes bore into Sam's, conveying her unbreakable resolve. She would not rest until Lucy's spirit was at peace.

He rose from his chair and gestured towards the door. "If you have anything, please do not hesitate to call or come see me," he stated before opening the door for her to exit.

Teresa rose from her seat, a whirlwind of emotions churning inside her. Sam's words had been meant to temper her, but they only stoked the flames of her determination.

She strode towards the exit, fists clenched at her sides. How could Sam not see the importance of finding justice for Lucy? That necklace was the first real piece of evidence linking Steve to Tom's accident. It had to mean something.

Walking out of the office, Teresa noticed that Officer Jenkins was walking toward her. He turned the corner and walked into Sam's office. She wondered if this was a sign of some news in the case. Teresa slowly turned back towards the office and stood outside listening. Sam held the necklace up to Jenkins, who had a huge smile on his face. Sam was explaining that they had found another piece of evidence that showed Steve was in the area on Tom's death. She could not make out every word that was spoke but knew it had to be good news,

She stepped out into the brilliant daylight and started heading home with a resolute stride—finding closure for Lucy was going to be her mission no matter what it took.

Lucy's soft voice seemed to echo in Teresa's ears. "Don't give up, Mama. Keep fighting for me."

Teresa gazed up at the sun, unshed tears glistening in her eyes. "I won't stop until he pays, Lucy. I promise you that."

She would gather the proof Sam needed to make an arrest, no matter what it took. Teresa refused to let Lucy's killer walk free for another night. The time had come to take matters into her own hands.

Teresa pulled her coat tighter against a chill that came over her as she made her way down the empty street. The click of her heels on the pavement seemed unnaturally loud in the stillness of the empty street. She paused in front of the library; this is where she would start.

The old library was empty except for a few students in the corner studying. Most people do their research and reading at home now. Libraries are becoming outdated. Teresa always enjoyed having the books in her hands, reading from a computer was not natural to her.

Teresa walked up to the desk where Mary, an average looking woman was checking in a stack of books. She was a shy woman with dark hair. Her voice was soft and angelic. "What can I help you with."

"Hello, I am wanting to do research on a person, I am not sure where to start. Can you send me in the right direction?"

"Sure, we are a small community, so we have all the city records stored here as well. Follow me I will get you set up." Mary took Teresa over to one of the computers in the back room. She explained that all public records were stored in this room. She logged her in and showed her to the search engine. Teresa would be on her own form here,

Teresa thanked Mary as she walked back to the front desk. She thought back to her conversation with Sam. He had suggested looking into Steve's background and known associates. She began her search by typing in Steve's name and his last known address. As she sifted through the results, she noticed a name that kept popping up - a man named Tony.

Teresa's curiosity was piqued. Who was Tony, and how did he know Steve? She dug deeper, searching for any information she could find on Tony. After a few minutes of scrolling through public records, she found a phone number linked to his name. Without hesitation, she dialed the number, hoping someone would answer.

To her surprise, a gruff voice answered on the other end of the line. "Hello?"

"Hi, my name is Teresa. I'm trying to gather information on a person named Steve Bird, and I noticed your name came up in my search," she explained.

There was a long pause before the voice spoke again. "Steve Bird is a pretty common name. Are you sure you have the right one?"

Teresa describe Steve's physicals characters to the man on the phone. She also told him of what town she believed Steve was from and about what family she thought he had. "I am not sure if any of it is true, I am just trying to find out if he has any family for sure."

"Well, I can't be sure, but it sounds like my brother. I haven't talk to him in over ten years. I have no idea what he is doing or where he is. But if it is him, best to stay away." Tony voice was rough, he didn't seem to want to engage any further.

"Can you tell me if your parents are alive?"

"Listen lady, just leave things alone and go about your business." Tony hung up the phone.

Teresa was excited, she had her first lead. But she couldn't shake the feeling of apprehension Tony's words left her with. What did he mean by "stay away"? And why did he seem so unwilling to talk about Steve?

Despite her reservations, Teresa continued digging for information on Tony and his relationship with Steve. She spent hours poring over public records, social media profiles, and any other sources she could find. As she dug deeper, she found more and more troubling details about Tony's past.

Teresa's instincts told her to back off, but her curiosity got the better of her. She decided to try calling Tony again, hoping he would be more forthcoming with information this time.

To her surprise, he answered almost immediately. "What do you want?" he snapped.

"I'm sorry to bother you again, Tony," Teresa said, trying to keep her voice steady. "But I really need to find out more about Steve. Can you tell me anything else?"

There was a long pause on the other end of the line. Teresa heard what sounded like quiet muttering before Tony spoke again.

"I will tell you one thing and you lose my number. Check into the family money." Again, the line went dead. Tony had hung up the phone.

Family money? Teresa thought Steve didn't have any money, she knew this. He lost his house due to bank foreclosure before they married. Teresa had spoken with an attorney to make certain that their marriage would not put her responsible for his debts. She had enough of her own.

Teresa pulled birth certificates to find the family names, after putting together a small family tree only going back two generations, she found it. His maternal grandmother was Bella Francis Rosa. She came from old money in the Midwest. She had two children, Rose, and Thomas Bird.

Thomas became a well-known banker and married into even more money. They had four children, all doing well and living in the same area in Texas.

Rose, on the other hand, chose to marry for love. She bid farewell to her home in Texas and wed a farmer from Kansas City. Thomas Anthony Bird owned a tiny farm outside Kansas City, where he grew wheat and kept a small herd of cattle. In the early years of marriage, Bella Rosa disinherited Rose due to her decisions. The terms of Bella's will stated that Rose's portion of the fortune would be distributed among her grandchildren, but only if they achieved financial success.

Rose and Thomas had two sons. Anthony was the oldest, and only a year after his birth, Thomas came along. For several years, they enjoyed a loving family life without worrying about the inheritance that would remain untouched for years to come.

Thomas died from a tragic accident on the farm when the boys were just teenagers. Rose, not growing up or learning much about the farm lost it due to financial difficulties soon after. The two boys were left to fend for themselves with no direct contact with their extended family.

Anthony became a mechanic, never married now at age 42. Steven had married twice but no children were created from either marriage.

Teresa's mind was swirling with all the information was able to find. There were a number of newspaper articles about the family and the dynamics surrounding the money that has been left unclaimed.

Teresa wrote down names and addresses of the family she found. She also found the contact information of the family that had bought the property in Kansas City. She was going to do some detailed digging. On her own, she would piece together who the man she married was.

CHAPTER 13

When Teresa arrived home at the end of a tiresome day, her head was spinning with all the new knowledge she had gained. She planned to start on a quest of exploration first thing in the morning. She thought she could easily travel the country on this journey in a few days' time. Fortunately, she had set aside funds for when times were tough, which they certainly are now. It was enough to cover her expenses until the storm passed and things returned to normal for Lucy and Tom. She had to uncover the answers.

She had not been home much in the last couple of days, with church on Sunday and all day at the library today, she wondered if Lucy was still presence in the house. The house was still, the air calm, not usual from the last month.

"Lucy, are you here?" Teresa almost felt an ache from her presence missing in the house.

"I am here, mom. You are on the right path." Lucy was present but there was no need for her to disturb her mother. Teresa was working toward finding the answers Lucy was looking for.

The morning sun came piercing into the bedroom window, two days in row the sun woke Teresa from a peaceful sleep. Teresa lay in bed thinking how she was going to pull off this adventure. She needed to contact Maggie and Elizabeth and reschedule their weekly lunch. Father Michael was supposed to be over this week, which would be an easy phone call. Sam? That is going to be the fun one. How is he going to take the idea of this trip? What can she tell him, so he won't worry?

She made her calls and talked to everyone before she had her morning coffee, though none of them were too pleased with her decision to go. The only person who didn't know the truth was Sam; if he found out, he'd no doubt try to talk her out of it. But she needed to do this on her own - after all, it was she that had married Steve without knowing his past history. That thought sent a chill down her spine. Was she doing the right thing?

Elizabeth and Maggie agreed to look after the house until Teresa called in each night. Elizabeth had scheduled for a medium to come by on Friday, which Maggie and Elizabeth would attend in Teresa's absence, and she could follow up with them when she got back for the weekend. With everything squared away, there was nothing to be concerned about.

She arrived in Kansas City in the late afternoon, feeling tired but determined. She checked into a motel on the outskirts of town, where she could park her car and plan her next moves. She spent the evening researching the Bird family, scouring online databases, public records, and news articles.

There was something eerie about this place, something that made her feel like an outsider. Maybe it was the vastness of the fields, or the emptiness of the sky, or the eerily quiet towns that dotted the landscape. Or maybe it was the memory of Rose's fate, and the warning that Tony had given her. Either way, Teresa knew that she had to tread carefully.

The next morning, Teresa woke not sure where she was. The night before had been a restless one full of anxious dreams and unsettling questions. Standing in the small bathroom, she took a long look at her face in the mirror. Was she doing the right thing? Were these people even going to speak with her?

With determination, she grabbed her bag and headed out to find some breakfast. Two cups of coffee and some scrambled eggs later, Teresa set off for the Bird family home. As she drove along the winding rural roads, Teresa kept a close eye on her surroundings. After about an hour of driving, she finally arrived at the address listed on website.

The house was an old farmhouse situated on top of a hill surrounded by acres of farmland. It was perched atop a hill that overlooked miles of wheat fields; it couldn't have been more different from Teresa's life back home. Seeing such beauty gave her strength to press forward as she got out of her car and slowly walked to the front door.

She knocked several times before anyone answered, so when the door opened to reveal an elderly woman wearing a worn crimson dress with white lace trim and gray hair tied up in a bun with two streaming ribbons, Teresa couldn't help but feel intimidated. The woman stared at her silently for what felt like eternity before Teresa could introduce herself.

Teresa steadied herself. "I'm sorry to bother you so late. My name is Teresa Thompson. I was wondering if I could ask you some questions about the previous owner of this your farm - Thomas Bird."

The woman studied Teresa's face, as if gauging her intentions. Finally, she nodded and opened the door wider.

"You'd better come in."

Teresa stepped inside the dimly lit home. The floral wallpaper and doilies gave the place an old-fashioned feel.

"I'm Martha, dear. Now what's this about Thomas?" Martha asked as she led Teresa to the living room.

Teresa perched on the edge of a lacy sofa. "I know this may sound strange, but I have reason to believe Thomas's son may have been involved in... something terrible." She chose her words carefully, not wanting to make direct accusations without proof.

Martha's eyes widened. "Steven or Tony? But they always seemed like such a nice young man. A bit quiet and kept to themselves, but..." Her voice trailed off.

Martha looked up, tears glistening in her eyes. "If they have done something wrong, they need to face the consequences." She took a shaky breath. "Let me start from the beginning..."

Teresa was listening carefully as Martha revealed the details of the Bird family. Thomas Anthony's sons had been getting in trouble with the law since they were young boys. After his death, their mother tried to be a good parent but could barely keep up with managing the farm and making sure her sons stayed in school. In desperation, she called on her family for help and some of them offered to take the boys to military school. Anthony balked at the suggestion, but Steve agreed to go for an entire year.

During this time, Rose sold their farm and moved back to Texas without taking Anthony along with her. Martha explained that she didn't know anything else beyond that, but she did mention that Steve had returned home a changed man. He was no longer the happy-go-lucky boy that left, but a stoic and reserved man who kept to himself.

Teresa scribbled notes on her notepad as Martha spoke. She tried to hide her excitement at the added information but couldn't help the thrill of uncovering a piece of the puzzle.

As she got up to leave, Martha handed her a faded photograph of the Bird family. "Take this with you. Maybe it will help you find what you're looking for."

Teresa smiled gratefully and left the farmhouse, feeling victorious in her mission. She finally had a lead and a glimmer of hope that she could solve the mystery of who Steve Bird really was.

The hour-long drive back to the motel gave Teresa time to think about the conversation she had with Martha. Small towns seem to carry gossip to a new level. She wondered what secrets were not written in the newspapers. What could she learn from the town's people? She quickly turned the car around and decided to have lunch and poke around a bit in town. She was sure if she hit the right small diner there would be plenty of stories to hear.

Teresa pulled her car into the small-town diner, feeling a wave of optimism. Gossip often traveled through small towns like wildfire, so she figured this was her best chance to learn more about Steve Bird.

She stepped inside and was greeted by the smell of fried chicken wafting through the air. She smiled as a few townsfolk greeted her warmly and took a seat at an empty table.

A young server came up to her and asked what she wanted. Teresa ordered iced tea and the special hot roast beef sandwich. Teresa pulled out her notebook with all the press clippings and began to read all of them again. The server a tall slender woman with blond hair pulled up into a bun, brought her iced tea to the table.

"Oh, what are you looking at?" The woman bent down to see the newspaper clippings more closely.

"I am an acquaintance of Steve Bird; he told me his family used to own a farm here in town. I am looking for more information about his family." Teresa was sure that the server was aware of his name by the way she looked at her.

"Sure, I know the family. They were a weird bunch."

The server began to tell Teresa stories about Steve Bird's family. She explained that Rose Bird was a tough woman who worked hard to keep up with managing the farm and making sure her sons stayed in school. Everyone had heard how she was a devout Christian and often brought both her boys to Bible study on Sundays at the local church. But when her husband passed away, she found it hard to continue working on the farm while also raising two teenage boys, Anthony, and Steve.

One night, Rose had a nightmare where both her sons were

walking different paths; Anthony was headed down the wrong road and got into trouble while Steve seemed to be slowly disappearing from her life. This nightmare prompted Rose to move away from the town in search of better opportunities for them all.

Anthony refused outright to leave, so he stayed behind while Steve agreed to go with his mother. After they moved to Texas, I think, Steve came back a changed man; no longer filled with laughter and joy as before but now more serious and secretive. He dated several women in town. He thought he was "the man" because of the money he was going to inherit. But no one in town wanted to be stuck with him. He had just become too needy. This was about 15 years ago. I think"

"That is interesting, so did he ever get his inherits? What did he need to do to get it?" Teresa asked the server for more information.

"I gotta get back to work, but you should talk to Dale over there." She pointed to an overweight man in the corner. "He is the lawyer in town. He was also a friend of Rose, if you know what I mean." The server gave Teresa a wink as she hurried off to the kitchen.

Teresa thanked the server and walked up to Dale's table. He was a bald man in his fifties with glasses that kept slipping off his face. After introducing herself, Teresa asked if he knew anything about Steve Bird's inheritance.

Dale looked at her suspiciously before finally replying, "Well yes, I did know something about it. The family set aside an inheritance for both of her sons Anthony and Steve as long as they fulfilled a certain condition." He hesitated for a few moments before continuing, "It seems that both boys failed to fulfill this condition in order to access the inheritance. Without it, they are not entitled to receive any money from the family."

"Interesting, I heard some of the requirements are having a family or children?"

"That's right, from what I know, neither of the boys has had any offspring."

"How about if they had stepchildren? Would that suffice?" Teresa felt her anxiety rising. Was she interrogating them too much? She didn't want to scare the locals into distrusting her presence.

"Who did you say you were? I'm not sure I should be

answering all of these questions?" The man seemed agitated now. Maybe it was time for Teresa to come clean and tell him who she really was.

"I apologize for the questions, I'm not here to cause trouble or anything. My name is Teresa Thompson, and I am actually Steve's soon to be ex-wife. I am not interested in the money. It is just that I have a daughter and I am concerned for her." Finally, she told Dale her real purpose in town, and he let out a long sigh of relief that it wasn't something more sinister.

"As I said before," Dale continued, "both boys were required to have children of their own or to be married with children if they wished to access the inheritance left by the family. If they fulfilled this condition, then Anthony and Steve would both be entitled to half of the estate." He paused for a moment as if he were waiting for a reaction, but none came.

"Perhaps I could help you with the technicalities of contacting the family?" he offered. "I have an old connection to the Bird family that I could use to speak on your behalf." He smiled warmly at Teresa, giving her some hope that things would turn out all right in the end.

"I have a flight out to Texas in the morning, I am not sure if the family will see me, but I need to try."

"Let me make a phone call for you. Give me your number, I will pass it along or I will call you after I speak with them." Dale seemed happy to help her. This was something she loved about small towns.

Teresa thanked Dale for the help and returned to the motel for the evening. The drive back through the countryside was eerily quiet. Teresa took the long way, so she had time to think and drive. There didn't seem to be any cars on the road.

Teresa arrived back at her motel in time for dinner, her mind spinning with thoughts of how best to approach the Bird family when she arrived in Texas. She had never met any of them before and wasn't sure if they would accept her on behalf of Steve and Anthony.

Her phone rang while she was at dinner. The caller ID showed a Texas area code. Teresa took a deep breath before answering. "Hello".

"Hello, is this Teresa Thompson?"

A TANGLED WEAVE: Death of a Child

"Yes, can I help you?"

" My name is Derek Franks; I am the attorney for the Bird family. I am told you are inquiring about Steven." The man on the phone was very pleasant.

Teresa's heart raced as she realized the call was from Texas. She explained her situation to Derek, and he seemed understanding. He agreed to arrange for a meeting between Teresa and the Bird family in person.

They arranged a date for the following evening when Teresa would finally have an opportunity to speak with the family face-to-face. Teresa felt both nervous and excited at this prospect - while she had no idea what to expect, she hoped that this meeting would provide answers about Steve.

*****

Elizabeth and Maggie walked into Teresa's house armed with candles, sage, rosemary, lavender, rose, and juniper in herb bundles to burn throughout the house. Elizabeth had explained to Maggie everything she had learned about the old house. Maggie had a great deal of knowledge about wicca and cleansing routines.

Maggie was fascinated by the stories Elizabeth had uncovered about the house and its former owner, Lucy Simms. She suggested that they could perform a house blessing in order to drive away any negative energy or spirits that may be lingering in the home. Elizabeth was intrigued and asked what materials would be needed for this ritual. Maggie explained that she would need all kinds of herbs and plants, but first she would need to create bundles out of them for the blessing.

They gathered together cedar, sage, thyme, lavender, rosemary, and other herbs and plants. Maggie carefully bundled them into small sachets which were then hung up around the house. As she lit each bundle of herbs, Maggie intoned words of blessings in a faint voice while walking through each room; her words filled the space with peace and harmony.

Afterwards, Maggie told Elizabeth that when someone enters a home where a house blessing has been performed, they will feel more connected to the deity or spirit chosen for protection as well as an overall sense of peace and protection within the home itself. Elizabeth thanked Maggie for her help and set about creating rituals for Teresa to do every day in order to protect her home from any unpleasant energies or unwelcome spirits.

Maggie knew that if they continued to perform these rituals it would keep Teresa's home safe from any dark forces. With renewed confidence they both left knowing that things were going to be alright now that their home was blessed by favorable energies brought by their ritual work together.

When we meet with the medium, we can explain what we have done. They both agreed to keep this to themselves until it was necessary to involve Teresa.

CHAPTER 14

The following morning, Teresa arrived at the airport earlier than expected. She had not phoned Elizabeth like they had arranged; yesterday had been a long day and she was too exhausted when she finally got to bed. Knowing that it was important to contact her friend to let her know she was all right, Teresa reached for her phone.

"Oh my gosh, Teresa, thank goodness! I'd been so worried about you. Why didn't you call last night?" Elizabeth picked up on the first ring - it seemed that she had been sitting right next to the phone waiting for it to ring.

Teresa went through everything that had happened the previous day before explaining that she was currently at the airport awaiting her flight. In addition, they discussed whether or not it was still possible for her to make it on time for the planned medium appointment later in the week.

After their call ended, Teresa promised to ring Elizabeth again after she finished with the Bird family meeting and try to get a flight back as soon as possible. But before Teresa could even say goodbye, another call came in from the Birds' attorney.

"Excuse me for a moment, Elizabeth. I have to take this."

"Ms. Thompson, just wanted to let you know that a car will pick you up when you land in Dallas. The family would prefer not to prolong your visit," Derek said in a straightforward but still pleasant voice.

Teresa agreed and hung up with Elizabeth. She couldn't wait to deliver the news that Elizabeth would be home even sooner than she had thought.

When Teresa landed in Dallas, a car was waiting for her as promised. The car drove in silence to the Bird home located just outside of town. As they turned up the long driveway leading to the house, Teresa could see the large two-story property looming ahead of her. Her heart raced with anticipation as she wondered what awaited her inside.

The door was opened to welcome her by Thomas and Clara Bird, Steve's cousin, and cousin-in-law. After introducing themselves, they invited Teresa into their home and showed her to their living room where Bella Bird sat in a wheelchair. Bella introduced herself as Steve's grandmother and remarked that it had been too long since anyone from the family had spoken on behalf of Steve or Anthony regarding their birthright inheritance.

Thomas told Teresa that Steve had contacted them about a year ago about claiming his inheritance from his grandmother but that he could not do so unless Lucy accepted him. He said that they were still awaiting a response from him.

Bella spoke up at this point and told Teresa that first Lucy needed to call him Dad before any decisions could be made regarding inheritance claims or future plans to allow him access to the money.

Teresa assured the family that the money was not what she was after. She explained about her marriage to Steve and about the death of Lucy. With a somber expression, she told them that Steve had changed since Lucy's death. He had become withdrawn and angry.

Thomas and Clara looked at each other with understanding while Bella's weathered face softened in sympathy for Teresa's situation. Thomas cleared his throat and spoke slowly.

"We have not heard from him in a year, but we assume," Thomas said. "We have been following your story. We are terribly sorry for your loss. Lucy was a beautiful child."

Teresa only then looked around the room. There was a large fireplace in the corner, on the mantel above was a picture of Lucy. She stood and walked to the photo.

She hadn't expected the Bird family to be so open-hearted towards her after all she knew nothing about them, but their words of comfort gave her hope for the future.

"Tell me what do you know of my baby girl? Did you know when we were married? Or before? I don't understand any of this?" Teresa was streaming down her face. The confusion of this family she knew nothing about, but they knew her.

Thomas rose to his feet, his eyes sympathetic as he walked over to Teresa and stood beside her, looking at the photo of Lucy. "We knew of Lucy, yes. Bella recognized her immediately from the pictures Steve had shown her," he explained. "But we didn't know the extent of your marriage or Lucy's death until later. Steve didn't speak to us often, and when he did, it was clear that your marriage was a sore subject for him."

"I just want all my grandchildren to be happy." You could see the pain in Bella's eyes as she spoke. "I need to lay down, if I don't see you before you leave, please stay in touch. Thomas has instructions to help you with whatever in need. My child, I am sorry you have been brought into this." One of the servants appeared and walked Bella to the back of the house.

Teresa felt a pang of sadness at Bella's words. It was clear that the Bird family had their own struggles and secrets to bear.

"But what about the inheritance?" Teresa asked, turning back to Thomas. "I don't want anything. That isn't why I am here. Please tell me about Steve."

Thomas paused before answering, and Teresa sensed that there was more to this story than anyone was letting on. "Come back over here and sit down, I will try and give you all the information I have."

Teresa sat in the chair across from Thomas and next to his wife Clara.

Thomas took a deep breath and began." Steve has been married three times, including you. His first wife was not able to have children and they could not afford to adopt. So, they were divorced within five years. His second wife had two children but was not willing to have a third with him. She died in an accident not long after they were married, and the children went to live with their biological father."

Teresa was astonished at how Steve seemed to marry only for the children. He must have been fixated on the money. Thomas continues to explain about the family and how Bella was terribly upset about Rose, Steve's mother, they talked for few hours about Steve and how he was determined to get his inheritance at any cost.

Teresa wondered about his second wife and how she died. She was afraid to implicate him in a murder, but there was her Tom to think about.

As Thomas went on, Teresa felt her mind drifting away from the conversation. She couldn't stop thinking about Steve's second wife and how she had died in an accident. It all seemed too convenient, as if someone had planned it all out. She couldn't help but wonder if Steve was involved somehow.

"Excuse me, Thomas," Teresa interrupted him. "Do you know any details about how Steve's second wife died?"

Thomas looked at her skeptically. "Why do you ask?"

"I don't know," Teresa hedged. "It just seems like such a tragic coincidence, that's all. I was wondering if there was any more information about the incident."

Thomas sighed and leaned back in his chair. "I suppose there's no harm in telling you. The official story is that she died in a car crash. But there was always something off about the whole thing. No one knows for sure what really happened."

Teresa felt a chill run down her spine. She knew she was treading into dangerous territory, but she couldn't shake the feeling that there was more to the story. "Do the police suspect anyone?"

Thomas shrugged. "Not that I know of. It was ruled an accident, and the case was closed. But like I said, there's always been something fishy about it. Steve was devastated, of course, but he moved on pretty quickly after that. Almost too quickly, if you know what I mean."

Teresa nodded, her mind racing with thoughts. She needed to find out more about Steve's second wife, and she needed to do it without raising any suspicions. She was determined to find the underlying cause of this.

"You know about my first husband, right? Lucy's father. it seems a bit too close to home." Teresa tried to focus; she was not sure what kind of reaction she would get from this family.

Thomas's expression softened as he looked at Teresa. "Yes, I remember hearing about him. I'm so sorry for your loss."

Teresa nodded, grateful for the sympathy. "Thank you. It's been a difficult road, but Lucy keeps me going." She paused, thinking of how to approach her next question. "Do you think Steve could have had any involvement in his wife's death?"

Thomas leaned forward; his voice lowered to a whisper. "I can't say for sure, but there were rumors floating around back then. No one ever came forward with any tangible evidence, though. And like I said, the police ruled it an accident."

Teresa felt a pang of disappointment. She had hoped for more concrete information. "Do you know of anyone who might have more information? Maybe someone who was closer to Steve's second wife?"

Thomas shook his head. "Sorry, Teresa. I wish I could be more help. But I don't know anyone who was close to her. Steve was always very private about his personal life." He paused, then added, "Just be careful, okay? You don't want to get caught up in something dangerous."

Teresa nodded, feeling a sense of determination. She would find out the truth, even if it meant putting herself in harm's way. As she left the Bird home and headed back to her motel room, her mind raced with thoughts of Steve, his second wife, and the mysterious circumstances surrounding her death. She would have to tread carefully, but she was determined to find the underlying cause of this.

CHAPTER 15

After coming home from her trip, Teresa was drained. Her attempt to uncover the truth had only led to more questions. She had scheduled a meeting with Sam in the morning to explain what she had found out. Elizabeth and Maggie were eager that she was back in town to connect with the medium.

Now she just needed Steve to show up. Teresa had called him from the airport asking him to come pick up some of his things. He happily agreed. Teresa was prepared; she asked him to arrive at the same time as Elizabeth, Maggie, and the medium, so she wouldn't have to be alone with him.

Teresa was motionless on the sofa, examining the faded wallpaper in front of her. The ticking of the clock on the mantel seemed extra loud in the tense quiet. A mix of guilt and fear coursed through her body, like waves eroding away a distant shoreline. She wanted revenge for Lucy's death and to fill up the emptiness within her heart. But dread kept her from confronting him.

The chill in the air seemed to intensify as Teresa heard a knock at the door. She hoped it was Elizabeth and Maggie arriving first, but as she walked slowly towards the front door, her heart sank when she saw Steve standing outside.

"Hey," he said sheepishly. "You called me?"

Teresa tried to keep her composure but inside her head was spinning. She managed to let him in, and Steve made his way to the living room where she had set up a few chairs for the group. He looked around nervously, clearly uncomfortable with his visit here.

"I have a box of your things; I would like for you to take them." Teresa voice shacking with fear and anger.

Steve nodded silently and stepped towards the kitchen, but before he could get too far, the doorbell chimed. Teresa practically ran to the front door. She opened it to reveal Elizabeth and Maggie standing on the welcome mat with a petite woman between them. Teresa felt a wave of relief wash over her; now she wouldn't have to face Steve alone.

Elizabeth embraced Teresa tightly as they stepped into the

house, trying to break the uneasy quiet. "I am so glad you made it back in time for this."

Maggie bustled in and made her way to Steve. "I hope you're prepared for this!"

"Prepared for what? You people are insane," Steve replied with a hint of anxiety in his voice. He was unsure of what was about to go down. But seeing the medium standing next to Elizbeth he knew something was up.

The medium walked slowly around the living room. A crisp cool feeling filled the atmosphere. The petite woman, appearing to be in her forties, stood before them with auburn hair pulled back into a gentle braid that tumbled down to the center of her back. Her voice was serene and lovely.

The sense of anticipation was unmistakable now and everyone seemed to be holding their breath in anticipation as Teresa began talking about Lucy's death and her memories surrounding it. Steve nervously avoided eye contact with Teresa throughout it all, making her feel like he wasn't willing to tell her everything he knew. In turn, this just added fuel to her already burning desire for retribution against him for being involved in Lucy's death in some way or another.

Steve spoke up, breaking the stillness in the room. "What's going on here? Where is this box you mentioned?" He glanced around at all the women present.

"So how was your trip to Teresa? Did you find out what you were looking for?" Elizabeth continued pressing buttons that made Teresa a bit uncertain.

"The box is over there." Teresa pointed to corner beside the old clock. She turned to Elizabeth, her gaze toward her showed resentment. "We can talk about that later, okay?"

Steve knew that this was his cue to leave. He slowly rose from his seat and went over to collect the box, his expression unreadable. He grabbed it without a word and hurried out the door, making sure each of the ladies knew he was not happy about all of them being there.

As he stepped outside, Teresa watched as Steve walked away with a sense of closure rushing through her veins; she finally felt like she had gotten what she wanted when it came to Steve- justice for Lucy's death. She shut the door behind him with relief and turned back towards Maggie, Elizabeth and the medium who were still in her living room. Now Teresa could find out whatever they had come for- Lucy's truth- at last.

As they all gathered in the kitchen, Maggie made the proper introductions. "Teresa, this is Joanna, I have worked with her before. She is very capable of seeing things that are not visible to most of us."

Joanna held her hand out to Teresa, "I know you are scared; I am here to help you see the truth." Joanna held her hand for a few moments before digging into her bag. She pulled out candles and began to place them throughout the kitchen and around the table.

As Joanna began to light the candles, a calmness seemed to settle over the group. She then told Teresa to close her eyes and focus on Lucy, so that she could connect with her energy and spirit. Teresa complied and felt her muscles relax as she homed in on the memories of Lucy, allowing them to flood through her mind.

Joanna began speaking in a faint voice that was both comforting and yet still commanding. She asked Teresa to share all of her emotions of pain, anger, sadness, and confusion regarding Lucy's death. As Teresa opened up about how helpless she felt when it happened, tears welled up in her eyes.

Suddenly, the room began to feel strange, and Teresa felt a cool breeze brushing against her skin, a quiet presence that seemed to move around the kitchen. Her friends and Joanna were all looking around with wide eyes and she knew that Lucy's spirit had been invited into the room.

The candles flickered wildly as tendrils of smoke rose up from them. The glass cabinets in the kitchen rattled uncontrollably and the spoon resting on the counter was flung across the room. Everyone was too scared to move or speak, their eyes glued to the spectacle before them.

And then it stopped just as abruptly as it began- saving everyone from having a heart attack in Teresa's kitchen. Silence filled the air for a few moments before someone finally broke it by uttering two words: "Thank you." It was Joanna, expressing her gratitude for Lucy's presence being known and acknowledged that evening. "Now, Lucy, help us understand, where do we go from here?"

The air was still and silent, as the group waited for a response. Suddenly, a faint whisper could be heard, until it was a clear and distinct voice. It was Lucy's voice, but it sounded different, like she was speaking from beyond the grave.

"Be careful mommy," the voice said, and the candles flickered once again. "I am watching over you."

Teresa's heart was pounding in her chest. She had never believed in this sort of thing before, but now she was convinced that Lucy's spirit was truly there with them. She looked at Joanna, who nodded her head as if to say, "I know what we have to do."

Joanna stood up and closed her eyes, her hands raised above her head. She began chanting in a language that Teresa did not recognize, and the room filled with an otherworldly energy. The candles burned brighter, and the temperature dropped several degrees. Suddenly, Joanna stopped chanting and opened her eyes.

"I have made contact with Lucy's spirit," she said, her voice shaking slightly. "She has given us a clue to her killer's identity."

Everyone leaned in closer, their eyes fixed on Joanna.

"She says that her killer is someone that she knew well," Joanna continued. "Someone who was close to her, someone who she trusted."

Teresa's mind raced as she tried to think of who it could be. She was just a child, she trusted everyone. "I don't know, it has to be Steve."

"Close your eyes, Teresa. Think of a moment in time when all was pleasant when laughter filled your heart." Joanna held her hand softly. She needed Teresa to clear her mind of the agony in her heart. She needed to be focused on the life of Lucy not her death.

Teresa closed her eyes, seeking escape. She retreated deep into her memories, to a sunny afternoon long ago.

She was in the backyard with Tom and little Lucy, who giggled as Tom pushed her on the creaky swing set. Teresa smiled as she watched them, heart swelling with love.

Tom's laughter filled the air as he swooped a squealing Lucy into his arms. "Let's go on an adventure!" he declared, hoisting Lucy onto his shoulders. They set off marching across the lawn, Lucy waving a stick she'd declared her magic wand.

Tom played along, pretending to be a fearsome dragon as Lucy "battled" him. Teresa chuckled, wishing she could freeze this moment and live in it forever.

The golden afternoon sunlight warmed her skin as she

watched her little family play. For now, no darkness could touch them here. The memory grounded her, reminding her of the light she still carried within. She clung to it like a lifeline, using its warmth to bolster her courage.

Teresa opened her eyes as the memory faded, the ghost of Tom's laughter still ringing in her ears. She was back in her dim kitchen, with her friends seated all around her.

"That is, it, hold that memory," Joanna again tried to reach Lucy. "I am sorry, she is gone but I am feeling a strong presence of a man. He is watching over Lucy, but he needs Lucy to move on, but she is determined to stay here with you."

"That must be Tom." Teresa sat straight up in the chair, her mind swirling with the thought that they were together. This gave her comfort knowing Lucy was not alone.

"I am sorry, this is all I have for tonight." Joanna began blowing out the remaining candles.

"How about some tea?" Maggie stood and walked to the sink to fill the kettle.

"That would be nice." All the women were in agreement. It was time to settle back and enjoy each other's company without the heavy weight of the otherworldly on their shoulders.

As the kettle began to boil, they all chatted and laughed about mundane things – the weather, the latest gossip in town, and new recipes they wanted to try. It was a welcome break from the intensity of their previous conversation.

But as they sipped on their tea and exchanged lighthearted banter, Teresa couldn't shake the feeling that something was off. It was as if the lingering presence of Lucy and Tom had cast a shadow over their gathering, reminding them that there were still unanswered questions and unresolved issues at play.

Sensing this shift in energy, Joanna spoke up. "I know we were hoping for more answers tonight, but sometimes these things take time. We'll keep trying to communicate with Lucy and Tom, and hopefully, they will lead us to the truth."

Teresa felt a sense of gratitude wash over her. Despite the weight of their investigation, she was grateful for the support of her friends and the unwavering determination of Joanna. She knew that they would get to the bottom of Lucy's murder, no matter what it took.

Elizabeth's voice pulled her back to the present. "I wish I could stay, but I've got to run. Call me if you need anything, okay?"

Teresa nodded, swallowing the lump in her throat. As the door closed behind them, the silence returned like a heavy weight. She stood motionless, lost in the past's gentle embrace. But the present was always waiting, cold and bleak. And she still had no idea how to escape its darkness.

Teresa sank down onto the couch, her body heavy with exhaustion. She stared blankly at the faded wallpaper, absently tracing the floral pattern with her finger.

How did I get here? She wondered. When did this become my life?

She thought back to the early days with Tom, when the future seemed to stretch before them, bright and full of promise. They were going to grow old together, watch their grandchildren play in this very house. But fate had intervened, stealing Tom away and leaving her utterly alone.

And now this new tragedy with Lucy. Teresa pressed her palms against her eyes, as if she could somehow push the images from her mind. But she could still see her daughter's body crumpled in the yard, could still feel the coldness of her skin as Teresa begged her to wake up.

Rage simmered within her, hot and acidic. She wanted to confront Steve, to unleash the full fury of her pain and make him understand what he had done. But she was paralyzed by fear, by the helplessness of her situation.

Teresa hugged herself tightly, rocking back and forth on the couch. She had never felt so powerless, so trapped by the darkness surrounding her. This struggle was changing her, hardening her heart, and stealing what little hope she had left.

She didn't know how to keep going down this bleak path. The future loomed before her, vast and terrifying in its uncertainty. All she could do was take it one moment at a time and pray that the light would someday find its way back to her.

CHAPTER 16

The chill had seeped into the air and Teresa knew she must move forward without Lucy, but she couldn't seem to take her first step. She felt like a child again, helpless, and scared. Tears streamed down her face as she felt Tom's presence close by.

Suddenly, Lucy appeared beside her, seemingly out of thin air. She was translucent and shimmering in the light, yet still so very real to Teresa. In that moment, Teresa felt a surge of love overwhelm her and all of her sadness seemed to evaporate in its presence.

Lucy looked up at her mother with love in her eyes, silently communicating her desire for Teresa to find peace and solace without her physical presence. She wanted more than anything for Teresa to move forward.

Tom stood close by and watched this exchange with awe and reverence; he too wanted nothing more than for Teresa to let go of Lucy so that she could feel the joy of the next stage of life.

"It is okay mommy, I am here" Lucy could feel the pain that was cursing through her mother's body. She needed it to go away.

"Lucy, this is not helping your mother. You need to come with, there is so much more for you to see." Tom understood the longing to stay. You remained with his family after his death until he first seen Teresa laugh. At that time, he knew they would be okay with him.

"I can't leave her, I have been quite like you asked, but I can't leave my mommy." Lucy was confused and pulled between being with her dad and her mom. She wanted both.

"Let me show you something, you can come back and check on you mom after." Tom held out his to his daughter as they floated through the house and into the night.

The two floated high in the sky. Lucy looked around as she was flying with stars, each glimmered in assorted colors. The air was warm and light, dancing on a cloud. "This is my heaven, Lucy; I want you share my world with you."

As they soared through the sky, Lucy marveled at the stars that twinkling in a dazzling array of colors around her. Each one shone with its own unique hue, creating a kaleidoscopic display of light. The warm breeze lifted her up, and she felt as if she were dancing on a cloud. "This is all mine," said Tom, gazing down at Lucy with a smile. "And I want to share it with you." They landed in a large meadow filled with soft, plush grass. In the distance was a vast house beside a gently flowing stream. Lucy recognized it immediately; it was hers, but it stood alone in the middle of nowhere, surrounded by nothing but open space.

Tom smiled and took Lucy's small hand in his, leading her to the door of the house. He looked down at her with a loving gaze and said, "This is our home, Lucy. This is where I live now. Would you like to come inside and have a look around?"

Lucy's eyes lit up as she took in the scene before her—the warm sunlight filtering through the trees, the birdsong in the air, and their house standing tall in the middle. She could almost imagine it was just like it had been when they were all together as a family.

Tom opened the door to the house, and they stepped into the foyer. Little Lucy's artwork was displayed on the walls, reminding Tom of his daughter's creative soul and lust for life. The hallway was illuminated in a spectrum of hues, showing off colorful pictures she had made while she was alive, all of them exuding energy.

As they walked around the house, Lucy saw a study lined with bookshelves filled with Lucy's favorite stories, she could tell it was a special place that Tom went to whenever he needed to feel closer to his little girl.

They laughed together at all of Lucy's silly memories written on notes tacked up onto the fridge—reminders of happy days gone by that were now frozen in time forever.

It felt like coming home again for both Tom and Lucy; here together, under one roof once more—finally reunited after so many years apart. Tears rolled down Tom's face as he watched his daughter take in this new journey ahead of them both without hesitation or fear; it filled him with joy knowing how strong she still was despite it all.

"Now come out here." Tom walked through the kitchen and out the back door. There stood the old oak tree. The same tree that Lucy would sit under, where she would draw, her masterpieces.

Tom watched as Lucy's eyes widened in amazement at the sight of the tree, its sturdy branches looming tall overhead and casting a dappled shade on the grass below. As they approached, Tom reached out to take Lucy's hand in his once more, the gentle pressure reassuring her that he was there for her.

"Come on," he said, his voice soft and gentle. "Let's sit down and talk for a while."

Lucy nodded, and they settled down on the grass under the tree, the cool blades tickling their skin. The warmth of the sun enveloped them as they sat in comfortable silence, each lost in their own thoughts.

Lucy felt a sense of peace wash over her, as though a weight had been lifted off her shoulders. She leaned against her father's shoulder, feeling safe and protected in his embrace.

The two talked about the memories they shared. They discussed Lucy's school friends, her teachers, all the things that Lucy had done after Tom had left her.

"How do you know all the things that I have done? You were not with mommy and me."

"I will show you later, but for now you have visitors. Look over there." Tom pointed off towards the creek.

Lucy's eyes widened in surprise. She hadn't expected anyone else to be there. Tom smiled as he watched his daughter take it all in. He had arranged this gathering ahead of time, to give Lucy the chance to make new friends and learn more about her past.

The children were delighted to meet Lucy and welcomed her with open arms. Together they played tag, splashed in the creek, and told stories around the bonfire. Lucy laughed with delight as she saw some familiar faces—family she had known years ago before Tom had left her.

As night fell, Tom gave each child a hug goodbye and thanked them for coming. With the sun setting on their special day together, Lucy felt contentment in knowing that she was still capable of making new friends—even if it was different than what she remembered from when she was younger.

Tom tapped her gently on the shoulder—"Come on," he said, "Let's go home." Taking one last look at the stars glimmering above them both, Lucy followed her father back up to the house.

Back inside, Tom went to retrieve something from his bedroom while Lucy stood admiring the notes attached to the fridge by magnets—her memories pinned up like precious works of art for all eternity.

Tom came back into the room carrying a small tablet. He placed the tablet on kitchen table. "Let's see what your mom is doing."

Lucy jumped with excitement. "I can see mom for here. What is she doing?"

They huddle together, their eyes glued to the screen as if it were a window into another world. Tom explained to Lucy that when they watch the tablet, it's like seeing what's happening without delay. She could relive any moment in her life, no matter how small or insignificant it may seem.

They watched as Teresa, Elizabeth, and Maggie laughed and talked as they headed out for a girls' night. They went to dinner, then the movies. Tom and Lucy marveled at everything they saw—the way Teresa hugged Maggie after she spilled her popcorn, the hug shared between Elizabeth and Teresa when their favorite movie ended—it was like being right there in the theater with them.

As they watched, Tom and Lucy smiled at each other. They could feel the love and friendship that radiated from the love they shared, even though they were miles apart. Lucy looked up at her father with contentment written all over her face; she felt blessed to be able to witness such special moments in life.

It was later into the night when Teresa's group made it back home but even in darkness Tom and Lucy continued to watch with fascination until finally it was too late for Lucy to stay awake any longer.

Tom tucked him into bed with a kiss on the forehead, knowing full well that this was only just a glimpse into his daughter's world of learning.

As morning broke, Tom suggested to Lucy that should do something special, "Anything, name anything you want to do?' Tome tried to push his daughter into thinking big.

"I want to see mom again."

"We can do that later, think Lucy if you could go anywhere in the world or do anything you wanted."

"Okay, how about Disney World?" Lucy just spoke up; it was not like she was really even thinking she wanted to go there.

Tom opened the back door, the door that led to all oak tree, now was opening to Disney World. Lucy's eyes widened as she stepped through the threshold, and suddenly found herself transported to the Happiest Place on Earth. She could hear the joyful screams of children and the delightful tunes of Disney songs all around her.

Tom smiled at his daughter's reaction, and they both began walking down Main Street USA, taking in the sights and sounds of the park. Lucy pointed to all her favorite rides and attractions, and Tom made sure they went on every single one.

As they wandered through Fantasyland, Lucy spotted a princess walking by and ran up to her for a hug. The princess giggled and took a photo with the young girl, making Lucy's day even brighter.

After a long day of rides, shows, and character meet-and-greets, Tom and Lucy sat down to watch the Disney fireworks. The sky lit up in a dazzling display of colors and shapes, and Lucy could hardly contain her excitement. As the fireworks ended, Tom turned to Lucy and said, "Now, why don't we go see your mom?"

Lucy nodded eagerly, feeling grateful for her father's willingness to make her dreams come true. As they stepped back into the oak tree portal, Lucy felt a sense of contentment wash over her. She knew that no matter where she was or what she was doing, her family would always be there to support her and make her happy.

"Is lifelike this every day? Lucy began to understand what her heaven could be.

"Yes, Lucy. This is heaven, your heart has always been true. Your mind is always filled with happy moments. This is what you are missing. The more time you spend in your old life, the worst is on your mom.

Tom trailed off; his voice filled with concern. Lucy looked up at him, confused.

"What do you mean?" she asked.

"Well, your mom has been struggling a lot lately," Tom explained. "She misses you so much, and it's been really hard for her to cope with your passing. We thought that maybe, if we could help you find some peace and happiness here in heaven, it would make things easier for her."

Lucy felt a pang of guilt in her chest. She had never considered how her death was affecting her mother. She had been too caught up in her own pain to think about anyone else's.

"I'm sorry, Dad," she whispered. "I didn't know. I'll try to be happy here, for Mom's sake."

Tom smiled warmly at her. "I know you will, sweetheart. And I promise, we'll always be here for you, no matter what. Besides, we can watch mom whenever we want" Tom knew that Lucy would soon learn the ways of heaven, but he hoped he could keep her here long enough for Teresa to find peace.

Lucy nodded, feeling a sense of warmth and love radiating from her father. She knew that, even in death, their bond was unbreakable. And as she looked out at the endless possibilities of heaven, she began to feel a glimmer of hope for the first time since her passing.

Maybe this was not such a bad place after all.

CHAPTER 17

The sun had just begun to peek over the horizon as Teresa hurried towards the police station. She had stayed up late the night before, talking with Joanna and her friends about her vision, and she was already exhausted. But she had a plan that could possibly lead them to some answers, and so she put aside her weariness and pressed on.

When she arrived, Sam was already in his office. He shot her a surprised glance as she walked in without knocking.

"I heard you were out town. Did you find what you were looking for?" He asked.

"A lot more than I expected," Teresa said with a sigh. "I went to Steve's family home, and I got some information that might be helpful in your investigation."

Sam leaned forward in his chair, eager for more details. He knew she should not have gone, but in truth he knew she would. Teresa explained everything that happened in Kansas City and Texas. She told him of the family money and how Steve was determined to get it. When she was done speaking, Sam sat back in his chair and sighed heavily.

"You should not have gone, you know that." Sam voice had become sterner. "We know about his family. Why didn't you come to me? I could help you through all this.

"You knew, why didn't you tell me?" Teresa was becoming enraged. How could he keep something like this from her? She had the right to know.

Sam could see the mixture of anger and hurt in Teresa's eyes, and he knew he had to tread carefully. "I'm sorry, Teresa. I should have told you earlier. But I didn't want to put you in harm's way."

Teresa shook her head, not satisfied with his answer. "I'm a part of this investigation too, Sam. I deserve to know everything that's going on. How can we solve Lucy's murder if we're not working together?"

Sam leaned forward; his expression serious. "You're right, Teresa. We need to work together. And I promise you, from now on,

I won't keep anything from you."

Feeling slightly mollified, Teresa took a deep breath and nodded. "Okay. So, what's our next move?"

Sam picked up a file from his desk and handed it to her. "This is the case file on Steve's family. You can go through it and see if you can find anything different from what you found out."

Teresa flipped through the file, studying the names and dates. She felt a chill run down her spine as she saw the names of several people who had died under suspicious circumstances. "This is...this is a lot," she said, her voice trembling slightly.

"I know," Sam said grimly. "We have enough that we are picking him up for Tom's death. I cannot tie him into Lucy at this time, but it is a start."

"I understand, this does puzzle me, why would he kill Lucy, she would be his ticket to the inheritance." Teresa still flipping through the files looked up at Sam. Teresa spoke, her words more analytical than emotional.

"That is the situation as of now. I shall visit again once he has gone through questioning." Sam led Teresa out of the station, he was trying to get her out before Steve was brought in.

Sam stood by the entrance of the station, holding the door open as the vehicle with Steve restrained in its rear drove up. Steve could see Teresa's face through the window of the car, her gaze locked on him. Her expression was unreadable, but Sam could see that she was trying to remain composed.

The car stopped and two officers stepped out. They opened the back door and carefully guided Steve out of the car. Sam motioned for them to bring him inside and they complied, leading him through the station's hallway towards an interrogation room.

Steve had a smug look on his face, like he was confident that he wouldn't be charged with anything. This made Teresa even angrier, and she started walking towards him. Sam quickly grabbed her arm and pulled her back before she could reach him.

"Teresa, let me handle this," Sam said firmly. "I don't want you getting hurt."

Teresa reluctantly allowed herself to be pulled back as she watched Steve being taken inside with a resentful glare. She wanted nothing more than to rip him apart for what he had done, but she knew that wouldn't help anyone right now, so she stayed quiet.

A TANGLED WEAVE: Death of a Child

All Teresa wanted was justice for Lucy's death and Tom- no matter what it took - and if that meant going head-to-head with Steve then so be it.

****

Detective Davis stood alone in the dimly lit observation room; his piercing blue eyes focused intently on the necklace he held between his fingers. The cold metal felt like a haunting reminder of the cruelty that had befallen Tom Thompson and his family. He carefully studied the intricate design, noting the patterns of leaves and vines that intertwined around a small, tarnished pendant. It was as though the very essence of nature had been captured and preserved within this unassuming piece of jewelry.

As he jotted down his observations in a worn leather notebook, Detective Davis couldn't help but think about the inexorable forces that had led them all to this moment – the relentless passage of time, the unforgiving power of nature, and the inevitability of destiny itself. Every decision, every action, every twist and turn of fate had brought them to this crossroads where justice would finally be served.

The door to the interrogation room creaked open, its hinges protesting with an eerie groan that sent a shiver down Sam's spine. He stepped into the stark room, immediately feeling the weight of Steve's gaze upon him. The man's eyes, dark with fear and guilt, darted nervously from side to side as if searching for some form of refuge from the storm that was brewing within him.

"Hello, Steve" Detective Davis began slowly. "I thought this would be a better place to talk, than your motel room. Don't you agree? Sam placed a folder on the table and sat across from Steve. His eyes never pieced on Steve's.

"Nature has a way of revealing our darkest secrets, Steve," Detective Davis continued, his voice tinged with a hint of sadness. "The roots of ancient trees will eventually break through the earth's surface, no matter how deep they are buried. And just like those roots, the truth always finds a way to come to light."

As the words settled in the air between them, Steve felt the weight of his guilt pressing down on him, trapping him within the confines of the interrogation room. The walls seemed to close in

A TANGLED WEAVE: Death of a Child

around him, the relentless pursuit of justice suffocating him as the inevitable storm of consequences loomed ever closer.

Detective Davis allowed the silence to stretch out, his piercing blue eyes trained on Steve's face. The man's chest heaved with each shallow breath, his hands trembling in his lap. The tension in the air was palpable, a living creature tightening its grip around the room.

"So is there anything you would like to share before we get started."

"I have told you everything. I would never have hurt Lucy. Besides, I was not home, I was at the bar, you know this."

"You are correct about being at the bar, but we are not here to discuss Lucy right now." Sam confidence was building up. He was determined to discover the truth. "We are here to talk about Tom, Lucy's father. You remember him, right?"

The cold, sterile walls of the police station's interrogation room seemed to close in on Steve as he sat nervously at the table. The metal chair beneath him was a stark reminder of his current predicament. His hands trembled, betraying his attempts to appear calm. He couldn't shake the overwhelming feeling that his life would never be the same.

"Steve Michael Bird," Detective Davis began, his voice steady yet stern, "We have reason to believe you were at the scene of the accident that took Tom Thompson's life." He held up the necklace for Steve to see, its silver chain glinting ominously under the harsh fluorescent lights.

"Where did you find that?" Steve stammered, his eyes widening with shock and disbelief. But within the depths of those eyes, the flicker of guilt betrayed him.

"Right where you left it, Steve," Detective Davis replied, his gaze never wavering from the suspect. "At the scene of the car crash that killed Tom. A place you had no business being."

Steve's heart raced, threatening to burst from his chest as the inevitability of his fate loomed over him like a merciless storm. He knew the power of nature was unforgiving, but he hadn't anticipated the relentless pursuit of justice. The truth had a way of making itself known, much like the unyielding roots of ancient trees, breaking through the earth's surface no matter how deep they were buried.

"Steve Michael Bird," Detective Davis began, his voice steady

A TANGLED WEAVE: Death of a Child

yet stern, "Go ahead, take a look at this necklace." He held up the silver chain for Steve to see, allowing the fluorescent lights above to cast ominous shadows across the walls of the cramped room.

"Where... where did you find that?" Steve stammered, beads of sweat forming on his brow as his heart raced beneath the thin fabric of his shirt.

"I told you, right where you left it," Detective Davis replied matter-of-factly, his gaze never wavering from the man before him. "At the scene of the car crash that killed Tom Thompson."

Steve's mouth opened and closed like a fish gasping for air, but no sound escaped his lips. His mind raced with thoughts of the life he had tried so hard to build, now crumbling around him as the truth threatened to swallow him whole.

The silver pendant glinted under the harsh fluorescent lights, its intricate designs casting eerie shadows on the table between them. "This, Mr. Bird, is what ties you to the scene of Tom Thompson's accident."

Steve's gaze darted to the necklace and away, his eyes wide with fear as he struggled to find the right words. "I - I've never seen that before in my life," he stammered, but the tremor in his voice betrayed him. He knew, deep down, that denying the truth would only make things worse.

"Really?" Detective Davis asked, arching an eyebrow skeptically. "Because this very necklace was found tangled near the wreckage of the car, Steve. It's almost as if it was trying to tell us something, don't you think?"

The room seemed to spin as Steve stared at the damning piece of evidence, the weight of his guilt pressing down on him like the heavy hand of fate. He tried to suppress the memories that threatened to surface - the jealousy, the rage, the desperate need to control - but they clawed their way to the forefront of his mind, demanding to be acknowledged.

"The spirits of the ancestors are watching us, Steve," Detective Davis whispered, his voice low and somber. "They see our actions, our choices, and they know the truth of our hearts. You can't outrun your destiny, no matter how hard you try."

A bead of sweat trickled down Steve's temple, his heart pounding like a war drum in his chest. He clenched his fists, the nails digging into his palms as he tried to hold onto the last remnants of his crumbling facade.

"Detective, I swear, I don't know anything about that necklace," Steve insisted, desperation seeping into his voice. "You have to believe me."

But even as the words left his lips, he knew it was futile. The truth had been unearthed, and there was no escaping its grasp. As the tendrils of fate closed around him, Steve could only stare at the necklace on the table, an ominous reminder of the price he would pay for his actions.

The air in the interrogation room was thick with tension, the fluorescent lights casting stark shadows on the worn linoleum floor. Steve could feel the weight of Sam's gaze upon him, as heavy and oppressive as a storm cloud.

"Steve," Sam began, his voice measured and controlled like the calm before the tempest. "We found some gas receipts from the day of the crash as well, all from stations close to the scene." He slid the incriminating evidence across the table, each scrap of paper fluttering like autumn leaves caught in the wind.

"Anyone could have filled up at those stations," Steve retorted, anger and fear surging within him like a river breaking free from its banks. But even as he spoke, his mind raced with memories - the scent of gasoline, the cold metal of the pump in his hand, the foreboding whispers of the wind as it rustled through the trees.

"True, but how do you explain this?" Detective Davis pressed, a steely glint in his blue eyes that seemed to pierce straight through to Steve's soul. "The last receipt shows a purchase just moments before the accident occurred."

"Look, I... I don't know what you're talking about!" Steve stammered, his heart pounding like a desperate animal trapped in the jaws of fate. "I wasn't even there!"

"Your guilt is written on your face, Steve," Detective Davis replied, his voice low and relentless as the distant rumble of thunder. "The spirits of the ancestors see it, and they will not be silenced."

"Enough with the spirits!" Steve barked, his voice cracking like the ice beneath his feet. "You can't prove anything based on some stupid receipts!"

"Perhaps not," Detective Davis conceded, his words slow and deliberate like the creeping tide. "But combined with the necklace, it paints a rather damning picture, don't you think?"

Steve's jaw clenched as he stared at the damning evidence before him, his thoughts a whirlwind of fear and regret. He knew the power of the spirits - they could not be denied or defied, only appeased. And now, it seemed, their judgment had come for him, carried on the wings of fate.

"Steve," Detective Davis said softly, his voice echoing like the call of a bird through the silent forest. "It's time to stop running from the truth. It's time to face what you've done."

The room seemed to close in around Steve, the shadows clawing in his mind like hungry beasts. His hands shook as he looked up at the stoic face of Detective Davis, knowing that there would be no escape from the storm that was about to descend upon him.

"You have nothing on me, why would I have done this. He was my friend." Steve voice was shaking, the evidence they have was all circumstantial. They could not prove anything.

The interrogation room was an eerie place, despite the bright fluorescent lights that shone from the ceiling. The atmosphere was oppressive, and it seemed to Teresa like they were being watched by some entity that could never be seen.

Sam and Steve had been going back and forth for several hours now, but Steve still denied any involvement in Tom's death. He insisted he was innocent and had nothing to do with either of them.

Suddenly, as if on cue, the lights in the room began to flicker as though a spark was being ignited. The air grew cold, an eerie feeling settled down in the small, enclosed room. Neither Sam nor Steve was aware of the presence that hovered above them.

The cloud remained motionless for a few seconds before drifting into sight, moving forward towards Steve who slouched uncomfortably against his chair as if afraid to move due to its proximity. The cloud then slowly fell just above Steve's head.

Steve suddenly panicked and tried to move away from it, but he could not escape his fate- he had been caught red-handed by whatever this strange object was trying to prove its point! Sam too noticed what was happening but couldn't take his eyes away from Steve's reaction.

The cloud began to move slowly, forming a misty white barrier between Steve and Sam. It then gradually expanded into an image of the night Tom had been killed. Steve quickly became filled with guilt, pain, and sorrow as he remembered what he had done.

A TANGLED WEAVE: Death of a Child

The scene played out so clearly in Steve's mind- Tom's cries for help and his desperate final words. Steve had acted quickly with the knife, cutting through the brake lines of the car they were in. Then he'd made an excuse to remain behind at the station, aware that there was no more brake fluid left in the car.

As soon as this vision faded away, Steve froze in his own mind, and was still denying the truth. The cloud faded leaving Sam with a feeling of amazement. He made an excuse to leave the room.

Sam returned to the observation room where Officer Jenkins was watching the interrogation. He had a look of awe, disbelief, and confusion all at once. Sam knew exactly what he had seen but also knew that it would be hard to explain to anyone else.

"Did you see that?" Sam asked Jenkins in an urgent tone. "Play back the last 15 minutes of the video."

Officer Jenkins nodded and rewound the recording back to where Steve had become increasingly uncomfortable until the mysterious misty cloud appeared and seemed to be accusing him of something. Everyone was witness to his body language which said far more than he would ever confess aloud.

They watched, but the video footage revealed no clues to Steve's actions - his body language was all that gave away something was in that room. Sam retreated to a chair in the corner of the room, attempting to compose himself. He was certain something had happened inside there, yet the video showed nothing. What unknown force had taken place?

"What is it, Sam? What did you witness?" Jenkins could tell something was wrong by Steve's response. He couldn't quite place what the other man had seen, but he noticed Steve's hands flailing desperately in the air as if trying to grab at something that wasn't there.

The two decided it was time for a break, they could leave Steve to stew in his own mind. The mind that knew the truth about Tom's death but would not confess. Sam and Jenkins stepped out of the observation room and closed the door behind them. They needed to talk about what they had just seen in private.

As soon as they were alone, Jenkins turned to Sam and asked, "What did you see in there?"

Sam took a deep breath before beginning to recount his experience. "I saw a vision of Tom's death. Steve was there, and he cut the brake lines of the car they were in. He then made an excuse to stay behind at the station and let Tom die. Tom begged for his life, crying out for help, but Steve wouldn't listen."

Jenkins sat down heavily on a nearby chair, processing the information he had just heard. "That's a pretty damning vision. But we still need concrete evidence to prove it was Steve who killed Tom."

Sam nodded in agreement. "I know. But I can't ignore what I just saw. There's something in that room with him, accusing him of the crime. And he knows it too, which is why he's so defensive."

Jenkins rubbed his chin thoughtfully. "We need to find that evidence, whatever it takes. Maybe a closer investigation of the car will reveal something."

"The car has been gone for years, there is nothing to see there." Sam sat in his own thoughts.

Suddenly, an idea struck him. "But what about Steve's belongings? Maybe he kept something there that could incriminate him."

Jenkins looked at Sam with a spark of hope in his eyes. "That's a good idea. Let's go check it out. We still have the court order for the motel, we can see if we can add the Thompson home. "

They quickly made their way to Steve's motel, hoping to find something that could finally prove his guilt. As they searched through his belongings, they stumbled upon box he picked up from Teresa's the night before. Inside, they found a small metal box. Jenkins pried it open and gasped in shock at its contents.

"This...this is it. This is the evidence we've been searching for," he whispered.

Sam leaned in to take a closer look, his eyes widening as he saw what was inside the box. There was a folded piece of paper with a note from Bella Thompson in Steve's handwriting, as well as several photographs of him with Lucy.

Jenkins felt a sense of relief wash over him as he realized they finally had enough to put Steve behind bars for what he had done. They quickly gathered up the evidence and made their way back to the station.

As Sam re-entered the room, he was reminded how Steve had accomplished his goal of getting rid of Tom. His desire to have Teresa and Lucy all for himself had come true, allowing him to finally gain access to his inheritance money. He needed Steve to confess, it would be the easiest. It would prevent Teresa from having to relive this nightmare.

Sam's piercing blue eyes bore into Steve, demanding the truth with a steely resolve that seemed to pierce through his very soul. The air in the interrogation room was heavy with the weight of guilt and impending justice.

"How you are doing now, Steve?" Sam's confidence was stronger than ever. His strength of mind unwilling to accept anything but the truth.

"You need to get me out of here" Steve's eyes were bloodshot, the perspiration on his brow was dripping into his eyes. His hands bound to the table with handcuffs preventing him from wiping the sweat from his face. "I think it is time for me to call an attorney, I want my phone call."

Sam laughed as he sat down at the table. "Sure, I will have a phone brought in for you." He raised his hand above his head motioning to Jenkins in the observation room. "While we wait how about I just talk to you."

Sam laid out all the evidence in front Steve from the pictures, the necklace, the handwritten note to Bella, his grandmother. Sam knew he didn't stand a chance even with a lawyer. He sat in silence waiting for Jenkins to bring in the phone.

Steve made his call, and as he hung up the phone a sense of calm rushed over him. Steve was misled that all would be taken care of. The two men sat in silence waiting for his attorney to arrive. Sam knew that it was pointless, and Steve believed that all was circumstantial.

"So, Steve, while we wait. I was wondering how your family is doing. Have you spoken with them lately? I hear Bella is still as strong as ever." Sam knew he could not question him, but he could try to carry on a conversation. "I am not sure if I would genuinely want to live as long as she has. But one thing for sure, at least she is still around to watch her great grandchildren grow up. How old do you think she is anyway?"

Steve stayed quiet as he waited for his lawyer to arrive. When the attorney finally appeared, it was clear that the proof against Steve was considerable. The lawyer insisted on having a private conversation with Steve, so Sam left the room to provide an opportunity for discussion. He felt that Teresa deserved some sort of resolution, even if it wasn't for Lucy but for Tom.

It was not long before the door opened, and the attorney motioned for Sam to come back into the room.

"Let's just throw everything out here so we know what we are looking at." The attorney was straight forward, Sam appreciated that. He was getting tired after dealing with Steve all day.

Sam went over everything that was laid out in front of him. "Let's just jump to key points, we know the receipts and the necklace are circumstantial. But let us take a look at the family inheritance. This gives us the motive, with the letter Steve wrote to Bella and the photograph, this is a sure bet. Then we can move to phone calls placed within the last five years to family home. The Thompson family is ready to testify. I don't believe we need to go any further, do we Steve?"

As Steve stared into the unwavering gaze of Detective Davis, a sense of inevitability settled over him, like a raven perched atop a gravestone. He realized there would be no escape from the tangled web of fate he had woven for himself, no shelter from the relentless storm of retribution that was fast approaching.

"I..." he began, the word catching in his throat like a sob. His hands trembled, as if they too were struggling to come to terms with the gravity of his actions. "I can't... I can't..."

"Take a deep breath, Steve," Detective Davis urged, his voice both gentle and firm like the whisper of the wind through the trees. "Tell me the truth. It's time."

Tears brimmed in Steve's eyes, spilling down his cheeks like the first drops of rain in a long-awaited storm. The walls he had built around his guilt began to crumble, leaving him exposed and vulnerable before the unrelenting force of justice.

"Steve," Detective Davis said firmly, every syllable a hammer blow against the fragile wall of lies that surrounded Steve's crimes. "I need you to be honest with me. I need a confession."

"Alright," he choked out, each syllable a plea for mercy in the face of destiny's judgment. "I did it. I was there that night. I... I couldn't stop myself."

"Thank you, Steve," Detective Davis replied, his eyes never leaving the broken man before him. "Now we can begin to set things right."

A TANGLED WEAVE: Death of a Child

The plea struck a chord within Steve, resonating with the dark melody of fear and guilt that had haunted him since that fateful night. He swallowed hard, feeling the enormity of his actions pressing down upon him like a storm cloud ready to burst.

"Look, Detective," he stammered, desperation clawing at the edges of his voice. "You have to understand, I didn't want any of this to happen. I just... I couldn't control myself."

"Your inability to control yourself doesn't change what you've done, Steve," Detective Davis replied, unyielding as the great oak in the face of a raging storm. "Face your actions and accept the consequences."

"Thank you for being honest, Steve," Detective Davis said softly, never breaking eye contact as he bore witness to the man's surrender to fate. "Now we can begin the process of setting things right."

Detective Davis stood, his piercing blue eyes never leaving Steve's tear-streaked face. The room seemed to close in around them, the walls whispering silent secrets as the weight of the truth bore down upon them both. "You have the right to remain silent," he began, the words resonating like a solemn oath.

"Anything you say can and will be used against you in a court of law." Steve's breath hitched at the finality of the statement, the reality of his situation sinking in like a stone cast into a dark, unfathomable lake. "You have the right to an attorney. If you cannot afford one, one will be provided for you." Detective Davis's voice was steady, each word a reminder of the inevitable march of justice. He placed a comforting hand on Steve's trembling shoulder, an anchor amidst the turbulent sea of emotions that had consumed him.

"Do you understand these rights I have just read to you?" Detective Davis asked, his gaze unwavering as it searched deep within Steve's soul, seeking the fragments of remorse and hope hidden beneath the layers of guilt and fear.

Steve swallowed hard, his throat raw from the onslaught of tears and despair that had threatened to choke him moments before. "Yes," he breathed, the single syllable laden with the weight of a thousand unspoken regrets.

"Alright then, let's go." Detective Davis gently guided Steve to his feet, his firm grip a testament to his dedication to protecting those who had been wronged by fate's cruel hand. Together, they crossed the threshold of the interrogation room, leaving behind the shadows of the past to face the uncertain future that lay ahead.

The hallway stretched out before them like a winding path through a dense forest, its twists and turns obscured by the enveloping darkness. As they moved forward, Steve could feel the heavy silence pressing in on him, suffocating him with the knowledge that his fate was no longer his own. In the back of his mind, Steve thought, at least they don't know about my second wife, or he didn't dare think it.

CHAPTER 18

Sam made his way to Teresa's house, feeling a sense of dread as he walked up the steps. He had dreaded this moment ever since they had started their investigation into Steve. Now, not only did he have to tell her about Steve's arrest, but he also had to tell her that they still hadn't been able to find Lucy's killer.

He took a deep breath before knocking on the door. Teresa opened the door with a sigh of relief when she saw Sam standing there. She knew it must be shocking news if he was here and welcomed him in without saying a word.

Sam sat down in the living room and cleared his throat before speaking. He explained all that had happened and told Teresa that Steve had been arrested and confessed to Tom's murder as well as several other charges related to his inheritance money from the Thompson family.

"I'm so sorry," he murmured apologetically before adding, "We have Steve for Tom's murder. He has confessed." Sam took a deep breath, before continuing, "His alibi for Lucy's murder is solid. I don't think he killed her, with the inheritance written they was it is... It would not be in his best interest to kill her. There must be something we are missing. I have not given up; we will find however did this."

Teresa looked away from Sam and stared into space for what seemed like an eternity before responding. Finally, she nodded slowly as tears began streaming down her face and spoke in a soft, yet strong voice: "Thank you for doing your best."

Sam gave her an understanding smile before standing up and heading towards the door. As his hand touched the doorknob, Teresa spoke again: "Find them," she said firmly. "Find whoever did this."

Sam nodded solemnly in agreement before leaving Theresa's home that day; determined to find justice for both Tom and Lucy.

He began reaching out to the people closest to Lucy. He called her friends and family members, looking for any clues that could lead him to her killer.

A TANGLED WEAVE: Death of a Child

******

Elizabeth and Maggie joined Teresa in her kitchen, to plan for a candlelight ceremony honoring Tom's life. It was now clear his accident wasn't an accident at all, but rather murder. Teresa wanted to announce to the community that she was still there, standing firm and ready to find out what happened to Lucy through whatever means necessary.

The ladies concluded that they should post on social media, spread the news in their church, and distribute flyers to the places the family used to frequent. Elizabeth proposed asking for donations to help Teresa make ends meet; since Steve had left, she was struggling to keep up with bills from only one source of income. Teresa had been working less frequently in recent months, as she found it hard to think of anything other than her own problems.

Teresa agreed to the donations, she could use the help. Elizabeth agreed to talk to Father Michael about borrowing tables and chairs for the ceremony from the church. Teresa wants everything held at the house.

Maggie, on the other hand, wasn't too thrilled about hosting the event at their house. "What if Lucy shows up during the ceremony?" she asked.

"It might not be a bad thing," Elizabeth replied. "At least it will let people know that Teresa has someone powerful standing by her side."

Teresa felt a pang of loneliness when she did not sense Lucy's presence in the house, but she was comforted by the thought that Tom and Lucy were together. She assumed this must have been all that Lucy needed to find resolution. After all, Teresa had just returned home from her visit with Steve's family.

"I am not worried about Lucy; I have not felt her spirit in the house since I got back from the trip to see Steve's family. Maybe that is all she needed, for resolution for Tom."

Maggie, Elizabeth, and Teresa spent the next few days preparing for the candlelight vigil; setting up tables and chairs, planting flowers in the yard, and writing invitations for all their friends and family to come celebrate Tom's life.

The day of the ceremony came quickly, and people from all

over town showed up to pay their respects. As they lit the candles one by one, a familiar presence made itself known. It was Lucy. Everyone could feel her presence in the room as if she were there with them that day. Tears filled Teresa's eyes as she thought of Tom and all that he had been through only to have his life taken away far too soon.

Father Michael greeted the attendees, "It's wonderful to see all of you here to support Tom, Lucy, and Teresa. Those of you I already know from church or our local community, it is nice to see your faces. For those who do not know me, I want to let you know that we are all family here. Tom was a dear friend to me and a deacon in our church. I don't plan to give a full sermon, but instead I'd like each one of you to take time to share stories about Tom and Lucy. We have a recorder running if anyone wants Teresa to listen to their reminiscences later on. Just let us know if you would prefer this conversation not to be recorded. Now, who would like to go first?"

Elizabeth stood up and spoke first, describing how she had known Lucy since she was a baby. Elizabeth talked about how kind and selfless Lucy always was, putting others before herself without a thought. Her words brought both comfort and sadness to Teresa - comfort that her daughter had been so beloved, but sadness at knowing she would never be able to hug Lucy again.

Maggie was next, talking about how amazing it was to witness Lucy grow up in their small town. She spoke of how proud she was of Lucy's for her drawings. She spoke about how her drawings would always make people smile Maggie's words were a bittersweet reminder of what could have been if not for this tragedy.

A shy woman in the back of the room slowly raised her hand. Father Michael nodded to her and invited her to come up to the front.

"I didn't know Tom very well," the woman began, her voice trembling slightly. "But I remember the first time I met him. It was at a church potluck, and I was a new member of the congregation. Tom saw that I was sitting alone and came over to talk to me. He made me feel so welcome and included. From that day on, he always made a point to say hello to me and check in on how I was doing. Even though I didn't know him well, he left a lasting impact on me, and I will always be grateful for his kindness."

The backyard was silent for a moment before a man from

across the room spoke up. "Tom and I went to high school together," he said. "We played football together, and let me tell you, Tom was one tough son of a gun on the field. But off the field, he had the biggest heart of anyone I knew. He was always willing to help out a friend, no matter what. And when Lucy came into his life, it was like a light turned on in him. He was so happy with her, and you could see how much he loved her. It's not fair that he was taken from us so soon, but I know he's up there watching over us, just like he watched over us on the football field."

As more people shared their memories of Tom and Lucy, Teresa felt a sense of peace come over her. She realized that Tom had touched so many lives.

George moved to the front of the crowd. The old man that Lucy had grown so fond of was now speaking. "I didn't know Tom, I met Lucy after he passed away. She was such a delight in my life. We spent many afternoons at the library where I would read to her, and she would sketch pictures for me. She was always so cheerful and full of joy - she told me once that all she ever wanted was to be close to her father," tears running down his face as he glanced towards the sky, "Now I believe you have your wish, my dear; our town will take good care of your mother.

This moment put tears into Teresa's eyes, she could no longer control her anguish and sadness. She had lost her husband and now her daughter was gone too. It was too much to bear. She stood up and walked towards the house where George was standing. He looked at her with a sympathetic expression.

"I'm sorry for your loss," he said, placing a hand on her shoulder.

Teresa couldn't hold back the tears any longer. She broke down crying, feeling like she had lost everything that mattered to her.

George hugged her tightly. "It's okay, let it out."

As she cried in George's arms, memories of Lucy flooded her mind. She remembered the way Lucy used to sing around the house and dance in the living room. She remembered their weekend trips to the river, fishing, camping, and roasting marshmallows by the fire.

But most of all, she remembered the love that Lucy had for her. Even in her darkest moments, Lucy had always been there to support her and make her feel better. And now, with Lucy gone, Teresa didn't know how she was going to move on.

But as George held her, Teresa realized that she wasn't alone. She had friends and family members who loved her and would be there for her no matter what. And even though Lucy was gone, her memory would live on in the hearts of those who loved her.

With that realization, Teresa slowly began to breathe again. The pain was still there, but it was bearable now. She would get through this, one day at a time. And somehow, she knew that Lucy would be proud of her strength.

Several others stood up to speak that night including Jenkins and Sam. The ceremony ran late into the evening. Once everyone had left, Teresa took a moment to reflect on all that had happened since Lucy had gone missing. Despite her sadness and loss, she had gained strength from her friends and family together supporting her mission of finding out who was responsible for taking away so many innocent lives.

Teresa was just shutting off the lights when there was a soft knock at the door. Lucy turned on the hallway light before opening the door for Sam.

"I know it is very late, I did not want to disturb you," Sam paused for a moment looking into the house. "It was a beautiful ceremony tonight. I only wanted to make sure you were okay. I know it was a hard night."

"I am okay, just very tired. Do you need anything?"

"No, like I said, I am just checking on you." Sam knew it was late. He was not sure why he stopped. "Have a good night, call me if you need anything."

Walking away from the house, Sam could kick himself for coming back so late. He really had no idea why he was there. Something just told him to stop.

CHAPTER 19

The wind rustles the trees like crumpled paper, crunching its torn leaves with a symphony of emptiness. The night air was crisp and cool, and Teresa couldn't help but shiver as she walked to her car. She didn't want to go home just yet, her drives through the countryside were her way to relax. She needed time to be alone with her thoughts. She wished that Lucy was there, she almost missed the objects moving around the house, the sudden coolness in the room, the whispers of her voice.

The next morning, Teresa woke with a heavy heart. She lay in bed thinking of the last time she had seen Lucy, and all the memories they had shared. She remembered the spaghetti that Lucy always loved to eat for dinner, and the conversation they had about Steve, the man who had murdered Tom.

Tears began streaming down her face as she thought of the pain that her daughter must have endured before her death. She wished she could do something to bring Lucy back, to make things right again. But it was too late now. All she could do was grieve and move forward with her life without her baby girl.

Slowly, Teresa got out of bed and made her way downstairs. The house felt unusually cold and quiet, like it was missing something essential to its lifeblood. She grabbed a blanket off the couch and wrapped it around herself tightly, trying to ward off the chill that seemed to permeate everything around her.

Outside, the tree branches beat against the windows with a clatter, making a ghostly sound that scratched across the glass. Teresa shivered in fear as she remembered how fragile life really was, how one moment she had been living in joyous bliss with Lucy by her side, only for it all to be snatched away from them in an instant by someone else's hand—someone who seemed beyond justice or retribution.

It had been almost a year since her death, Teresa was frozen in time, unable to move forward. The first six months were built in with trying to get by day by day. The next six months were discovery, Lucy's presence in the house, the discovery of Steve's family and the accident that was ultimately his murder. Teresa was pleased that Steve was behind bars. She needed the closure but now Lucy. Was it going to be another six months? Or was she going to have to wait years like she did with Tom?

******

Father Michael waited outside Teresa's home, he needed to find the courage to knock on the door. He knew that the previous night was extremely hard on her. He hated to see his congregation suffer. Suffering over the loss of a child could be the worst. He knew the best way he could help her was to find a way to get her to move on with her life.

Teresa was on her third cup of coffee when Father Michael finally knocked at the door. As Teresa rose to answer it, her mind wondered over the night before. It was a pleasing to have the community behind her. She was not feeling at peace, if she could just find out who took her child from her, she could continue to live.

"Hello, Father Michael, I was not aware you were coming over this morning. Please come in." Lucy opened the door.

"I wanted to speak to you about the library." Father Michael had talked with George the night before. George was still spending his afternoons at the library. He thought if he could bring these two closers that could be a key to bringing Teresa back into the world of the living.

"Okay, what about?

"I thought maybe doing some volunteer work would be good for you. You should lean on your community right now, Lucy. We are here to help you." Father Michael was always sincere in his words. Teresa knew that he meant to help.

Father Michael could see that Teresa was hesitant. He knew it could take some time for her to be comfortable going out and interacting with the world again. Just like he told her, it might just take some time.

"It's alright if you don't feel ready yet, Teresa. You can just come to the library when you are feeling better, even just for an hour or two. You will find solace in reading books and maybe when those memories come back, you can leave them there on the shelves where they belong. I will ensure that the library provides whatever materials you need to read.

"Seeing the light in Teresa's eyes, Father Michael knew she was considering his suggestion. With a smile, he handed her a leaflet containing information about volunteering at the library and walked toward the front door.

Opening the front door, a delivery driver was in the process of knocking with a package for Teresa that needed signing. She wrote down her name before bidding farewell to the priest.

With box in hand, Teresa headed over to the kitchen. The town listed on the package's return address was the same place of Steve's family; she assumed it had come from his relatives.

Teresa held the mysterious package with both hands, wondering what it could be. She had no idea where and who it was from - all that was written on the return address was a Texas postcode. If it was from Steve's family, why did they only send it to her? What if the parcel contained something she didn't want to see?

Taking a deep breath, she slowly opened the box and almost gasped when she saw what was inside. There were several items: a letter, some photos, and even a small toy that appeared to be handmade. Carefully picking up the letter, Teresa read its contents with tears in her eyes:

Dear Teresa,

We are sorry for your loss. We know this must be a challenging time for you and we wanted to let you know that you're not alone. We only wish we could have met you and Lucy sooner. Enclosed are some drawings that Steve had sent to us. We hope these will bring you comfort. Please consider us family, if you need anything at all, we are here.

We have enclosed a piece of the family's estate. The crystal rocking horse was meant to be a gift for Lucy if we ever got a chance to meet her. As a family, we felt this should go to you. Please take this in her name as a gesture of our condolences.

We love you and will always be here for you if ever need anything. Please take care of yourself.
Sincerely,
Bella

A TANGLED WEAVE: Death of a Child

Overwhelmed with emotions, Teresa read the letter with tears streaming down her face as she realized how much they all missed Lucy. In realization too of what really happened - that Steve had taken away their grandchild - guilt and sadness came crashing over Teresa like a wave. But at the same time, she was grateful for being able to read these heartfelt letters and connect with them in some way despite not being able to see them physically.

As the tears continued to run down Teresa's cheeks, she finished reading the letter; she had felt warmth in the idea that this family would think of her at this time. They had to know that Steve was in jail, that she helped put him there. She hugged the letter close to her chest as she looked at the other items in the box. The rocking horse must have been worth a fortune. They did not have to do that, but she was incredibly grateful that they did.

Teresa thought about this gift, if this family could put aside their grief to send her such an amazing gift maybe she could give a gift to community that had been here for her. Maybe Father Michael was right, maybe she should start small by doing some volunteer work. It would get her out of the house and in a small way give her a purpose again.

The thought of helping others in the name of Lucy gave Teresa a newfound sense of purpose. This could be her way of honoring her, even though she was no longer here. She knew that this wouldn't bring her back, but it would certainly help bring some happiness into the lives of others and that mattered most.

The library would be the perfect place, it was where Lucy found so much happiness. She enjoyed spending days walking the isles and looking at all the different books. Many of her drawings were of books, stacked in unusual ways, propped up in corners, or just laying open on the tables. There more Teresa thought amount this, the more she knew she had to do it.

The next morning, Teresa woke with a newfound determination. She had to put her life back together, for the sake of Lucy. She had no idea how she was going to do it, but she was determined to try. After taking a hot shower and having some breakfast, she set out for the library - a place where she used to spend time with Steve.

When Teresa arrived at the library, it had not yet opened its doors. A small crowd had mustered outside, and when she mentioned she was there to volunteer, one of the younger women asked if she could help her find a couple books once they got inside. She was surprised by how useful she was already feeling before even entering the building.

When the library finally opened its doors, Teresa stepped inside with a newfound sense of purpose. The young librarian behind the desk gave her a warm welcome as she explained her daily tasks and showed Teresa around the facility. She could tell she was excited to have someone help her during her shifts; someone she could talk to about books or just chat about life in general while they worked.

Throughout that day, Teresa worked hard alongside her new friend, helping her organize books on shelves and restock any supplies that were running low while also being available for customers who needed assistance finding certain titles or required information about their local library services. By the end of her shift, Teresa felt accomplished - like she had made a difference in someone else's life today - even though it was only a small contribution compared with all of Tom's wonderful work in their community before his passing.

That night as Teresa lay in bed thinking about her day at the library - all that she had done and how much more she wanted to accomplish - she smiled contentedly knowing that Lucy would be proud of what she was doing if she were here.

As she fell asleep, not even noticing the storm outside, her dreams took to her to happier times. In her dreams, she woke up to the sound of Tom's voice, telling her they had to hurry if they were going to make it to the river before sunrise. She felt a surge of joy and excitement as she remembered how they used to sneak out of their houses early in the morning just to watch the sunrise by the shore.

She got dressed quickly and ran outside to find Tom waiting for her, holding two bicycles. He had a mischievous grin on his face as he handed her one of the bikes and they rode off together, their laughter ringing through the empty streets.

As they reached the river, the sun was barely starting to peek above the horizon and the sky was painted in shades of pink and orange. They left their bikes aside and sat on the sand, watching the fish jump in the water.

Tom put his arm around her, and she leaned her head on his

shoulder, feeling safe and loved. For a moment, everything was perfect, and there was no pain or sadness in her heart.

Suddenly, a loud noise broke through her dream, making her jolt awake. She realized it was thunder - the storm outside was growing stronger. She sat up in bed and looked out the window, watching as lightning illuminated the sky.

Then she noticed something else - a message written on the glass, seemingly drawn by someone's finger. It said: "I miss you, Mom. Love, Lucy."

Teresa's heart swelled with love and gratitude as tears filled her eyes. She knew that Lucy was with her, even if she couldn't see her, and that she would always be there to support her.

CHAPTER 20

As the leaves began to change color and the nights grew colder, Teresa found that her life was slowly starting to move forward. She continued her volunteer at the library, helping people with their research and organizing bookshelves and catalogs. Her evenings were spent in an unusual way - she had started hanging Lucy's drawings all over the house, tucking them into every nook and corner that could hold a frame or paper.

It gave her some comfort to see Lucy's artwork around her, as if it made their home warmer somehow. Although Lucy wasn't around physically, Teresa felt like she was still there in spirit.

She also made an effort to stay connected with Elizabeth, Maggie, and Father Michael on a regular basis. They had become a source of support for her during this grim time, making sure she was taking care of herself and not falling into despair. Elizabeth even took her out for lunch once a week, just so they could talk about anything other than what had happened.

Despite all of this, Teresa still needed closure – she still needed answers as to who had taken Lucy away from her. She kept thinking of different scenarios and ideas as to what might have happened that night, but nothing seemed concrete enough. It was frustrating knowing that no one had any idea where Lucy could be or who could have taken her - it made it seem like she had simply vanished into thin air without leaving any traces behind.

This thought haunted Teresa late at night while she tried to sleep - but every morning when the sun came up again, hope renewed itself inside of her heart and she knew that someday soon she would have all the answers she needed.

On a chilly morning, there was a knock at the front door, Teresa was shocked to see Sam and Office Jenkins at her doorstep. Sam's tall, sturdy figure stood strong and resolute. A determined look glimmered in his eyes. It had already been a month since she had last spoken to him; the investigation had gone cold, and Tom had already taken a plea bargain with a 25-year sentence. There were no more leads to follow.

But something had changed for Sam, and he was now

convinced that Lucy's murder had been a targeted hit. He told her about his suspicions concerning Steve's brother; how they had recently discovered he was in town that night. Teresa was taken aback by this latest information - could it be true? Was there really someone out there who wanted to hurt Lucy so badly?

"Teresa, just would just take a minute. There are some interviews being held as we speak, and we need to bring you up to date." Jenkins' voice was more authoritative than normal.

"Sure, come in. Would you like some coffee?" Teresa led the pair into the kitchen and poured them coffee before sitting at the table.

Sam began to explain the discoveries of Steve's brother being in town the night of Lucy's death. Sam was convinced that Lucy's murder had been a targeted hit. He told her about his suspicions concerning Steve's brother; how they had recently discovered he was in town that night. Teresa was taken aback by this added information - could it be true? Was there really someone out there who wanted to hurt Lucy so badly?

Sam continued to explain that the night of Lucy's murder, he had tracked Tony to an old motel north of town. He had checked the guest register and discovered Tony had booked a room there a few weeks prior. He had also spoken to some of the staff at the bar and they confirmed that both Steve and Tony were there that night - but Steve failed to mention his brother when asked for his alibi.

It was then that Sam realized something was off - what if Tony had slipped out that night? What if he had murdered Lucy and then gone back to the bar? Teresa was shocked by this new revelation - could it be true? Was someone out there who wanted to hurt Lucy so badly?

"Sam, please don't get ahead of yourself." Jenkins interrupted Sam for a moment. "Teresa, the Kansas City police are questioning Tony at this time. We are here to make you aware of the findings. There is no physical evidence at this time tying Tony to the crime."

Sam began to move over nervously in his seat before standing up. "May I use your restroom."

"Yes, of course, you know where it is." Teresa was concerned about the way Sam was acting. It was not normal for him to be so blunt and rattled.

As Sam left, Jenkins revealed his concern for his partner's

wellbeing. He noticed that Sam was getting more distant from the police force, dedicating too many hours to investigate Lucy's death on his own. Jenkins was concerned about the strain this case had taken on his mental health.

"Jenkins, I appreciated you looking out for Sam, he has been a good friend through all this." Teresa was now concerned about Sam too. "When we will know anything for sure, about Tony, I mean?"

"Hopefully, very soon." Jenkins watched as Sam walked back into the room.

"Sam, why would Tony kill, Lucy? What would he have to gain?" Teresa remembered meeting Tony during her trip to see Steve's family. He was a rough man. but she didn't see him as being that violent. Teresa told Sam and Jenkins about her visit to him. She explained the conversation. He had not mentioned to her that he was in town or that he had spoken to Steve that night.

Sam leaned forward; his eyes intense. "Maybe he had a grudge against Lucy. Maybe he saw her as a threat to his part of the inheritance. Or maybe it was just a random act of violence."
Teresa shuddered at the thought of someone wanting to hurt Lucy for no reason. She couldn't wrap her head around the idea that there were people out there who were capable of such evil acts.

Jenkins noticed the troubled expression on Sam's face and placed a comforting hand on his shoulder. "We'll get to the bottom of this, Sam. We won't rest until we find whoever is responsible for Lucy's death."

Sam nodded silently, grateful for his friend's support. He knew that he couldn't let his emotions cloud his judgement. He needed to focus on finding the killer and bringing them to justice.

Teresa questioned the two officers, trying to get them to reveal more information. "What did Steve have to say about those phone calls? Can you tell us what they discussed?"

"Only that he was trying to reunite with his brother. Steve thought the inheritance coming to him would give both the brothers a chance at a clean slate. Steve was planning on sharing the money with him." Sam couldn't help but feel a pang of guilt. He had investigated the relationship between Tony and Steve, He knew it was a strained kinship, but he had never taken the time to delve deeper into the issue. Now, it seemed as though that neglect may have cost precious time to go by.

A TANGLED WEAVE: Death of a Child

Jenkins' phone rang and he stepped out of the room. Teresa looked at Sam and could see the pain in his eyes. "What are you thinking?" she asked him softly.

Sam let out a deep sigh. "I'm thinking that I should have made more of an effort to understand Steve's relationship with his brother. Maybe then we would have been able to move forward more quickly."

Teresa shook her head. "Don't blame yourself, Sam. You couldn't have known that something like this would happen."

Sam looked up at her, his eyes filled with emotion. "I just can't shake the feeling that there was something more going on between the brothers. Why would Tony come back after all these years if he had no interest in reconciling with Steve?"

A cold gust of air swept through the kitchen, and Teresa knew Sam felt it too. The burst of air filled the room with a swirling mist, a fog of tiny particles that glowed in the faint light from the outside streetlamps. As they danced around the room, they cast frightening shadows on the walls and furniture. The wind pounded against the backdoor, making it shake in its frame. The air carried with it the smell of rain and earth, an aroma that was both comforting and melancholy. There was also a hint of something sweet, like wildflowers in bloom, but the smell vanished as quickly as it had come. It was Lucy's, Teresa would remember the smell of her daughter forever. Suddenly, the lights flickered off and a thick darkness descended on the room.

Sam leapt from his chair in surprise. "Don't worry Sam, it's just Lucy. She wants us to know she is here with us," Teresa said calmly. She was used to her daughter's visits now; not as often as before, but she still enjoyed them on the days they came. Knowing today was the anniversary of Lucy's death made her certain that she'd make an appearance.

Jenkins hung up his phone and walked into the kitchen in the middle of the scene, "What the hell is going on in here?" He had witnessed something very strange. He watched as Sam jumped from his seat. He seen a cloud move through the kitchen. "Is this what you saw during the interview with Steve?" Jenkins was shaking not knowing how to react.

"We need to go, there is a conversance call schedule at the station with Kansas City, we need to prepare for." Still shaking, Jenkins lead Sam towards the door.

"Are you going to be okay here?" Sam turns to Teresa; he was now showing the same concern she felt during the months before.

"I am fine, please let me know what you find out." Teresa held the door and watched as the two stepped off the porch and walked to their car. They both continued looking back at the house. Not sure what they had just witnessed.

******

It was the day of Lucy's passing; Teresa knew that there would be activity in the house. The visit from Jenkins and Sam in the morning was surprising to say the least. Teresa thought about the visit with Tony, he seemed to be an okay person, a bit rough on the edges. She knew he had been in jail, but murder just didn't make sense.

Lucy picked up the phone and dialed the Bird home. "Hello, this is Teresa. Is Bella available." There was a short pause on the other end of the phone.

"I am sorry, Teresa, but Bella passed this morning. The family is not taking phone calls now. I can give them a message for you."

Teresa had spoken with Bella a couple of times since she received the crystal rocking horse. It was just a nice gesture; Teresa tried to call and check on them once a week. "Please just tell them I called, and my thoughts are with them." As Teresa hung up the phone the breeze had returned in the house.

"Lucy, I am here. Did you know about Bella? She would have been your great grandmother." Teresa spoke to Lucy like one day she would answer. She knew it would never truly happen, but it brought her peace.

Teresa sat on the old sofa waiting for another sign of Lucy's presence. The air grew colder, but this was a different feeling, it was not the calm that Lucy would give her. It was mysterious, dark quite dark but chilling. Teresa stood up and began walking through the house.

Teresa stood paralyzed in the hallway, her legs refusing to move. The shadows that moved around the walls began to take on a sinister form. She could feel a presence within them, an ancient and powerful force that had been summoned by something, or someone.

Suddenly there was a loud crash and all of the pictures on the walls were ripped down, their frames smashed against the floor. Teresa gasped in horror as she felt a chill run through her body. What was going on? Who or what was doing this?

Teresa gasped in horror as she felt a chill run through her body. She knew it was Lucy, coming to tell her something. She tried to control her breathing, but it felt like she could barely move.

The sound of a chair crashing into a wall filled the house and Teresa heard Lucy's scream of agony. Teresa felt a bolt of fear shoot through her. She had never heard such a bloodcurdling scream before. It was as if Lucy was being tortured by something beyond this world. She stumbled forward, the floorboards creaking beneath her feet. She reached the end of the hallway and peered into the room where the noise had come from. What she saw made her heart sink?

In front of her, the rocking horse was moving back and forth on its own. It was as if Lucy's spirit had taken over the toy and was trying to communicate with Teresa. The room was freezing cold, and Teresa felt herself shiver uncontrollably. The air around her seemed to be charged with energy, and she could feel an unseen force pulling at her. As she took a step forward, the rocking horse suddenly stopped moving.

"Lucy? Why are you doing this?" Teresa wailed in distress. The destructive behavior continued as Teresa fought through the chaos to reach the front door. She tugged and yanked, but it wouldn't open. Teresa reluctantly crawled to the phone on the floor, defeated.

Teresa sat paralyzed in the hallway, her legs refusing to move. The shadows that moved around the walls began to take on a sinister form. She could feel a presence within them, an ancient and powerful force that had been summoned by something, or someone.

Her first thought was to call Elizabeth and Maggie for support; she knew they would understand what she was going through. She dialed their number hoping that they could come quick enough to help her out of this situation.

The phone felt hot to the touch as if to burn her hand. Tears streaming down her face, Teresa stammered out an urgent plea for assistance. "Help! Lucy is tearing up the house. Please, hurry!"

Elizabeth could hear the terror in her friends' voice, "I am on my way." Elizabeth could hear the cries in the background. It was like that of a thousand voices carried inside fog horns, it moaned and groaned, it roared. The voices on the phone were unrecognizable.

A TANGLED WEAVE: Death of a Child

Elizabeth was terrible as she hung up the phone, running out of the house to help her friend.

Elizabeth and Maggie stood outside the house staring at what could not be described. They had tried every door and window to get into the house. Running from front to back, there was no way to enter. They arrived at a surreal sight, there was a huge dark cloud hovering above the house. The lights were frantically flashing through all the windows. The streams coming from inside the house were echoing into the night.

Elizabeth and Maggie exchanged nervous glances, wondering what they should do. They had never encountered anything like this before. They knew they had to stay strong for Teresa, but how?

Suddenly, they heard a shrill scream coming from inside the house. It was Teresa! Without thinking, Elizabeth and Maggie ran towards the back of the house, where the scream had come from. As they reached the backyard, they saw something that made their blood run cold.

Lucy was hovering under the old oak tree, her body twisted and contorted in unnatural ways. Her eyes were glowing red, and her mouth was open wide as if she were screaming, but no sound came out. Elizabeth and Maggie stood frozen in terror as Lucy's body began to convulse violently.

"Lucy, please stop!" Teresa's voice rang out from somewhere inside the house. "Whatever you're doing, it's not too late to stop!"

But Lucy didn't seem to hear her. Her body continued to thrash around in mid-air, causing the ground beneath them to shake. The sky above them grew dark, and a feeling of dread settled over the three friends like a heavy fog.

Then, just as suddenly as the chaos had begun, it stopped. Lucy's body disappeared, and the sky cleared up. Elizabeth and Maggie rushed to the backdoor, checking to see if Teresa was okay. She was kneeling on the floor with several of Lucy's drawings crumpled in her hands.

They decided it wasn't safe for Teresa to stay alone so they called Father Michael. He waited for the three in the church sanctuary. Elizabeth and Maggie comforted Teresa and said prayers Father Michael asked about how long this had been going on and why the women had not mentioned it before.

"Nothing like this has happened before, Lucy has always

been a comfort to me." Teresa was calm but still unnerved by what was happening in the house.

"Are you sure this is Lucy? It could be someone else, or Lucy could be changing with the amount of time she is not at rest."

When Father Michael appeared at the door, Elizabeth, and Maggie both exhaled in relief. He had been an immense help to their family before, especially Elizabeth and Teresa. After they explained what had happened with Lucy, Father Michael was astonished—he had heard of other priests encountering spirits, but never anything like this.

"I am going to make some calls," he said gravely. "Teresa, you should not return home tonight. Can you stay here with Elizabeth?"

Without hesitation, Teresa nodded her head in agreement; she was still shaken by the night's events. As Father Michael began making his calls to seek assistance, Elizabeth and Maggie discussed the cleansing ritual they had implemented while Teresa was away from the house. Father Michael paid close attention; his eyebrows pulled together as he intently listened. They were all waiting for an answer and putting their trust in God's plan.

"It's a possibility that the ritual you conducted earlier only made the spirits angry," he said. "It could have been their way of warning you about what happened tonight."

Elizabeth narrated the details of what she had discovered about the old house, about its prior occupants. Elizabeth and Maggie shared an apprehensive glance. "What should we do now?" Elizabeth asked.

Father Michael stood up; his demeanor solemn. "We need to carry out a more extensive purification ritual," he declared. "And we need to bring in an authority who can help us identify exactly what we're facing."

"No!" Teresa shouted in alarm, "There has to be another alternative. Lucy needs her rest; I don't want her harmed! I will not have strangers chanting inside my home." Teresa was grief-stricken by the suggestion of burning personal items. "If these are bad spirits, they must be associated with something here." Teresa described the attic to Father Michael—where they had placed everything when they had moved in—and suggested that maybe they could get rid of everything by setting fire to it.

The group ultimately decided that they would investigate the attic the following day; for now, they agreed it was best to stay away from the premises.

CHAPTER 21

Tom's heaven had grown cold, the sky had turned grey and dark. Tom stepped out of his paradise home to find Lucy staring at the tablet. He had asked her several times not to watch it unless the two were together. Tom knew that Lucy needed to find peace, he was trying but she was stuck in the house with Teresa.

Tom sat beside his daughter, "You do not fully understand what you are doing Lucy. You must be at peace so that you can have your heavenly home. This is only going to end up bad for you."

"But look at what they are doing daddy, they don't understand me." Lucy's anger was escalating. "I have tried to tell them, but they won't listen."

"Lucy, are you not happy here?" Tom's fear of what could happen if his daughter could not find peace was growing. He knew that no good would come of her actions. He knew that punishment for interacting too much with the living was dangerous. He needed to find a way to show this to Lucy before it was too late.

Tom sat there in silence, contemplating his next move. He knew he had to talk to Lucy about the dangers of what she was doing, but he didn't know how to approach the topic without upsetting her. Finally, he took a deep breath and turned to her.

"Lucy, honey, I need to talk to you about something important."

Lucy looked up from the tablet, her eyes flashing with anger. "What is it, Dad? Can't you see I'm busy trying to help mommy?"

Tom hesitated for a moment, gathering his thoughts. "I know you want to help, sweetheart. But what you're doing...it's not safe. You could get into trouble."

Lucy rolled her eyes. "I'm already dead, Dad. What are they going to do, kill me again?"

Tom winced at his daughter's callous remark. He knew that Lucy was struggling to come to terms with her death, but he couldn't let her continue down this dangerous path.

"Lucy, you don't understand. You're putting yourself and

others in danger by meddling with the living. The consequences could be severe."

Lucy's expression softened, and she looked at her father with new understanding. "What do you mean, Dad? What consequences?"

Tom took a deep breath, trying to find the right words. "There are rules in the afterlife, Lucy. Rules we have to follow. And one of those rules is that we can't interfere with the living. If we do, there can be...consequences. And they're not pleasant."

Lucy frowned, clearly unconvinced. "But what about Mommy? Don't I have a right to help her?"

Tom sighed, his heart breaking for his daughter. "I know you do, sweetheart. And I understand how hard it is to let go. But we have to trust that your mother will find her own peace, in her own time and in her own way. We can't force it."

Lucy's eyes welled up with tears. "But what if she never finds peace, Dad? What if she's stuck here forever?"

Tom took his daughter's hands in his own, looking deep into her eyes. "We have to have faith, Lucy. Faith that everything happens for a reason. That even when we don't understand why things happen, there is a greater plan at work. Your mother's soul is on its own journey, just like ours. And we have to trust that she will find her way."

Lucy nodded slowly, her tears still flowing. "I...I'll try, Dad. I'll try to trust you."

Tom took the tablet from his daughters' hands and walked back to the house.

"I am not done watching mommy, she is talking to people she shouldn't be talking too." Lucy had instantly become enraged as Tom continued to walk into the house.

As Tom stands at the threshold, he gazes at his daughter with regret and says, "I'm sorry Lucy, you cannot go down this road." He shuts the door firmly behind him as he hopes that she will come to her senses. He takes a seat at the table and unlocks his tablet, intending to keep an eye on his wife while she rests.

But instead of seeing evidence of Lucy not calming down, Tom's fear for both his daughter and wife spirals up inside him.

As he looks at the tablet's screen, Tom notices that the images of his wife are growing distorted and blurry. The view inside the room flickers on and off, as if someone is deliberately tampering

A TANGLED WEAVE: Death of a Child

with it.

Tom's heart races as he tries to make sense of what's going on. He knows that something is terribly wrong.

"Daddy, please help me," she begs, her voice quiet and low with trembling vibrations. "I'm trapped here, unable to move on. You have to help me find my way."

Tom's mind races as he tries to produce a plan. He knows that he shouldn't interfere with the living, but he can't bear to see his daughter suffer any longer.

Taking a deep breath, he offers her his hand. "I'll do whatever it takes, honey. I'll help you find your way out of here." Tom stops the agony of what Lucy was doing to his wife. But he knew that this would not be the last time he would have to interfere. He needed to find a solution.

He would have to contact the living himself. Tom would find a way. He would have to contact the living himself. He knew it would be dangerous, he would have to perfect timing to make this right. He had to find a way to communicate with the living, and Bella could be his only hope.

Bella listened intently as Tom spoke. She knew it was unusual for the dead to communicate with the living, but she also believed that anything was possible with the grace of God. Bella had just arrived in her heaven; she was at peace. She had all the knowledge given to her and understood her place. But knowing that her Lucy was in danger of not finding her peace, she agreed to help.

Tom breathed a sigh of relief. He knew he couldn't do this alone. He needed someone who could guide him on the right path.

"Tom, you are a good man. Lucy will find her way to you once more." Bella being able to live her life out had the knowledge that those who passed early did not. She knew that Lucy's time walking among the living would soon end. "She will be at peace soon."

"What about Teresa, will she ever learn what her destiny is?" Tom knew that Teresa had suffered great lose because she was meant for greater things. Without the loss she would never have the strength to carry out was she was meant to do.

"She will my son, now you should rest and be at ease." Bella would stay by Tom's side and watch the future unfold with him.

*****

It was shortly after 3AM when Teresa and Elizabeth reached

the house. Teresa peered down the street towards her own home, wishing she could go to check on it, but knowing it wouldn't be a wise move.

Elizabeth's house was neat and outfitted with all the stylish items of a 1970s living space. Brown and yellow flowers decorated the furniture. Homemade blankets draped across the bed, large pillows filled up the sofas, and plenty of porcelain dolls lined the room.

Elizabeth laid out a pillow and bed sheets on the couch for her to sleep on. Teresa didn't believe she would be able to get much rest, but lying down would at least allow her to relax. When Elizabeth finished setting up the makeshift bed, she asked Teresa if she would like something hot to drink, like tea. They both went into the kitchen and Elizabeth put some water in the kettle. Sitting at the table, they waited for it to boil.

"I know this must be quite a lot to take in." Elizabeth tried to make light conversation to help Teresa feel more at ease. "You're going to get through this just fine."

"I know, I just don't understand why Lucy was so angry today. She can go days without talking to me or seeing me." Teresa's exhaustion had begun to cloud her rationality. "I'm sorry Elizabeth; I think I'll just lie down for a bit. I'm going to give your tea a pass."

Elizabeth nodded and turned off the kettle, "If you need anything, I'll be down the hall."

Teresa drifted off to sleep on the couch while her dreams were filled with images of her family. Tom and Lucy were in the backyard underneath the large oak tree, laughing as they played together. But then everything changed when Lucy glared at Teresa and asked in a stern voice, "Why do you still do this? You should know the truth by now!" With that, Lucy turned away and went back to having fun with Tom.

Teresa was the spectator; she was not in a dream but watching it like family movies that would roll over and over again. They would play for a few minutes and then Lucy's glare would interrupt the happy moment. Over and over in an endless loop, she watched as Lucy and Tom played in the yard until Lucy would stop, turn, and glare at her.

The dream began to feel like a movie. A seemingly never-ending loop that would play out the same scene repeatedly. Teresa watched from a safe distance, feeling powerless to do anything but watch as Lucy and Tom laughed and played beneath the large oak tree in their backyard.

But inevitably, Lucy's glare would appear, her expression one of intense anger and disappointment. She seemed to know something that Teresa didn't. The dream had an air of finality about it; it felt like whatever the truth was, if it were revealed to Teresa, it would change her life forever.

Suddenly, a voice broke through the silence and snapped Teresa out of her trance. It was Father Michael's voice calling her name from outside the house. He said that he had been searching for her all night long, following traces of energy that he felt lingering in the air nearby.

Father Michael told her not to worry; he said that he could help them find a solution if they'd be willing to trust him with their secrets. He said that he could talk to spirits on their behalf and get answers they wouldn't be able to find on their own.

With a hard look, Lucy dragged Teresa back to the old oak tree. Terror was coursing through her veins and Teresa could feel her heart cracking with every breath she took.

The sound of a dog barking outside pulled Teresa from her slumber. As she drifted back to sleep, she found herself dreaming about Tom. She was in the kitchen of their home, cooking dinner when he spoke to her from the living room, "It's time, Teresa. Let the others take on the case."

Confused by his words, Teresa replied, "What case? I thought it was time for dinner. Can you get Lucy?" She smiled with contentment in this dreamlike moment when everything seemed as it once was.

Tom stepped up behind her and hugged her tightly. But his embrace felt different; cold and lifeless. He whispered in her ear, "Lucy is gone. It's time to move on." When Teresa turned around to face him, she saw that his body had decayed like he had been buried for years - Tom was now a ghost.

The dream had left Teresa feeling shaken and disturbed. She sat up from the couch, her body trembling from the intensity of the vision. She was covered in sweat and her heart was pounding fiercely in her chest.

Thoughts raced through her mind as she tried to make sense

of what she had seen. Could it be a sign? Was Tom trying to tell Teresa something? If so, what was it?

CHAPTER 22

Although filled with fear and apprehension, Teresa knew that she had to find out the truth. She got dressed quickly and hurried outside, determined to find Father Michael, and finally get some answers. The morning air was warm for a September morning, Teresa thought maybe this was a good sign. The warmth envelope her as she rushed next door.

She found him, Elizabeth and Maggie standing beneath the old oak tree in her backyard, gazing up at its branches as if communing with something unseen. Father Michael smiled warmly when he saw Teresa approach and he seemed to already know why she had come.

Without a word, Father Michael motioned for them to sit down beneath the tree so they could talk privately away from prying eyes. He listened intently while Teresa recounted all of her visions from that night - including the eerie dream of Tom's ghostly figure - before offering his advice on how they could uncover the truth that they sought.

"I need to find out if Lucy is still there," She looked up towards the house, her home, her family home. Her heart felt like it would break in two as she stood outside the with her friends, desperate to know if her child was still there. Lucy was gone from this world and the next, and Teresa had to find out for sure if she was gone from this one too.

"We can go in but know this could be another trigger. We need to be prepared to get out quickly." Father Michael led the women into the house.

The house was as warm as if nothing had happened the night before. All signs of Lucy's outburst were gone - a miraculous sight. Teresa slowly walked throughout each room, looking for any evidence that either Tom or Lucy had been there - to no avail.

Everything was in its place; all the furniture stood where it once did and the drawings hung back on the walls, untouched.

Teresa looked up at the others, "I know what happened here, it was not my imagination."

Maggie stood near the backdoor in the kitchen, her gaze stopping at the refrigerator. She walked over and pulled a drawing from it – one she hadn't seen before. She looked closer, recognizing Tom's face and clothes in the picture. A smile slowly spread across her features; it was Tom cleaning the house!

With excitement building, she handed it to Teresa, who stared at it briefly before starting to laugh and cry at the same time. It was true – Tom had been here last night! He had come back to take care of Lucy's mess, just as he had always done for his family.

Father Michael stepped closer and gently took the picture from Teresa's hands. He smiled sadly and nodded his head towards the door leading upstairs. "Shall we go?"

The women followed Father Michael as he slowly ascended the stairs, treading carefully as if they were not welcome visitors but ghosts themselves. At the top of the stairs, they gathered together in a huddle around Lucy's bedroom door - afraid yet determined to open it and find out what lies inside.

They were ready to face whatever they would find in the attic, but they knew it wouldn't be easy. The events of the previous night were still fresh in their minds, and they knew that they were dealing with a force unlike anything they had ever encountered before.

As they climbed up the stairs and into the attic, they were greeted by the musty smell of old belongings. The walls were lined with shelves, and there were boxes stacked on top of each other. Teresa led them to a corner of the attic where she had placed everything that they had not yet unpacked since moving in.

Father Michael took out his crucifix and began to walk around the room, murmuring prayers under his breath. Elizabeth and Maggie started to go through the boxes, trying to find anything that might be connected to the spirits that were haunting Teresa's home.

They were about halfway through the boxes when Elizabeth let out a gasp. She had found an old journal among the belongings. As she began to read through its pages, her hands began to shake.

"This belonged to the previous owner," she said, passing it to Father Michael. "It's filled with pages and pages of dark thoughts and rituals. He was trying to summon something.

"Father Michael took the journal and started to read through it himself. His brow furrowed as he saw just how deep the previous owner's obsession with the occult had been."

We need to burn this journal," he said finally. "And we need to do it now."

Teresa hesitated for a moment, but ultimately trusted Father Michael's expertise. They gathered up all the other items from the attic into a pile and took them to the backyard. Then they doused the pile with gasoline and set it ablaze.

As the flames engulfed the objects, they could feel a sense of peace and lightness wash over them. Father Michael led them all in prayer, and they could feel the power and protection of God around them.

When the fire died down, they all breathed a sigh of relief. It was over, and they had successfully cleansed Teresa's home of the evil that had been lurking within it, but as they turned to go back inside, they heard a sound coming from the bushes near the edge of the yard. Elizabeth felt a shiver run down her spine as she saw movement amongst the leaves.

"Father Michael, look!" she exclaimed, pointing towards the bushes. He turned to see what Elizabeth was referring to, and as he did so, a figure emerged from the bushes.

It was a woman, her face softened into an expression of peace. Her eyes were bright with an otherworldly glow, and her hair was whipping around her head as if in a fierce wind. Teresa recognized her immediately. It was Bella. "This is over," she murmured to the other.

The woman advanced towards them, and Father Michael stepped forward to meet her. He brandished his sacred emblem and began intoning prayers, calling on the strength of God to aid him in this fight.

Teresa put out her arm to stop Father Michael, "Hold on, that is Bella. It's Steve's grandma." Bella stopped and then faded back into the foliage. Teresa sensed a warmth in her. She was sure with Tom and Bella attending and Lucy everything would come right in the end.

A TANGLED WEAVE: Death of a Child

*****

Lucy stirred beneath the giant oak tree in Tom's heaven. She was weak, lightheaded, and disoriented. Her small body lay on the ground as she attempted to lift herself up, but her legs wouldn't move. She called out for her father yet received no reply. She was alone and scared.

The ground she lay on was covered with dirty leaves, her small body was shivering from the cold. It was cold enough to see her own breath, so Lucy hugged her knees to her chest, trying in vain to keep warm. It was not the place she had been playing in for weeks. She was happy in that place.

Lucy slowly raised her head, gradually taking in her new surroundings. She felt a wave of despair flush through her being as she realized she was no longer in the familiar place where she spent most of her days. Nothing here resembled the safety and comfort of home – only the gentle rustle of leaves and an eerie stillness shrouded the area.

She started to remember what had happened the night before, the fear and anger that had consumed her mind as she trashed her own mother's house. The guilt came flooding back too, making Lucy want to curl up in a ball and cry until it all went away. But as hard as she tried, nothing could alleviate this sense of sadness that now lingered in her heart.

Then suddenly something caught her eye – a small glimmer of light coming from somewhere nearby. Intrigued, Lucy cautiously made her way over to investigate further. As she got closer, she saw that it was a child she had played with earlier. Lucy finally stood and walked slowly to her friend. The friend's voice was like soft angelic song. She explained that true peace come from within - from accepting herself for who she is, living with compassion and kindness towards others regardless of their own actions or beliefs.

"Lucy, this is not your father's version of heaven, this is yours. The shadows and chill come from the depths of your heart." The young girl standing across from her was a few years older; her ebony locks fluttered in the breeze, while her eyes shimmered, resembling small black pearls that transformed in the light.

"Where is my dad?" Lucy's tears flowed down her cheeks.

The tears created a glistening teardrop, catching the light in a prismatic display. She looked on worriedly as the droplet splattered against the ground, sending tiny ripples across the surface of the light.

"Lucy, your father won't be able to come see you anymore. Tom tried to bring you calmness, but instead you are destroying his serenity. He can't help you any longer; it's up to you now to find your own inner peace." The girl took Lucy's hand, let me show you something. "My name is Maria, you know me, when the calmness comes you will remember."

The tears created a glistening teardrop, catching the light in a prismatic display. She looked on worriedly as the droplet splattered against the ground, sending tiny ripples across the surface of the light.

As Maria held Lucy's hand, she guided her through the trees and out into an open field. From this vantage point, Lucy could see hundreds of children running and laughing. The playfulness of the kids brought a great peace to her heart; it was something she had not felt in a long time.

The scene before her was beautiful - the sun shone brightly, casting an array of oranges and yellows onto the lush green grass. The flurry of activity was mesmerizing - kids were picking flowers, playing tag, kicking around balls or just lying back on the warm grass enjoying the day.

Lucy felt relaxed as she watched them all joyfully embracing life without fear or worry. She recognized many of them from around town but yet here they were different – they seemed so free from judgment or expectation; with each giggle or smile Lucy felt a bit lighter inside.

"This is what Heaven should look like," Maria said, her voice gentle but firm as if echoing Lucy's thoughts aloud. "True peace is within accepting yourself for who you are and having compassion and kindness for everyone around you."

Lucy was embraced by warmth and love. Her body eased as she walked slowly. She wanted to join the children, so she looked to Maria for guidance. Maria stood still with a smile and pointed towards the field; but Lucy's gaze shifted beyond her friend, and she saw a vision of her mom before quickly kneeling beneath the oak tree.

"Lucy, we will be here when you are ready," Maria's voice echoed in her.

A TANGLED WEAVE: Death of a Child

*****

As Sam stepped out of his house on the September morning, he could feel that it was quite a bit warmer than usual. As he walked towards the police station, the sun had already made its way far up the sky. He couldn't contain his excitement at hearing what Tony told the police in the interview; he was certain they were finally close to solving it.

The station house was busting with activity from calls from the night before. "What happened last night?" Sam was confused at the calls coming in from a normal peaceful town.

"We had several calls from townspeople saying they heard strange noises and saw strange lights in the sky." Jenkins replied as he rifled through a stack of papers on his desk. "It appears to be something otherworldly that is happening in our town. There has never been anything like this before."

The police officers were befuddled by the mysterious reports that had come in and didn't know how to proceed. Sam discussed the odd phone calls with his colleagues, wondering if they could somehow be linked.

Suddenly, Sam pulled Jenkins' arm, "We have a call to take care of." Jenkins glanced at his partner with surprise, aware that the peculiar messages could wait. He was sure there were plenty of other officers who could handle it.

"Yes, I already booked us a room." Jenkins surveyed the area and rested a stack of folders on another officer's desk.

The two pulled out their laptops and placed all the reports on the table in front of them as they placed the call to Kansas City police department.

Sargent Timms was handling the interview with Tony. Sam had spoken to him several times in the last week about Lucy's case. Timms knew Tony well, as he had been in and out of trouble for many years.

"Good morning gentleman, I hope you had a good night's sleep. Things here have gotten very weird." Timms voice was hurried. "Our entire station in up in arms over some strange lights and sounds being reported since around midnight last night."

Jenkins spoke up, "Really, we have the same thing going on

here as well."

"It is the bizarre thing." Timms continued, "We have been trying to investigate the source of these lights and sounds, but we haven't been successful so far.

Sam interrupted, he had only one case on his mind, "So not to change the subject, but how did the interview go with Tony?"

Timms spent several hours questioning Tony, but Tony's alibi checked out. He had only been in town for one night to visit Steve, and then he left on an early flight that night. According to Tony, he went to see Steve to tell him that he wanted nothing to do with the inheritance or the family. The money seemed like a curse to him, and he had no interest in being a part of it. Furthermore, Tony claimed that he would have been gone before Lucy's death.

"I have checked with the taxicab that picked him up from the bar. The cab picked him up at 10:15pm and drove him to the airport where he took an 11:30pm flight back to here." Timms felt bad he could not help with the case against Tony. He would have been all too happy to see Tony behind bars.

"Okay, so we are back to step one, thanks for the time Timms." Jenkins hung up the phone and turned to Sam. "We will figure this out."

Sam pounded his fist on the table before storming out of the room.

CHAPTER 23

As Teresa sat in her kitchen, memories of the last year began to float back. She remembered the heartbreaking news that her beloved husband Tom had been taken from her due to an act of violence rather than an accident. He had been her soulmate, the father of their beautiful daughter and a perfect partner in every sense of the word.

After the passing of Tom, she thought Steve would be her rock. She was convinced he'd be a great father to Lucy and a husband that would provide for them. He wasn't the savior she believed him to be. She trusted Steve to be a fatherly figure for Lucy and provide for them as a husband would. Instead, he turned out to be the very monster that shattered her life.

She thought of Lucy, who could bring such joy to any child she met. Lucy had a zest for life that glowed in her smile and laughter. Teresa's hopes had been that Lucy and Steve would have connected better; instead, it was Tom who deeply held the key to her heart. Teresa couldn't help but smile when she thought about the bond between them. Tom always held an especially deep place in her heart, even from when Lucy was just a baby.

Teresa reflected on the job at the hospital she was unable to make herself return to. She had been fond of the people she worked with and relished helping others who were suffering, providing a bit of solace during their illness or discomfort. Her financial resources had been depleted and she knew she needed to go back, but her emotional turmoil was halting her progress.

She thought about the library, the only place now that brings her any solace or peace. She thought about the times there with Lucy. The two of them would spend hours in the children's section engrossed in books and stories, a place where they could forget about the outside world for a little while. It was the one place where Teresa could find some comfort in knowing that Lucy was safe from the world and the dangers that lurked around every corner.

As she sat there lost in her thoughts, she heard the knock at the front door. She quickly wiped away the tears that had formed in her eyes and composed herself as best she could. She opened the door to see Sam, dressed not in his normal suit and tie, but in blue jeans and T-shirt. He looked completely different; he had a sadness in him that she had not seen before.

"Sam, I didn't expect you this morning. Come in would like some coffee." Teresa opened the door so that he could walk through the house.

"Yes, please, that would be great."

"How did it go in Kansas City? Did Tony really kill Lucy? Is this all over now?" Teresa's insistent curiosity about her daughter had taken over any pretense of politeness. "I apologize, I'm just so caught up in all of this." She offered a cup of coffee to Sam as he sat across from her at the table.

"It's alright, I get it." Sam accepted the hot beverage and began explaining his conversation with the police department in Kansas City. There was no conceivable way that Tony could have done it, he said, apologizing for bringing her into this mess without being certain of all the facts first.

Sam felt guilty about bringing her pain in the situation. He needed to be professional, but it was ridiculously hard for him with the situation that Teresa was in. "Teresa, I want you to understand that this case had become very personal for me." He stopped and took a sip of coffee before continuing. "Lucy has touched my heart in no way any other child has. I have always been able to give closure to the family. This is my first case that has be stumped."

"I am trying to understand, I really am, but who could have done such a terrible thing in this community." Tears were beginning to flow down her cheeks once again. Teresa was trying hard to control her emotions. "Our community is small, things like this don't happen here."

"I know, this is why I moved here to begin with. The big cities are full of crime, I was ready to find a peaceful place to hopefully retire in." Sam took another sip of coffee, "I want you to know I will not stop until I find what has happened to Lucy."

They sat in silence, until there was another knock at the door. "I need to be going," Sam stood and walked to the door alongside Teresa.

Teresa opened the door to the mail carrier, "I have a certified letter for you, Teresa."

Teresa looked at the mail carrier with a surprised look on her face. She had the same carrier for years. Everyone in town knew Teresa. She wondered what it was. "Who is from?"

"It's from Steve's family." As Teresa took the clipboard to sign for the letter, he gave her his condolence. "I am very sorry, for everything you are going through, if you need anything, I am here for you."

"Thank You, here you go," she handed the clipboard back to him and took the letter.

"Oh, I almost forgot, my daughter wanted to me to tell you that she loves you being at the library. It is nice that she enjoys going there now that you are there. You are making an impact on your stories you are reading to the children." His smile turning away from her brought a smile to Teresa's face.

Sam and Teresa stood and watched as he returned to his route. "That feels good, to hear the children like the books I pick for them." Teresa thought about the happiness she had at the library.

Sam took a step closer to the door, "I should really be going."

"No, please stay a while, I don't want to be alone right now. Besides, I am not sure what this is, and I would like someone here while I open it."

The two walked back to the kitchen, there was an awkward silence between the two as Teresa stared at the envelope. It was from Steve's family she knew it was. Teresa felt the sadness of Bella's passing and wondered what the family must be thinking of her now. With Steve in prison, the police pulling Tony in for questioning, was it her that was destroying their family?

"Well, are you going to open it?" Sam finally broke the silence.

"Yes, I was just thinking about Steve's family. This must be terrible for them, knowing that one of their own had taken a life." Teresa began to open the letter and stopped; she looked up at Sam. "Do you think I am tearing their family apart; with everything they have been through."

"No, I think they are in just as much pain as you are." Sam could feel the pain Teresa was feeling. She was a caring person. He hated he had not been able to bring her closure.

Teresa unsealed the envelope, which was from an attorney of Steve's family assets. Her eyes widened upon realizing that she had been included on the list of recipients. The letter requested that Teresa visit a legal representative to learn more about their decision.

"What could this about?" Teresa hands the letter over to Sam.

"I have a friend that you could contact, he can help sort out whatever the family has for you. The family has a large estate, it could be just letter you know that they are thinking off you by leaving a small gesture." Sam handed the letter back to her. He pulled out his phone and sent her a contact for a local attorney. "I would not get your hopes up for a fortune, but it nice that they thought of you."

Teresa gave Sam her word that she would be in touch with the office later. With a nod, Sam strode from the kitchen, already running late for his next meeting. He left Teresa behind, seated alone in the room.

Once more, Teresa was assigned the task of entertaining her own mind. However, thanks to Sam's visit, the mailman's arrival, and the letter she had just received, she now had a reason to push herself into action. Quickly getting dressed, Teresa rushed out of the house and made her first stop the library - she wanted to plan her schedule for the week. She felt that if she wrote down certain times and dates instead of simply showing up to volunteer whenever she felt like it, she would be much more motivated when it came time for her to contribute.

When Teresa arrived at the library, she found Mary in the historical aisle restocking books. The strain was obvious on her face—dark circles lined her eyes, and her expression was puffy with fatigue.

"Good morning, Mary, how are you doing?"

Mary lifted her head and gave a tired smile. "I am so glad you are here. Are you coming to work today or tomorrow? I could really use a break."

"I came to schedule some time working here, if that's alright." Teresa felt a pang of guilt. If she didn't have an appointment with an attorney or visit the hospital, she would stay and help today as well.

"Great! Why don't you come in tomorrow and we'll set up a schedule for you then?" Mary seemed relieved at the thought of getting some extra help around the library.

Teresa and Mary exchanged warm smiles before Teresa

started towards the doors of the library. Teresa could see that Mary had a lot going on in her life, but she was too overwhelmed to offer any help. It was out of character for her to be so wrapped up in her own pain that she couldn't step outside of it for a moment and lend an ear or a shoulder when needed. She knew she had to try and work on this.

Before reaching the doors, Teresa noticed George coming out of one of the offices. She had not spoken to him since the memorial at the house. "Hello, George how are you doing?" She tried to be pleasant hoping it would be a passing conversation.

"I'm doing great! I got a new book today; Lucy would've been over the moon for it. You should consider reading it to the kids here when you return, right? You are coming back, aren't you?" George was always so passionate. Even in the middle of a conversation, he spoke quickly, as if afraid of something—but that's just the way he had always been.

"Yes, I will be here tomorrow." Teresa started walking away just as he was continuing to talk. "I am sorry, George. I have an appointment I cannot miss. I will talk with you soon." Lucy would laugh at the way he spoke; she thought it was amusing how he could keep all his thought together and speak so quickly. This thought put a smile on her face as she continued out the door and down the street.

Second on her list for the day was to schedule a meeting with the lawyer to see what was left to her in Bella's will. She pondered this for a moment before thinking about the crystal rocking horse that had been sent to her daughter, Lucy. It would be nice to have something else small to display in her living room. While it was hard having reminders of Steve around, she wished Lucy could have met his grandmother, Bella. Teresa thought she could have been significant role model for her daughter, and her advice would have allowed Lucy to blossom into an amazing person.

As Teresa strolled through her little hometown, she took in the scenery around her. She and Tom had decided to move here shortly after graduating college. The two of them wanted to start a family, but big cities felt far too dangerous - they desired somewhere peaceful and safe for their children to play and grow up. Little towns like this one had less crime than metropolitan areas, which was just what Teresa and Tom were hoping for.

The old buildings contained not only family-owned

businesses but small apartments as well. Although the town was much smaller than the city, it still had all amenities one could ask for. The library was in the middle of town and next to the courthouse. Across from the library was the park which had recently been upgraded with modern facilities. Teresa thought Lucy would have enjoyed playing there.

As she made her way to the lawyer, she paused by the jewelry store that was advertising a Christmas special a few months away. She smiled as she remembered how time seemed to stop in this small town. She had many friends among the shop owners; they often held events together and had no sense of competition between them.

Teresa stood outside of the law office, looking at a sign painted on the window. It read "Philip Stein, Attorney of Law. Serving all your domestic and criminal needs." She doubted that Philip's clients were as plentiful as the promises on his banner suggested. Teresa pushed open the door to see a tasteful reception desk with a few chairs, along with some end tables and magazines. The walls were adorned with artwork featuring birds during flight—their wings spread across the canvas as if they wanted to soar away in a hurry. With the letter in her hand, she stepped inside.

Behind the reception desk was Margaret, Teresa knew her from church. She was an elderly woman that lost her husband about the same time she had lost Tom. She was always a great comfort to her but also the town gossip. Teresa felt bad that she did not stay connected with her as much as she should have. But they were both going through grief at the same time. Margaret had been married for 35 years; her grief was very different to hers.

"Well, hello Teresa, it has been a long time. It is so good to see you." The woman walked around the desk and embraced Teresa.

"I didn't realize you worked here; it is good to see you too." Teressa was astonished that she would receive this kind of welcome from the woman. It made her feel even more guilty for not staying in touch.

"Oh, silly, I don't work here. This is my son's office. I just help out every now and then. It keeps me busy and makes Philip think he has a busting business." Margaret chuckled and moved Teresa towards the chairs to sit down. "I am so sorry for not keeping up with you these last few years. My children have been keeping me busy." They think since I am getting old, I need activity in my life."

Margaret stood and walked toward the little coffee stations along the back wall. "Do you want some coffee? I drink it all day since it is here."

"Yes, that would be great," Teresa was relieved to know that Margaret did hold a grudge about her absence.

"I heard about what happed with little Lucy and that dreadful man you married after Tom. Steve was his man, right? "

Teresa squirmed a bit in her chair, she didn't want to get into a huge conversation about this with her. "It has been a rough year. But I am handling everything okay. So, uhm... I need to make an appointment to see your son. Can you set that up for me?" She discreetly wanted to change the conversation.

"Well of course I can." Margaret walked over to the desk and pulled out the appointment calendar. There was not much written on it. Only a few dates had plans written down. "How about tomorrow morning, first thing?

"That would be great, I need to be at the library by 9am, can I come by around 8."

"Sure, I heard you volunteering there. Did you hear about what is going on with Mary, the little librarian? Her and husband are getting a divorce. I know because her husband is in here every day. It is just a sad situation." Margaret continued to carry on as Teresa stood, she thanked Margaret and walked toward the door.

"I will see you tomorrow, okay. I have so much more to get done today but thank you." Teresa was exhausted by the encounter. It also brought a quirky smile at the thought that the woman was interested in everyone else's life. Teresa wondered what her life must be like. She thought of the poor woman who lost her husband after 35 years. How could that feel? What would she have left in life? Maybe that is why she was so interested in others.

Glancing at the time, Teresa noted that she still had enough time to stop by the hospital and get lunch. Freda's place was on her way there; a small diner that sat on the main street and only served breakfast and lunch. The cozy atmosphere of Freda's made it one of Tom's favorite places to eat when Teresa worked at the hospital.

Tom and Teresa always took the table by the window so they could watch people while they ate. Teresa would observe them and make up different stories about where they were going or what was going through their minds. Tom would laugh at her wild imagination, often telling her she should write a book. Smiling fondly at the memory, Teresa opened the door to enter the diner.

The place was as busy as a small restaurant could be. There were only eight tables in the entire place. Most of Freda's business was to go orders because of her location in the middle of town. Many of the employees from the courthouse and surrounding offices would come in for sandwiches they could take back to work.

Teresa spotted an empty table by the window and quickly walked over to it. The seat had a view of Main Street and Teresa looked out into the hustle and bustle of the town center. It made her miss Tom more than ever before.

A server came up and greeted Teresa with a warm smile before offering her a menu, which she declined, knowing exactly what she wanted. She asked for one of Tom's favorite items: chicken salad wrap with potato chips on the side and an iced tea. After ordering, she sat at the table looking out onto Main Street, taking in every detail of her surroundings.

As people hurried from place to place in the busy town, she thought of their problems. Was anyone struggling with money or a failing marriage? Did any of them have ill kids or elderly parents? She had once aspired to help people during their challenging times, but now her own troubles filled her thoughts.

She used to dream of finding a community where she could embrace family and provide aid to others too. Nothing made her happier than making life easier for other people. Yet here she was, mired in her issues. One day at a time was all she could manage.
In days gone by, she had planned to find a place for herself that enabled her to be helpful to others. She only wanted to be surrounded by those she loved and brighten the lives of families beyond hers.

As Teresa was deep in thought, she noticed a familiar face walking down Main Street--it was Margaret from the attorney's office. Teresa thought back to their conversation and realized this must have been Margaret's daily routine; talking to all sorts of people while making her rounds in town.

Despite herself, Teresa couldn't help but feel admiration for Margaret's resilience despite all she had been through with losing her husband after 35 years together--she still persisted against all odds without any sign of giving up on life or joyfully engaging with others around her. Even though Teresa wished to slip away unnoticed, Margaret eventually spotted her sitting alone at the diner window table.

"Oh dear, you should not be eating alone." Margaret sat down before Teresa was able to say anything. "Now what are we having for lunch."

"I am sorry Margaret, I am meeting someone," Teresa noticed Maggie and Elizabeth had just opened the door and walked in. Teresa waved at the two as they were walking towards her.

"It is so good to see," Elizabeth moved over to give Teresa a short hug before turning to Margaret. "Are you joining as well? We will need to wait for a bigger table."

"Ah, I'm afraid I must be off to the office, but I wanted to check in on our dear Teresa first." Margaret stood up from her seat and offered it to Elizabeth. She gave Teresa an affectionate smile before heading up to the counter. Her order had already been prepared for pickup; Teresa watched as she paid for her purchase and stepped out into the street. She waved goodbye through the window before whirling around and walking back toward her son's office.

Maggie and Elizabeth took their seats, both ordering a club sandwich, and iced tea. It was refreshing to be away from Teresa's house. They asked how she was doing; in response, she told them about her appointment with the lawyer, revisiting the library, and going back to the hospital. Her two companions agreed that it was best for her to get out of her home—so they kept on conversing for multiple hours without even realizing the passing of time.

The conversations had nothing to do with what had been going on the last few days. They talked about the town and how it would be nice to see some improvements to the library and the town center. They talked about George, who was always someone that would listen to others. It wasn't until they started talking about the church and Father Michael that Teresa's mind wandered back to her own troubles.

Teresa became quiet, Elizabeth and Maggie both knew where her thoughts had trailed off too. It was only then that they noticed they were left alone in the diner. Freda was at the back table going through the day's receipts. They couldn't help but giggle as they realized how much time had passed without them noticing. Freda came over to their table with a smile.

"I didn't want to disturb you ladies; it looks like you all are having fun." She was a small woman with an enormous personality, that had been living in this town since before she married her husband. "I almost joined you once we closed up, but there was still some work to be done."

Teresa stood up and pulled another chair near the table. "Please join us; this has turned into a wonderful day! I can check my hospital schedule some other time."

Freda beamed as she lowered herself onto the chair that Teresa had brought over to the table. Freda could always find something clever and humorous to say - her smile seeming to contain a zest for life that Teresa admired.

"I'm happy to join you. It's rare that the diner is completely empty, so it's nice to have some company."

As they continued chatting and laughing, Teresa couldn't help but feel grateful for these women in her life. In the midst of all the chaos she had been dealing with, they were the only ones who knew how to deluge her with positive vibes and encouragement.

As Teresa listened to her friends discuss their plans to open a community center or establish an art gallery, she realized that she was incapable of ever achieving such dreams since Tom and Lucy's deaths. But then, as she looked at all of them that special day, she felt deep down that anything was possible again. She knew then that her shattered hopes could be pieced back together; here was where her most significant dreams could start taking shape.

The day was filled with chatter and laughter as the ladies shared their stories about growing up in the town and all the mischief they got into. They indulged in slices of pie and cups of coffee, but something felt amiss, somehow tainted by what had happened.

As the sun began to dip below the horizon, they decided to stop for the day and Teresa walked Freda back to her vehicle parked outside the diner. They exchanged farewells and Teresa watched as Freda's car drove away down the street.

Returning to her car, Teresa noticed George for the second time that day - a rare occurrence. He was striding down the street behind the library, with a stack of books in his arms. Nothing seemed out of the ordinary, but there was something unsettling about it; seeing him all alone in a town where the streets were filled with nothing but empty air.

CHAPTER 24

Welcoming the warmth of her home as she stepped inside, Teresa couldn't help but be overwhelmed with joy. While her day had been filled with social engagements and commitments, coming here made her feel more settled than she had in over a year. As she strolled through the living areas, she couldn't help but admire all the drawings her daughters had put up on the walls - though it still felt like something was holding her back from progressing. Taking a deep breath, Teresa started to take down the artworks; slowly but surely each room's walls were wiped clean as the pieces were stacked onto the table in the kitchen.

As Teresa sat at the kitchen table, she looked around her at all the drawings her daughters had created. She smiled as she remembered how much joy they had brought into the room and how proud she felt when their art was displayed on the walls. Taking a deep breath, Teresa opened a scrapbook and set about arranging each artwork into chronological order. As she placed each drawing in its place, memories of her time with them came flooding back to her; all those special moments shared together that would now be immortalized in this book.

Once the scrapbook was finished, Teresa put on a kettle for tea and settled down to reflect on all that had happened throughout her day. She thought about Freda and their conversation and how it reminded her of how valuable close friendships can be - even if it's just for a short while - and how lucky she was to have these people in her life.

As Teresa closed her eyes that night, she could not help but feel a strange sensation come over her - an unfamiliarity that enveloped her in a peacefulness she had not experienced in some time. With no dreams to awaken her, the night passed in near silence and Teresa slept better than she had on many nights.

Morning came soon after, and with it came the bustling of life and activity. As Teresa got ready for the day ahead, she felt a renewed sense of purpose and energy. She was determined to make the most of her Friday, both mentally and physically.

Strolling through town on her way to the attorney's office with a newfound appreciation for all around her, Teresa found herself drawn to a nearby park. There, she paused to take in the beauty of nature before continuing her way - admiring everything from the trees swaying gently in the breeze to the birds gracefully fluttering from branch to branch.

Teresa paused to observe the hustle and bustle of people around her, wondering if any of them had noticed the surroundings or taken a second to appreciate nature. As she started to make her way again, she spotted several children heading off to school and immediately thought of Lucy. Teresa imagined that they would visit the park often, making it part of their daily routine. She quickly shook off the thought and continued her journey; she had appointments she needed to keep.

Walking into the attorney's office, Margret was busy arranging the magazines and dusting off tables. "Hello, dear it is good to see you. My son is waiting for you, go on in. We can talk after,"

Teresa opened the door of the Philips office. The office is tastefully decorated with several framed degrees and certifications. There is a large mahogany desk with a matching chair to the side of the room. It stood in front of a wall of bookshelves and a window overlooking the street. There were papers strewn across the desk and scattered across the floor.

"Take a seat, Teresa. What can I help you with today?" Philip Stein was a large man with a muscular tone, a body built for hard manual work. His face was covered with a thick black beard with black hair neatly combed. He wore a tailored black suit that showed the muscle tones of his body. His voice was quiet not like you would think of from a man his size.

Teresa hands the letter from Steve's family to him. "I received this certified letter yesterday. Detective Sam Davis said you could help me with it."

Philip read the letter from the family attorney. "It does appear you have been named in the will. I will contact the family executor; it will start with just a phone call. "Would like to visit with my mom for a minute and I can do this now? It should be only a minute."

Teresa stood and walked toward the door, "Yes, thank you." That seemed all too easy, Teresa was not sure what to think of this man. He was nothing like his mother who could talk for hours never saying anything.

Outside the office, Margaret took a seat in the waiting room and handed Teresa her coffee from the office's coffee station. "I've made this cup especially for you," she said as she gestured for Teresa to sit beside her. Margaret had already conversed with her son about her visit today and realized that Teresa needed someone to help her get through the process of dealing with the will. She just needed an extra push to keep going on the path that would lead her to progress forward in life.

Teresa found it amusing how much this kind-hearted elderly woman seemed to know about everyone's life circumstances. She found the more she was around this woman the more she was beginning to warm to her outspoken personality.

It was not long before Philip stepped outside his office, "Do you want to step back in for a minute." Philip held the door as she took a seat in front of his desk. "I understand from my mom that you would like to keep this quiet for now. I understand this will remain confidential." Teresa looked at this man surprisingly, she had not mentioned anything to Margaret about why she was there.

"My mother has a knack at knowing things. Trust me, I understand your confusion." Philip handed the letter back to her. "I have everything set up for you. It looks like the family has taken part of Steve's portion of the will and divided it between yourself and his seconds wife family. We should know shortly what the inheritance is for you."

"How does your mother do that?" Teresa smiled as she thought the woman hand to be clairvoyant.

"Do not worry, my mother is just what you see. Her intentions are good even if her methods are a bit disconcerting." Philip stood again opening the door, "the family executor will contact me soon with all the information."

Teresa left the office not sure what had just happened. She looked back at the door and Margaret was standing inside with the strangest smile, waving goodbye. Her visit with Philip took only 15 minutes, she had time to stop at the hospital before meeting Mary at the library. Everything seemed to be falling into place.

Teresa trudged to the hospital, her mind weighed down with dejection and dread. She hated the idea of returning to the hospital, but she had no other option if she wanted to keep a roof over her head. She had been so fortunate that everyone in town had helped her out when Tom passed away, but she couldn't rely on them forever. Her savings were drained, and it was time for her to start making an income again.

When she reached the hospital, Teresa was greeted by the familiar faces of nurses and doctors that she used to work with. Despite the sadness of returning here, Teresa found some comfort in knowing that there were people around who knew and respected her and Tom. After speaking with the chief administrator, Teresa was offered a job as a medical assistant starting whenever she was ready.

Grateful for the opportunity, Teresa accepted right away. It felt strange being back here after so long but thankfully all the staff were welcoming and understanding of her demanding situation. She told them she would contact them when she was ready to come back. She should have started immediately, but her thoughts drifted back to the inheritance. She wondered what they would be. What if she could choose what she wanted to do, instead of being forced to return to a job she didn't want?

As Teresa left the medical center, she hurried to make it in time for her appointment at the library. She had been there many times before with Lucy and remembered how much she enjoyed reading with George during story time. It warmed her heart to think about how those memories could continue as she could be the one to read to other children.

When Teresa arrived at the library, Mary was behind the reception desk taking in returned books; it was evident that she was wearing down from fatigue. Teresa thought about how hard it must be for someone so young to go through such stress and agony. Despite this, Mary still managed to smile as she saw Teresa approach, thanking her profusely for offering her much needed help.

The two of them discussed what days and times would be best for Teresa to volunteer at the library. They decided on three days a week, with Saturdays dedicated to story hour for children, and Monday/Tuesday so Mary could have some time away. With everything figured out, Mary asked what books Tom would read to the kids during story hour. It touched Teresa's heart when she found out that one of his favorite stories was "Cinderella," which he had read numerous times when his own daughter was younger and used to accompany him here at the library.

Teresa thanked Mary again and allowed her to leave the library, so she could go home and get some rest. Teresa insisted that Mary take the rest of the morning despite her headache and promised to come in later in the day to close. They talked about what needed to be done before the weekend before Mary expressed her gratitude one more time and then left.

When Saturday finally rolled around, Teresa was prepared and excited to meet the little children that were coming for story hour. She smiled at all their eager faces when they began to trickle in one by one, each of them more delightful than the last. The children waved at her as she set up her chair in the corner and opened the book of Cinderella.

Before she even had a chance to start reading, all her listeners were entranced with anticipation of what was about to come next. They all scooted closer to Teresa as she began talking about how Cinderella's life was full of sorrow after losing both parents but that didn't prevent her from believing in the power of dreams.

As Teresa continued with her storytelling, she could see each and every child absorbed in awe within their own imaginations; some eyes shining bright with tears, others curled up on chairs embracing themselves tight against fear or delight. Teresa noticed how no matter if it was laughter or crying that surfaced during her narration, nobody ever felt embarrassed around each other; it was like a peaceful sanctuary where everyone felt safe and accepted whatever came out.

By the time she reached the end of Cinderella's journey, everyone had a glimmering smile on their faces and clapped heartily at its conclusion. Before they went off back home, some brave children approached Teresa thanking her for bringing such an amazing story alive right before them - despite this being their first time meeting each other, it left them feeling connected through this shared experience.

Teresa watched fondly as these tiny people ran out into the streets free from worry with bright smiles on their faces, the magic of "Cinderella" still lingering in their hearts. She couldn't help but feel a sense of fulfillment and satisfaction knowing that she had introduced them to a world of wonder and imagination.

As she packed up her things, she noticed a man standing at the back of the room, observing quietly. He was tall with broad shoulders and a chiseled jawline that could cut through steel. But it

A TANGLED WEAVE: Death of a Child

was his eyes that caught Teresa's attention - deep, dark pools that seemed to hold secrets and mysteries.

"Can I help you with something?" she asked politely.

The man stepped forward, revealing a soft smile that made Teresa's heart skip a beat. "No, no, I was just passing by and heard the sound of children's laughter. It's a beautiful thing, isn't it? The innocence and purity of a child's mind."

Teresa nodded, feeling a strange pull towards this stranger. "Yes, it truly is. Do you have any kids of your own?"

The man's smile faltered for a moment before he regained his composure. "No, unfortunately not. But I've always been fascinated by the minds of children. Their ability to see the world in a different light."

Teresa chuckled, feeling a sudden warmth spread throughout her chest. "Maybe you should come back next week and hear another story. It might reignite your own sense of wonder."

The man's eyes sparkled with amusement as he leaned in closer to Teresa. "I might just take you up on that offer. My name is Jack, by the way."

"Teresa," she replied, feeling her heart race with wonder of who this man was. She didn't remember ever seeing him in town before. She thought she knew just about everyone.

Teresa rose to her feet, giving a polite nod before concluding the conversation. She filed away her belongings and prepared to depart for home.

CHAPTER 25

Teresa returned home to a peaceful house. Over the past week, she had organized and spiffed up every room until it felt like her own. She had finally gotten rid of Steve's stuff by donating them to the church, and she was proud of the neatly compiled scrapbook of Lucy's drawings that graced the coffee table in the living room. Her evenings were spent savoring their memories together through those pages. Unlike the other rooms, she couldn't bear to enter Lucy's bedroom yet; not until they had found the monster that ended her young life. For now, Teresa savored the peace and calmness of her own company.

As she pondered the unknown future, the phone sounded off. It was the hospital calling, and Teresa hesitated to pick it up. She knew she had to go back to work, but also yearned for something different. Tom and she had discussed their aspirations during college -Tom planned on starting his own business while Teresa wanted to be a stay-at-home mom and writer. Though she had received her degree in English, Teresa now feared that writing would not generate enough income for her to survive.

When Lucy's arrival came with a set of costs, that dream was slowly pushed aside, and reality began to take its place. Teresa realized that her dreams of being a stay-at-home mom and writer were slowly slipping away. She discussed her options with Tom who wanted to make sure they could live comfortably while still providing the best care possible for their daughter.

Although she was sad to leave her newborn baby, Teresa took the job at the hospital and began to adjust to working life again. It was hard at first since it felt like she was neglecting her daughter but soon enough, she found herself enjoying the little trips away from home. She even found solace in seeing other parents and children on the ward - knowing that somewhere out there were others going through similar struggles.

Tom was also supportive throughout this transition, shifting his working hours so he could look after Lucy when Teresa wasn't around. Despite their occasional disagreements on financial matters or parenting styles, Teresa couldn't help but admire Tom's dedication and bond he created with Lucy. Even though they rarely spoke about it, she knew they shared an unspoken bond which would eventually help them get through anything life throws their way.

Heading back to the hospital was a source of anguish for Teresa. That's where she had been when her child had been stolen from her, killed by a creature, a monster, she couldn't stop. She'd been forced to leave her precious child, to work at job she hated. The place she went to make money had taken away her reason for living. Brushing away the thoughts stirring in her head, Teresa rose and made her way to the kitchen. She boiled some water for a cup of tea before sleep.

As Sunday morning came around, Teresa dressed herself for church. She had been determined to make every Sunday service. With Elizabeth and Maggie at her side, she sat comfortably in the pews. Father Michael would often use Teresa as a source to show dedication of faith.

Once she arrived at Church, it didn't take long for Teresa's suspicions to be confirmed. Father Michael began his sermon with an announcement that he wanted to dedicate part of it to bring attention to a certain woman in attendance that day: Teresa herself. He praised her strength and bravery since Lucy had been taken from the earth and paid tribute to how she continued attending services each week despite feeling such loss and despair. Everyone in church clapped at his words while some even cried out of appreciation for her courage.

The sermon was moving and touching, but it was also calming for Teresa who suddenly felt at peace as she listened closely with tears rolling down her cheeks as Father Michael finished off his speech with a prayer for Lucy's soul to be at rest.

Afterwards, when they met in the dining hall everyone was in good spirits despite tearful eyes still lingering on their faces from earlier events at services. Elizabeth and Maggie had become a strength in Teresa's life. They had stood by her when everything seemed to fall apart.

"How are you doing, dear." Elizabeth knew that Father Michael's service had touched an open wound in Teresa's heart. She knew that Lucy was not at rest, even after that dreadful night, the note from Tom's spirit, there was still something lingering in Teresa's home.

Maggie could feel it too, as she approached the two women talking in the corner. "Teresa, is there any news from Sam."

Teresa turned to see Father Michael speaking to others in the congregation. He was looking up at her and she knew he was talking about her. Looking at the women that were helping her hold everything together, she just signed and told them she was ready to go home.

The ride was quiet on the way back and Teresa didn't say much despite Elizabeth and Maggie's attempts to bring cheerfulness into the conversation. One thing seemed clear though, there was something different about this Sunday. The women sat int the kitchen while Teresa put together a small lunch. There was a chill in air as fall was now behind them and winter was sneaking in. Elizabeth and Maggie were browsing through the scrapbook when there was a knock at the door.

Maggie stood and walked to the front door. It was Father Michael, he asked for Teresa and if she could spare a couple minutes for him and she obliged.

Once in her living room, Father Michael began talking about Lucy's death and what it really meant for her family or rather how it affected them all differently. Teresa listened silently as his soft-spoken voice filled the room with words of comfort and compassion. He spoke of divine love being so powerful that no matter how demanding times got, nothing could ever take away the bond between parent and child which had been formed during life.

He also spoke of strength gained from heartache as he reminded Teresa that even through pain comes beauty; reminding everyone to treasure moments shared with loved ones still alive for they are what make up our most cherished memories in time gone by.

After a lull in their conversation, he looked at Teresa one last time before standing up to leave while gently placing his hands around hers in an effort to send healing vibes in her direction before taking off into the sunlit sky once again as another day of service ended.

As soon as Father Michael walked to door to leave, the air in the room became colder than normal. Teresa felt the coldness swipe through her. Teresa felt a heaviness on her shoulders like never before. Maggie and Elizabeth joined them in the living room. "Did you feel that?" Maggie knew that there was something wrong.

A TANGLED WEAVE: Death of a Child

The four stood for several minutes, looking around the room, but no one made a move. They could all sense the presence that was in the house; it was almost as if the air were vibrating with energy. Teresa knew exactly what this meant—her daughter, Lucy, had come to visit her.

Maggie and Elizabeth both stepped closer to Teresa as she began to cry softly. Father Michael softly touched her shoulders and looked deep into her eyes with compassion and understanding. He spoke softly of Lucy's love for her family and how even death cannot separate them from each other or prevent them from being together in spirit.

At that moment, Teresa felt an immense warmth surrounding her and she knew that Lucy had come to be by her side once more, just like when they were together in life. She could feel the comfort of having a piece of Lucy with her again and it eased the pain she had been feeling since losing her daughter.

There was a crash in the kitchen that brought all of them out of the silence in the room. Then they all ran to see what had happened. They noticed the scrap book scattered on the floor. Teresa gasped at the all the labored work she had done putting it together. "Please, stop." Teresa burst into tears falling on the floor to pick up the drawings.

Father Michael was astounded by what he was feeling and seeing, "I would never of truly believed it, if I hadn't seen it with my own eyes."

"I thought, it had been quiet, what has brought this on." Maggie moved to help Teresa pick up the drawings. She reached down to pick up the one closest to her when it flew out of her hand and across the room. Maggie took a step back, "We need to call Joanna."

Elizabeth agreed as she pulled Teresa from the floor. They could all feel the energy in the room growing stronger with each passing moment. Something was definitely happening, and they needed to find out what it was before it escalated any further.

As they made their way towards the living room, Teresa suddenly stopped in her tracks. "What's wrong?" Elizabeth asked, concerned.

"I feel her," Teresa said softly. "Lucy... she's here."

Just then, a chill ran down Elizabeth's spine as she heard a whisper in her ear. She turned to see that no one was there, but the voice was unmistakably Lucy's. "Mommy, I'm here," she heard the voice say.

Father Michael could feel the hairs on the back of his neck stand up as he too felt the presence of Lucy. "She's trying to communicate with us," he said.

The group huddled together, trying to figure out what Lucy was trying to tell them. Suddenly, the room grew dark as the candles flickered out. They heard footsteps approaching, but no one could be seen.

"Maggie, give me your hand," Father Michael said. As Maggie complied, he began to pray aloud, asking for protection and guidance.

They could hear the sound of creaking floorboards coming from upstairs. As they climbed the stairs, the sense of dread that they had been feeling only grew stronger. They could feel the presence of Lucy all around them, but it was mixed with something else, something dark and malevolent that made the hairs on the back of their necks stand on end.

They reached the top of the stairs and saw that the door to Lucy's room was open. Slowly, they made their way towards it, each step feeling like it was taking an eternity to complete. Once they were close enough, they could see a faint light emanating from within the room.

Father Michael held up his cross and took a deep breath before pushing the door open. What they saw inside made them all freeze in terror?

There, in the center of the room, was Lucy's ghostly form, surrounded by a swirling vortex of darkness. Her eyes were a dark and the features of her face had changed, but it was Lucy.

When the lights flickered back on, the figure of Lucy was standing in front of them. She appeared to be older than she was when she died, and her eyes glowed with an otherworldly light. Maggie stepped forward, tears streaming down her face. "Oh, Lucy, we miss you so much," she said, her voice trembling.

Lucy smiled at her loved ones, and then spoke to them in a voice that was both familiar and strange voice. "Help me," and she was gone. Her figure had disappeared, the room began to warm, and they could all tell her presence was gone.

A TANGLED WEAVE: Death of a Child

They all stood in silence, not sure what to make of the appearance. Teresa held the hands of her friends while Father Michael walked around the room. His faith told him that what he seen was possible, the man in him was unsure. He had listened to Elizabeth and Maggie speak of this happening; he heard Teresa speak often about Lucy still being in the house. He thought it was her grief. Now he is forced to see it for himself. He could feel an energy emanating from the walls and he was sure that it was Lucy's presence.

"We should leave," he said finally. The group agreed and quickly began to make their way downstairs.

Once outside, they all looked up towards the house. The windows were dark, but it seemed as though something was watching them from inside. They all shivered in unison and silently made their way back to the car, Father Michael leading the way with a blessing on his lips.

Back at church, Father Michael gathered everyone in a circle and asked for guidance from above on what they had just experienced. They all shared their stories of Lucy's ghostly visitations and decided that it must have been her way of communicating with them after death. He also suggested that perhaps she wanted help finding peace in the afterlife or was looking for answers about life after death.

Again, Maggie and Elizabeth suggested contacting Joanna, Father Michael was not pleased about contacting a medium. It was not a sanctioned of the church. But under the circumstances he agreed. Maggie agreed to call her, until then they would go on as normal. Teresa agreed that if she felt threatened, she would go next door to Elizabeth's. She promised not to take too many risks.

CHAPTER 26

Returning to the house, Teresa did not feel Lucy's presence. She had stayed at Elizabeth until nightfall. The air was cold and light rain was beginning to fall. It was not cold enough for snow, but Teresa knew that time was coming. She was not looking forward to it. She was already missing the warmth of summer.

Walking into the house with just the light of the kitchen she was alone again. She had done so well at putting her life back together. Now she was back to feeling the loss that had enveloped her existence. She didn't bother with turning any lights on or making a cup of tea. Teresa went straight to bed. She had to get up early to be at the library before opening hours to prepare for the day.

The night was silent as Teresa tossed and turned in her sleep. Her mind was filled with worry and doubt, and she could feel Lucy's grief seeping into her subconscious. In her dreams, she saw dark figures lurking around the corner of every street, menacing shadows whispering to her from the distance. Everywhere she looked, there was an overwhelming sense of dread that caused her heart to ache with fear and sadness.

When Teresa finally opened her eyes, it was still dark outside. A chill ran down her spine as a wave of uneasiness swept over her. She felt like something bad was about to happen - something terrible that would affect not just Lucy but everyone in town. She had been living in a state of anxiety ever since Tom's death, but now it seemed to have reached a new level of intensity. Something had to be done before it was too late.

Teresa tried to push away these negative thoughts as she crawled out of bed. Even though things were difficult right now, there was still a glimmer of hope inside her; she could feel it urging her on despite the darkness that surrounded them all. With a few deep breaths, Teresa slowly began to regain control as hope filled up within her once again.

She quickly dressed and started to make breakfast, hoping that a few moments of activity would help her refocus her thoughts on the present. As she ate, she tried to put the events of the previous night out of her mind.

When it was time to go to work, she grabbed her coat and

keys and stepped outside into the crisp morning air. She took a deep breath, feeling somewhat refreshed by the frosty winter air.

At the library, Teresa immersed herself in her work. She chatted with visitors and parents looking for the right book, rearranged bookshelves, answered phone calls, and kept an eye on teenagers browsing through the stacks of books. It felt good to be useful and helping others find what they needed; it provided her with a sense of purpose in life again after all these months without Lucy.

By lunchtime, Teresa realized that she hadn't had a negative thought about Lucy since she arrived at work that morning. She smiled; perhaps this could be a turning point for her—maybe this job would help keep Lucy's memory alive without having to be constantly surrounded by reminders of what she lost.

Suddenly, Maggie came running up beside her with news: Joanna had agreed to come later that day for their session! Excitedly they discussed preparations before going back to their duties until closing time arrived later that evening.

At six o'clock sharp she locked up in the library before driving home in anticipation of Joanna's visit. Teresa's mind raced with thoughts as she walked to her car. She wondered what Joanna would be able to help this time. There was not much that came from her first visit. She was nervous but hopeful. As she arrived home, Teresa couldn't help but feel a pang in her chest as she walked past Lucy's bedroom.

Maggie and Father Michael were waiting for her at Elizabeth's house for her to get home from work. Once Teresa had changed clothes and took a moment to herself, she called them all over. Teresa was glad to see that they were waiting for her. She was not looking forward to this alone.

Joanna's arrival quickly took over her thoughts. When the doorbell rang, Teresa's heart skipped a beat. Father Michael answered the door, smiling warmly at Joanna as he welcomed her inside. As they entered the living room, Teresa couldn't help but notice the mysterious aura that surrounded Joanna. There was something different about her, something almost supernatural.

Father Michael asked about Joanna's credentials as well as how she felt about talking with someone who believed in communicating with spirits from beyond the grave—but none of them were overly concerned given what had happened at the house last night.

"Tonight, I want to try something a bit different. I want to see if Lucy can just answer the question as to why she is not at peace." Joanne confided in them that maybe with Lucy's age she does not understand what she is doing here. Maybe she just doesn't know where to go.

Teresa explained to Joanne what had happened on the terrible night that the house was trashed. She told her about the letter that was left by Tom. "How could she not know where to go, if she was with Tom?"

Joanne explained that when a child has passed away in circumstances such as these, they often struggle with the love they feel for those of the living and those of the deceased. In this particular case, it involved two parents which might make it a tougher transition for Lucy. "She is likely torn between you both, unable to move on until she finds solace in separating from you without closure."

Father Michael interrupted, "Our faith tells us that the deceased is met with open arms to their loved ones. Lucy should know that she is loved on both sides. Lucy's faith was strong for a child. She knew God would be waiting for her."

"God is not the one that waits to the deceased, it is a messenger that guides them. It could be a family member or could be just someone that they were ones close to." Joanne spoke calmly to Father Michael; she understood that sometimes the religious faith was different than the faithful.

Joanna sat on the couch, folding her hands neatly in her lap. "Shall we begin?" she asked softly. Teresa nodded, sitting across from her on the other side of the coffee table. Maggie sat on the armchair, observing quietly.

Joanna closed her eyes and placed her hands softly on the table. "Lucy, are you here?" she whispered.

For a moment, there was silence. Then, to Teresa's amazement, the temperature in the room dropped suddenly and drastically. A chill ran down her spine, and she felt the hairs on the back of her neck stand up.

Suddenly, Joanna's eyes opened, and she looked directly at Teresa. "She's here," she said firmly.

Teresa's heart leaped with joy. "Lucy? Are you here?" She

could feel Lucy's presence in the room. Her smell surrounded the room.

The silence was broken by a voice that sounded distant and small.

"Yes, Mom. It's me." Lucy voice was faint, she seemed drained of energy. Teresa could not see her, but she could feel her in the air.

"Lucy, what can I do for you?" Teresa asked anxiously.

"Don't forget about me. Will you help me?" Lucy's plea drifted away at the end of her sentence.

Joanne quickly interjected, "Stay with us Lucy; we have some questions for her." She then turned to Teresa and said, "Ask her why she is here and tell her you are alright."

"Sweetheart, please tell mommy why you are here. Mommy is safe, I need you to find peace." Tears began to swell up in her eyes. She could feel her world crashing down on her.

The candles in the room wavered as a gust of wind burst through the bay window, filling the house with clouds of dirt and dust. Father Michael ran to the window, attempting to push it closed against the formidable force. Maggie and Elizabeth held hands in fear, remembering all the strange stories that their friend Teresa had told them about this place. They'd felt a chill earlier but never expected it to be like this.

Father Michael finally got the window shut and they all gathered around him as he began to pray. "Lord, we come before you in need of your help and mercy. Please send us some guidance on how best to help our friend Teresa find her lost daughter Lucy. Help us to understand what she's trying to tell us from beyond this world."

"No, mother, not until I find daddy. You need to look in the right direction first." Lucy's voice began to fade off.

"What should I be looking for? What will help you out?" Teresa had no idea what Lucy meant by this.

"You're talking to the wrong people - go find the right ones! You should not let the bad near you. I have to keep you save until daddy comes." And then Lucy vanished again.

"Come back!" Teresa yelled after her daughter, but there was no reply anymore. Joanne stayed seated on the couch trying to reach out to Lucy, but there was still no response.

Teresa felt a deep ache in her chest as tears streamed down

her face. She had hoped for closure, but now she felt more lost than ever. She turned to Father Michael, hoping for some guidance.

The four of them bowed their heads in silence, each lost in their own memories of Lucy. Teresa thought back to the day Lucy was born, the first time she held her in her arms, and all the moments they shared together. She felt a sense of peace wash over her, knowing that although Lucy was gone, her love for her would never fade.

Teresa's eye filled with tears as she thought of her little girl who was lost. How could this be? How could she be lost when she was supposed to be with Tom? Father Michael tried to assure her that there had to be an explanation and they would find it. He thought of a young man he had meet at the conference last year.

"Let me make a call, I might have someone that can help us." Father Michael made his way to the door with Teresa following. "We will find her peace." He spoke with just certainty that Teresa felt the warmth in his heart. She knew he would help but was not sure what he could do.

Joanne approached the front door, expressing her sorrow at not being able to find Lucy. Teresa knew that she had put in her best effort, and that was what mattered most. Joanne spun round to address the women still present in the living room. "Teresa, you told me that there hadn't been any drama for a while now. What changed recently to bring Lucy back into your life? Who have you talked to that is different than before? The key is within you, you must find it."

"I've been tidying up Steve's possessions, and I collected Lucy's art in a scrapbook. I am also volunteering at the library. I'm thinking about going back to my job at the hospital, but my courage is failing me so far." Teresa was not sure what to make of what Lucy had said, but she knew she had to figure out the next step. For Lucy.

Joanne nodded to the other women before she left the house, wondering if Teresa had a plan by volunteering and reorganizing. The three women exchanged looks, all thinking the same thing—maybe Teresa was on to something. She had been trying to put her life back together these last few months. "I haven't had contact with Sam lately," she said aloud. "Perhaps I should call him tomorrow."

As the night went on, Teresa couldn't shake off the uneasy feeling she had about Lucy's appearance. Her mind wondered who she had been talking to too that had been different. There was no one, the lawyer, Margret? Maybe Lucy didn't want her to return to the hospital. Nothing made since.

As she sat on the couch staring at the scrapbook of Lucy's art, trying to find a clue as to what her daughter was talking about. She looked through the drawings of her school, the library, and the park. It was then that she noticed something strange in one of the drawings at the park.

In the corner of the page, there was a faint outline of a figure that appeared to be standing behind Lucy. Teresa squinted her eyes and leaned closer to the page, trying to make out the image. Suddenly, the figure became clearer, and she gasped in shock. It was George, the old man from the library and another man she didn't recognize at all.

Feeling overwhelmed and scared, Teresa decided to call Father Michael. He listened patiently as she recounted her experience with the scrapbook and the strange figure. After a moment of silence, Father Michael spoke up.

"Teresa, Lucy is trying to communicate with you from beyond the grave? It's not uncommon for loved ones to reach out to us through signs and symbols. Have faith, the answers will come. I think you should call the detective. Perhaps he will have some answers or at least do some more digging."

Teresa felt a chill run down her spine as she processed his words. But deep down, she knew that he was right. Lucy was always a creative child, and it wouldn't have been out of character for her to send a message through her art.

As Teresa hung up the phone, she thought about George. He was a kind man, a bit strange but always loved Lucy so much. It had also seemed strange that she was now seeing him more around town. It was getting late, but Teresa decided she needed to call Sam and ask about George, maybe he had given her some answers about him. Sam agreed to pull what he could on the old man.

*****

As Teresa got dressed in the morning, she had to remind herself to hurry—she wanted to get to the library before it opened but also needed to call Sam. As if on cue, her phone began to ring. It was him; it seemed they had a special connection since she had just been thinking about him. He asked to meet her for lunch, he has some news for her but not to get her hopes up about Lucy.

Teresa hung up the phone and called Mary asking if she could come in later so that she could make lunch with Sam. Mary was more than willing to come in. She had thought time off would be good for her, but instead it just gave her more time to think about her life. "I need to be busy." she told Teresa.

Teresa arrived a few minutes early at the diner. Freda's Diner was bustling with people as usual, all in a hurry to get the most out of their humble lunchtime. At the back table was a couple who were likely arguing, but Teresa couldn't make out what they were saying. Her thoughts drifted away from them and back to Lucy.

Freda took a few moments to say hi to Teresa. She was busy serving up orders for those picking up food, clearly making good money with all the customers coming into the cozy diner. Freda was always so cheerful; it was clear she enjoyed life a lot. It was wonderful stepping into a place she knew was going to be cheerful. Sometimes it is the tiny things in life that can bring you joy.

When Sam finally arrived, he was dressed in his usual business attire, a smart suit and tie, but there was something different about him today; he seemed more serious than usual. he ordered an iced tea and a club sandwich. As they waited for their orders to arrive, Sam filled Teresa in on what he had found out about George. It seemed that he couldn't have been connected to Lucy's death. Although disappointed, Teresa was glad that at least now she knew for sure that George wasn't involved in any way and could put her mind at ease.

Sam told Teresa he had someone he wanted her to meet. He was running late but wanted her to wait for him to arrive. Teresa could tell Sam had something on his mind but was struggling to say it. Sam kept making small talk and not getting to the subject.

"I know there is something else you want to talk about. Please, just say it." Teresa took the first step in moving the conversation along.

"I hate to say this, but we all have bosses. Mine is not always a compassionate one." Sam stalled again before continuing. "Lucy case is over a year old now and we have no more leads. My captain is asking me to put it on the back burner until something comes up."

"You mean Lucy is now going to be a cold case!" Teresa was

devastated, she felt her heart explode. How could this be happening, not now? Not with Lucy making contact again. "You promised to not let this go." Now Sam and Lucy were the ones arguing at the diner. Lucy thought to herself that Freda's was a happy place, there was no room for sad news here. But here it was.

Sam looked up and Teresa could feel the relief in his face as the man from the library walked up to the table.

"Sorry, I was so late, I ran into a bit of trouble," he took a seat at the table.

"Teresa, this is Jack Ellis, he is a dear friend of mine. " Sam tried to do the introductions not knowing that they had met earlier.

"We have met," Jack nodded to Teresa acknowledging her.

Sam began explaining the Jack was a private investigator from the city. They had worked on several cases together in the past.

Jack smiled at Teresa. "It's nice to meet you officially," he said, offering her his hand. She shook it firmly, feeling a little more at ease with the situation now that she knew who Jack was.

Sam began to explain why he had asked Jack to come. He told Teresa that he was not leaving the case but needed extra help. Jack would be able to step in and have a new set of eyes to move the investigation forward.

Jack declared that he could inquire about people who may have known Lucy and her family. Moreover, he proposed they research any unsolved cases similar to Lucy's as a way to discover connections or evidence related to her disappearance.

"Teresa," he said confidently, "I'm going to need you to help me in this endeavor. Will you accept?" Jack informed her he had contacts and access to information the police could not legally utilize. "As a private investigator, I can circumvent certain privacy laws—it permits progress to be made rapidly."

"Absolutely." Excited to begin the investigation, Teresa quickly accepted his offer and thanked Jack for coming over at such short notice.

Sam let us know that he had already copied and given Jack the files to review. He said he'd stay in contact but would be mostly out of the loop. Teresa and Jack arranged to gather at her house that night.

After saying goodbye to Sam and Jack, thanking Freda again for lunch, Teresa made her way back home pondering what all this meant. Now that she would be working with Jack, she could be more hands on in the investigation.

As Teresa walked home, her mind was racing with thoughts about the investigation. She felt a surge of excitement that she would finally be able to take a more active role in it. Her heart raced as she thought about what Jack had said about having access to information the police couldn't legally use.

She arrived home and immediately got to work. She started by looking up anyone who may have known Lucy or her family. She reached out to old classmates and acquaintances on social media and made some phone calls. She began piecing together the events leading up to Lucy's death.

As the night wore on, Jack arrived at Teresa's house. They sat down together with the files Sam had given them and began going through them one by one. Jack would point out details that Teresa may have missed, and Teresa would ask questions to clarify certain aspects of the case. They discussed any leads they had come across throughout the day and brainstormed possible connections to other unsolved cases.

Hours went by, but neither of them noticed. They were consumed by the investigation, fueled by their desire to find out what happened to Lucy. As they worked, they grew increasingly comfortable with each other, bonding over their shared determination to solve the case.

Eventually, they realized it was late and decided to call it a night. As Jack was packing up his things, he turned to Teresa. "You know," he said, "we make a pretty good team. Maybe we should work together more often."

Teresa smiled, feeling a warmth in her chest. She had enjoyed working with Jack and respected his talent as an investigator. She nodded in agreement, "I think that's a great idea, but right now. I need to put closure on this part of my life."

Jack agreed, "Okay then, I will see you in the morning. We will start going through Lucy's drawings and try to see what she has seen."

As Jack walked to his car, Teresa could feel the chill surrounding the house. Teresa looked around but the house was silent.

CHAPTER 27

Lucy watched closely as Jack walked into the house. She was not sure of this new man that her mother had brought into her home. She watched as they sat in the kitchen going over all the pictures of her dead body lying on the ground. She wondered who this man was.

Teresa pulled her drawings; she was showing this strange man her drawings. Lucy tried to pull the energy to stop them, but she was weak, she was not sure why she could not seem to do anything but watch.

Lucy tried to understand what Marie had said but her emotions were too strong. Marie was close, she could feel her, but she could not see her. She felt the tears streaming down her face and was determined not to give up. Taking a deep breath, Lucy composed herself before trying to speak again.

"Please, I need to see my dad," she begged. "I just need to know why he left me." Just then Marie appeared in front of her.

Marie looked deep into Lucy's eyes before answering. "Your father can not be here for you, but I believe if you can make peace with yourself first then you may be able to see him again." Marie pointed towards the field where the children continued to play. "Look to the sunshine Lucy, the sun begins a new day and new beginnings."

Lucy nodded slowly as she processed this information. She realized that if she could make peace with herself then perhaps, she could make peace with everything else in her death too, including finally helping her mother find closure with the unsolved mystery of her death.

Lucy thanked Marie before turning back to Jack and her mother in the kitchen. As she watched the two combing through the papers, she tried to contact them. She used all her strength to get her mother's attentions. But there was nothing. Why could she not make her mother feel her.

Lucy turned and began walking through the now overgrown garden, a thought suddenly occurred to Lucy: what if Jack hadn't been able to see or feel what she had done when they were going through her drawings? What if Jack couldn't see whatever energy Lucy was trying to control? The thought made sense; maybe this was why nothing happened, he was there to hurt her mother. She needed to stop him.

Lucy gasped as realization dawned on her; Jack wasn't looking for clues in those drawings; he was looking for clues about what happened after she died! With newfound hope in her heart, Lucy set off running back towards the house in search of more answers about what this new man in her mother's life was. Lucy became enraged, now she was using what energy she had left in her tiny soul.

*****

The night had become chilly, and Teresa shivered as she got up to go turn up the heat. Even though it was just a simple gesture, it brought her comfort. She missed Lucy's warm little body snuggled close to hers during cold nights like this.

She walked back to her bed and lay down but couldn't seem to sleep. She was still hoping that Lucy would come back home, and she could feel her presence around her, faint but there, nonetheless.

She thought about the night Lucy was murdered. She had been so young, so innocent, and taken in such a cruel way. It had been so hard for Teresa to cope with what had happened and she had often thought about how different life would have been if her little girl had been spared.

Teresa awoke in a daze, her eyes wet from tears. Tears streamed down Teresa's face as she drifted off in a fitful sleep, dreaming of the night Lucy was taken from her forever. In her dream she saw herself running towards where Lucy lay lifeless on the ground. She felt the weight and pain of Lucy's absence more deeply than ever before. She rose and stumbled to the window, pushing aside the curtains, and peering out into the darkness of night.

The moonlight illuminated a lonely figure standing in the shadows across from her house. By his shape, Teresa knew it was Tom. A deep sorrow overcame her as she called out to him, but it was too late - he had already gone. Desperate for answers, Teresa resolved to follow him, no matter what danger lay ahead.

She dressed quickly and dashed out into the night after Tom's retreating figure. As she ran down the street, a chill coursed through her veins; she had an eerie feeling that something was watching her every move. Suddenly, a gust of wind came sweeping through the trees nearby, taking her by surprise and causing her to stumble backwards onto the ground with a thud.

When Teresa looked up again, Father Michael appeared at her side. He put his hand on her shoulder and said softly: "Come now my child, be not afraid – I am here to guide you."

He beckoned for Teresa to follow her, and they began walking towards a small village on the outskirts of town. The streets were deserted except for a few shadowy figures lurking in alleyways or along walls; Father Michael held Teresa close as they made their way cautiously through this place of veiled secrets and whispers that seemed to have grown out of an ancient fear.

Teresa and Father Michael approached an old, abandoned church that had been boarded up years ago. When they drew near, Teresa noticed a large crack in the door and saw something glistening inside. With assistance from Father Michael, she pried it open to reveal an old chest filled with documents, which appeared to be related to Lucy's disappearance.

The documents were faded and yellowed with age, but Teresa managed to make out certain words that seemed familiar - words like "sinful", "adoption" and "scandal". Teresa thought what these words had to do with Lucy.

She looked up at Father Michael with hopeful eyes, the uncertainty of their future already forgotten in the face of this new discovery. He nodded faintly, before disappearing from her dream.

A loud crash woke Teresa from her dream, and she sat up in her bed, trying to shake off the images that still lingered in her mind. As she rubbed her eyes, she realized that the crash had come from her front door. She got out of bed and tiptoed to the door, peering through the peephole to see who was there. But it was dark, she slowly opened the door to find nothing but darkness.

Teresa knew she would not be able to go back to sleep, she made her way to the kitchen and started coffee. As she sat in the kitchen alone, she wondered if the dream was a clue or her mind reeling with all the events of the last few weeks. When the sun finally rose, Teresa was determined to find out the truth behind Lucy's murder. Maybe if they could finally get an answer, she could heal -

even though it seemed impossible right now - and bring some closure to this tragedy that changed her life forever.

She walked out the back door and sat under the oak tree. Sipping her coffee, she could hear the birds singing, the wind blowing through the trees, life goes on, she thought. She was going to make this a day of discovery.

She took another sip and looked around the yard, thinking about how much she had loved spending time outside with Lucy. They would play games, read books, and just enjoy each other's company. The memories were bittersweet now, but she couldn't help feeling grateful for them.

As she finished her coffee, she heard a car pull up in the driveway. Teresa's heart began to race as she got up from her seat and walked back into the house. She opened the door to find Jack standing on her front porch.

Jack had come a few hours earlier than expected, and the look of resolution in his eyes was all the answer Teresa needed. She placed a cup of coffee on the table in front of him. It was going to be all business today. They were going to find a new lead to follow.

With loads of enthusiasm, Jack and Teresa went through Lucy's artwork—each drawing bringing back fond memories, but also piercing Teresa's soul with sorrow. Her drawings were like a diary of her days, capturing her childhood, her thoughts and dreams, her adventures. It was almost too much to bear for her to look at them as a person she hardly knew.

Finally, after what felt like an eternity, they came across one last drawing that brought some peace to Teresa's heart. It was a picture of Tom and her embracing each other under the same oak tree where Teresa had just been sitting that morning. The drawing was filled with such love and tenderness that it seemed to bring her closer to Tom. She felt his presence in the house. Teresa knew it was Tom, the presence was strong, and she could smell him. His cologne lingered in the room.

Jack glanced up to Teresa with confusion. "Can you smell that?" he asked.

"Yes," she replied. "It's Tom. It's hard to describe, but I think he's just trying to give us a hand."

The phone rang, interrupting the awkward conversation. It was Margaret calling to ask Teresa to come into the office the next morning. Teresa asked if there was news about the inheritance, but Margaret couldn't give her any information. Teresa could feel weightlifting from her shoulders. What had Steve's family left for her? What would the conditions be? She thought about the way the will was sent up for Steve, to have a family. What was she going to have to have? Or was it going to be another figure like the crystal rocking horse.

Jack decided that it was late enough, they could pick up tomorrow afternoon. He asked if she could take the drawings back to his hotel for the night. Thinking, he could have undistracted time to review them. Teresa agreed if it was only for a night. She could not bear being without them longer.

CHAPTER 28

The next morning, Teresa arrived at the lawyer's office bright and early. She had no idea what was going to be discussed, but Margaret had seemed insistent that it couldn't wait. As she stepped inside, she was greeted by an elderly woman with a kind smile who introduced herself as Bella's lawyer. She said she had something important to discuss with her regarding Bella's will.

The lawyer welcomed Teresa into Philip's office and told her what had happened. Apparently, in the last days of Bella's life she wanted to add Teresa to the will. She hadn't had enough time to set up a trust fund in Lucy's name in case something happened to her, so instead, the family was giving the money left by Bella directly to Teresa - even though they were not legally obligated to do so, as Bella did not update her will with their decision. Nevertheless, they honored her wishes.

Teresa was speechless. She had never expected to inherit anything from Bella, not to mention such a generous sum of money. Tears welled up in her eyes as she thanked the lawyer and Philip for their generosity.

The lawyer assured Teresa that this was what Bella had wanted and asked if there were any questions she could answer. Teresa told her that she wanted to use some of the inheritance to help the library and maybe she could write a book. The lawyer applauded her idea, but also warned her to be careful with such a considerable sum of money and advised her to seek financial advice as soon as possible.

After the meeting, Teresa phoned Elizabeth and told her about the inheritance. Elizabeth was relieved that Teresa was going to have the means to care for herself without having to go back to work at the hospital. Elizabeth agreed to meet at the house when she returned to discuss options regarding the money.

The two of them discussed potential projects she could carry out with the money from the inheritance. Elizabeth told Teresa of the various expansion projects she could do at the local library, such as increasing seating and book capacity, creating a new computer lab, creating a children's section with toys and games, and offering more educational programming such as summer classes.

"We could name the project in Lucy's honor." Teresa was excited to have this was going to take. Her life was changing again. She had good friends on which she could lean. She had Sam and Jack to help her find closure for Lucy. And now she had the financial means to accomplish much more.

The next step was to discuss the money with a financial advisor. Teresa needed to make sure she planned well for the money Bella had given her. She met with the financial advisor and discussed stocks, bonds, investment options, and other ideas that would help her best manage the money. The financial advisor told her of various strategies and methods of investing, such as diversification over several stocks to manage risk. They discussed ways to establish an emergency fund so she wouldn't have to worry about unexpected expenses in the future. The advisor also suggested setting up a retirement plan for when Teresa wanted to retire from work one day.

The more Teresa talked about what she could do with the inheritance from Bella, it became clear that there were many possibilities out there - enough for her to create a legacy that embodied all of Lucy's spirit and love. As they wrapped up their conversation, Teresa thanked the financial advisor for his help and guidance in managing this sudden windfall. She couldn't wait to start designing plans around how best to use the money given by Bella.

First, she needed to contact the family, she wanted to find a way to thank them for her including her in the family. Teresa was touched by their kindness and needed to find a way to show them how kind this gesture was.

*****

After a long day of life-altering changes, Teresa sat in her kitchen reflecting on how she ended up here. Within the last decade, she'd lost her husband and soul mate, remarried for the security of herself and Lucy only to lose her daughter to murder. What's more, she discovered that her first husband was killed by her second, and today found out that she could now be considered a millionaire if it weren't for the events that changed everything. Though the wealth came with a price, Teresa would give it up in a heartbeat to have her life back before the tragedies.

As she sat there, lost in thought, Teresa's phone rang. It was a blocked number, and she didn't recognize the voice on the other end of the line at first. But as they spoke, Teresa's heart swelled with joy. It was an old friend from college, someone she hadn't spoken to in years.

They chattered away about their lives and rekindled their old friendship. And as they talked, Teresa slowly began to open about everything that had happened to her in the past few years - about losing Tom, and then Lucy, and about the inheritance she'd just received.

Her friend listened patiently, offering kind words of support and encouragement. And when Teresa told her about wanting to use the money to create a lasting legacy for Lucy, the friend suggested something extraordinary: a scholarship fund.

With tears in her eyes, Teresa realized this was the perfect way to honor her daughter's memory. There were so many ways to use this money to help the community. She was going to dedicate her life to Tom and Lucy's memory.

After hanging up the phone, Teresa cleaned up the kitchen and went to bed. Her minds swirling with the ideas of the scholarship, the library and most of all Lucy. She hoped that this might be another way to help her find peace.

The legacy Teresa wanted to create in their memory came flooding back to her. She had promised herself that she would use this money to do something meaningful, and now she knew exactly how she would do it. She would start a scholarship fund in Tom and Lucy's honor; one that would help children of all ages pursue higher education no matter what their financial situation or background may be.

Teresa was consumed with dreams once again that night. She dreamt of Tom desperately calling out to Lucy in some kind of ethereal space between the sky and the ground. He yelled her name as he roamed through the shadows. Tom begged her to come back to him, but she lingered over the house until her murder could be exposed.

Teresa woke in the morning to the sun already high in the sky. She pulled the blankets up covering her head while her thoughts of the day before came rushing back to her. She had so much planning to do, appointments to set and a murderer to find. She threw back to the covers and dressed hurriedly. Jack would be arriving at the house soon and she needed coffee.

Dressed and ready to start another day, Teresa headed towards the stairs. As she passed Lucy's room, a cold breeze wafted from under the door, and she paused before opening it. The chill inside was so intense, it was like someone had turned off all the heat in the room. She lifted the window curtains to check the vents and found warm air flowing through them. With tears in her eyes, Teresa took in the sight of beloved child's room - for her sake and Lucy's she needed closure on this sad mystery.

Teresa took a moment, she sat on Lucy's bed curled up with her favorite teddy bear, trying to calm herself down. She'd come a long way since Lucy's death, but she still couldn't shake the feeling of emptiness that consumed her heart. She closed her eyes and took a deep breath, taking in the familiar scent of Lucy's room.

As she opened her eyes, she saw something strange on Lucy's bed. There was a piece of paper, folded neatly and placed under her pillow. Teresa's heart raced as she reached out to grab it. When she unfolded the paper, she saw that it was a letter from Steve that she had never seen before.

Teresa's hands trembled as she seen the letter was from Bella. It was asking Steve to bring her and Lucy to Texas to meet the family. Teresa was taken back as she never knew anything about the family until after Lucy's death. Teresa sat with the letter in hand completely confused as to why this was in Lucy's room, she knew she needed to turn this over to the police or maybe just Jack.

Teresa folded the letter and continued down the stairs to start the coffee before Jack arrived. Sitting in the kitchen, with the letter in front of her, she wondered what else Steve had not told her. It did now make sense that Steve would not have killed Lucy, but who would?

The knock on the door brought Teresa back to reality. Jack came prepared with a notebook and several questions for Teresa. He asked about her teachers at school, anyone Steve worked with, and any places she would have gone alone.

Teresa did her best to answer all the questions. The teachers in the small town had been with the school district for ages. They were all local. The school tried to always hire within, so there had not been anyone new for several years. As for people Steve worked with, he worked from home, so he hardly had any contact with others except at the local bar. He was a frequent visitor there, but again they were also all local people.

Teresa thought about the times Lucy was alone. Teresa would not allow Lucy to be alone. She didn't find out until later that Steve left her home alone while he went to bar when she was working. Lucy did go to the library after school when Teresa could not pick her up. That was it, just the library.

After the questions, there was a moment of silence between them as Jack started pulling out the drawings. Lucy looking at the letter in front of her, finally handed it over to Jack.

"I found this in Lucy's room this morning." Teresa was not sure if it meant anything other than backing the story that Steve did not kill Lucy. "Bella was Steve's grandmother; she was the one that released Steve's inheritance."

"This is interesting, but why would it have been in Lucy's room. Wasn't the room searched before." Jack folded the letter and handed it back to Teresa.

"Yes, it was searched. But uh... things move over around a lot in this house." Teresa was not sure if she should share that Lucy's spirit was still in the house. That she believed Lucy was trying to tell her something, but she was sure what it was.

Jack noticed the pause, "It is okay, Sam has told me about things that have happened in the house. I do believe you; it is just not something we can take to court." Jack was right, there had to be evidence. "Hold onto this, it might be useful if we can tie it something else."

"Let's take a look at the drawings, I have a couple that I could not quite make out." Jack pulled a few of the drawings for his folder. "This one, it looks like she is at the library, but who are these people standing behind her."

Teresa pointed the people put as the librarian Mary, George the old man that would read to her, and Billy. "Billy is a couple of years older than Lucy. He lives a few blocks away with his grandmother. Nice boy, just very shy. Lucy never talked about him much, but he would stop at the library to visit George as well."

Jack then pulled the drawing that Sam was interested in with Steve yelling at Lucy. Teresa explained that Sam had gone over this drawing. It is what brought his attention to Steve to begin with.

"Okay but look at this." Jack pointed at the letter in his hands, "could that be the letter you just showed me." Jack didn't give Teresa a chance to answer as he pulled another drawing out. "These are in chronological order, correct? The next drawing is of Lucy crying at the library with George."

Teresa stared at Jack, she had not put that together, maybe George knows something. It was then that she remembered the drawing of the third man in the other drawing. Maybe, George knew who that man was? Or maybe, just maybe he was the key to all of this?

CHAPTER 29

George sat outside the library on the steps leading to the front door. He was bundled up in a few coats and socks on his hands creating mittens to keep his hands warm. Jack stood across the street watching him for several minutes. George only sat and watched as people walked by not even noticing the old man witting.

Jack couldn't help but feel a pang of sympathy for the old man. The public records revealed that George had served in Vietnam from 1965 to 1969, eventually being honorably discharged after sustaining a gunshot wound that left him with a disability. He married and had four children in 1974; however, his wife died during childbirth, and he tried to care for his children alone until 1985 when child services intervened due to neglect. His job at a steel mill in Pennsylvania was also lost, leading to a downward spiral of destitution which cost him his family.

He had looked over the police records of the old man by the name of George Lucus. He had been arrested several times, for shoplifting, public drunkenness, and loitering. Jack spoke to Sam about the charges; nothing indicated that he was a violent person. He was just a man trying to make it in a cruel world.

Sam explained that the charge of loitering was when George was sleeping in Margaret Stein's alleyway. Margaret was known as the town gossip. The incident happened soon after her husband passed away, and she became suspicious of everyone around her. The judge dropped the charge but allowed George to stay in the town jail for a few nights so that he could get some rest and a few good meals.

Jack thought about the many people in the world that were suffering from things out of their control. There was so much pain in the world. He thought the least he could do was take this man out for a healthy meal while he was talking with him.

Jack approached George slowly not wanting to scare him. "Hello George, my name is Jack. I was wondering if you could help me with a few things."

George looked up, "I know who you are. You are a friend of Teresa and Sam's."

"Yes, that is right." Jack moved his hand forward to shack hands with George.

George removed the sock from his hand before taking Jack's. "Any friend of the lady is a friend of mine. How can I help you?"

Jack asked if he would like to get some lunch so that they could talk about Teresa and Lucy. George was quick to accept standing up and saying he knew the perfect place. "We can walk over to Freda's."

"Thank sounds great, George but I am hoping to take you to some place a bit quieter. Do you know of another? I have a car we can drive someplace else." Jack needed George to focus, Freda's was too busy with the townspeople listening carefully about what they were going to be discussing.

"Oh, well yes, I guess. There is a restaurant out near the highway, but it is kind of expensive."

"Why don't you let me worry about that part." Jack led George over to his car and they drove out of town.

In the car, George removed his socks from his hands and replaced them with a comb for his hair and a wet wipe to clean his face. He joked to Jack that there were some places willing to turn away a homeless man like himself, but neither of them was concerned about what other people thought. George provided Jack with directions to the only steak house in the area, which pleased Jack as it had been quite some time since he'd enjoyed a good steak. They both took comfort in the fact that the parking lot was almost empty.

Inside the restaurant, Jack made sure that George could order whatever he wanted. The server came over and gave Jack a bewildered look at the company he was keeping. Jack insisted that they would make it worth her while to keep the bread and drinks full.

Jack explained to George who he was, and he was looking for anything that would help with finding out what happened to Lucy. He told George about the drawings and the one with her crying. He was hoping that George could tell him about that day.

"My poor Lucy, she was such a good girl. She liked spending time with me. She didn't care that I smelled bad either." George had a small tear in his eye. Jack knew this was going to be painful for the old man to remember.

"Take your time, why don't you just start by telling me about your relationship with her." Jack sat back and just let the old man talk.

George told Jack the story of how he and Lucy had met. It was a several months before Lucy died, when Lucy was sitting in the library trying to read Cinderella. She explained that her father used to read it to her every night, but he'd been gone for a while. George listened to Lucy conversation and offered to read it to her instead.

George and Lucy formed a strong bond over the pages of the book as they shared stories about their pasts and discussed what their futures may look like. From then on, whenever Lucy's mother, Teresa, packed her lunch for library day she would always include an extra sandwich for George.

Jack couldn't help but feel moved by their story, especially since George had opened up and shared his own personal struggles with him. He felt like he was getting an insight into George's life and seeing how kind-hearted he truly was.

Jack pulled out the drawing of Lucy crying, "Can you tell me about this?"

George told Jack how miserable Lucy was with Steve. He mentioned the way Steve treated her when Teresa wasn't around. "Lucy knew that he was only interested in the money she could bring him," George said. That day, Lucy had been crying because Steve forbade her from drawing pictures of her father.

"You need to understand, Lucy loved her mother, but her dad—that was something special. They were incredibly close. I think even after Tom had passed away, Lucy would spend hours playing with him, even though he wasn't actually there." George explained.

Jack listened intently to George, feeling a heavy sense of sadness for Lucy and what she must have gone through. He felt like he had gotten to know her even though they had never met.

Jack asked George if he had ever spoken to Teresa about what was going on with Lucy and Steve.

"Oh no, this was always just between Lucy and I," George said shaking his head. He explained that while he could see the struggle in her eyes, he understood that some things were too painful for her to share with anyone else. All she wanted was someone who listened and showed her attention, something that Steve wasn't providing. George told Jack that Lucy didn't want Teresa to know. Lucy knew that money was tight, and Steve's income helped her keep the house that her father bought for them.

George went on to tell Jack that Tom, Lucy's father, had given her a necklace. Steve took it away from Lucy and refused to give it back to her. On the day she died, George said she found it again but would not tell him where it was or who had it.

Jack was overcome with emotion at how cruel Steve had taken away something so special from Lucy. He encouraged George to talk to Teresa about what had been going on, hoping that perhaps this small gesture might help them both heal in some way.

"George, have you spoken to anyone about this?" Jack thought maybe with all that had happened maybe he needed someone to rely on.

George spoke fondly of Father Michael to Jack, mentioning how the priest always made sure he had a place to sleep on cold nights and would provide food for him when the soup kitchen was shut down. He further commented on the difficulty of being homeless in a small town, then voiced his fear that he wasn't strong enough to go back to the city where he could be vulnerable again.

After their meal at the steak house, Jack drove George home as promised and dropped him off outside the library. As they parted ways Jack made sure George knew that no matter what happened in the future, he would always be there for him as a friend.

As night fell upon them Jack knew that the key to finding Lucy's murder was to find the necklace. Sitting in the motel room, Jack studied Lucy's drawings again, he considered finding out what the necklace looked like and perhaps where it was. It was late in the night before he had seen it, a glint of silver in one of the sketches caught his eye. He leaned in closer and noticed that the necklace had a distinct pattern of interlocking links, almost like a chain. Jack sat back in his chair, deep in thought, wondering where he could start looking for such a distinctive piece of jewelry.

After a few moments of deliberation, Jack decided to start the investigation by interviewing Lucy's family and friends- the people who were closest to her. He began by compiling a list of everyone who knew her well enough to have seen or received the necklace. As he pored over the list, Jack realized that he had overlooked one important person. He checked his notes and retrieved an interview list that Sam had put together for him. As he went through the names on the list, some of them seemed unfamiliar while others jogged his memory. However, there was still one name missing: Father Michael.

Although it was evident that he was close to the family, why had he not been interviewed yet?

Jack lay in bed, his mind whirring with the meeting with George and why Father Michael had not been interviewed. He glanced at his watch; it was too late to call Sam, but he'd have to do that first thing in the morning.

The weight of George's situation bore heavily on him, reminding him of how easily any of them could be homeless. Memories of his ex-wife came to Jack—after their daughter's death, it had been difficult for them to keep the family unit together. Jack hadn't been a good husband at that point; he was in too much pain and had wished for the courage to take his own life, just so that he could be with his little girl again.

Jack stared up at the ceiling, remembering the pain of that night and all he'd lost. After Marie's death had left him completely broken, he'd been unable to stay in their home any longer. He had gone out on his own, searching for a way to make sense of everything that had happened. It was during this time that he met Sam who helped him find solace in his work as a private investigator.

A TANGLED WEAVE: Death of a Child

CHAPTER 30

When morning came Jack's thoughts returned to Father Michael and the necklace. He quickly showered and dressed before calling Sam to fill him in about George's situation. Sam agreed that it was important they visit Father Michael right away; with the priest being the only other person George had spoken with about Lucy, he was likely the only one who knew about the necklace.

Jack hung up the phone just as a knock sounded on his door—it was Georgie. "My mind was on Father Michael all night." It was obvious that George had not slept all night. Jack invited George in to warm up and have a cup of coffee.

George stepped into the motel room, looking at the sticking notes, photos, and newspaper clippings pinned to the wall. There was so much information, George was taken back at the work he had put into finding out who killed his special friend.

"This case means so much to me, George. You see, I have lost a child as well, it felt like a part of me was taken away too. I know what it is like to desperately want to have something back that you've lost—and I can feel Lucy's pain and her family's pain with every fiber of my being." A tear started to form in the corner of Jack's eyes. As have wiped it away, he told George his story of loss.

"We all have stories, Jack. The pain comes when we keep them to ourselves. Stories are meant to be told." George placed his hand on the shoulder of his new friend.

Jack investigated George's grief filled eyes. He could see the pain in his face, he understood what it meant and leaned forward in his chair, softly resting his hand upon George's shoulder. "I will do everything within my power to find justice for Lucy' he assured him—his voice calm but determined.

George nodded solemnly and stood from his chair, thanking Jack for the coffee and a bit of warmth before leaving the room. As Jack watched him walk slowly down the street under the dim morning glow of the horizon, he knew deep down that this was a case he would not take lightly; justice was coming for Lucy and Father Michael had all the answers that they needed.

Jack picked up his coat and headed toward the door, opening it up to see both Sam and George standing in front of his room.

Sam turned to Jack, "We are going with you."

"Sam you cannot come, if this does lead to something, it will interfere with a case in the courts." Jack turned back towards his room with the others following. "Why don't you two fill me in on Father Michael. Then we will figure out what comes next."

Georgie filled Jack in on all of Father Michael's background information; apparently, he had taken an interest in Lucy ever since she was quite young and had become like family to them over time. His kindness towards her was something special. Father Michael had been sent to town just before the death of Tom. He was quickly becoming part of the town, becoming involved quickly with its congregation.

"What about the previous priest? Do you know where he went or why he was replaced." Jack asked, sensing there was more to the story.

George hesitated for a moment before speaking. "Father Martin was transferred to another parish a couple years ago before Tom's death. There were rumors that it had to do with some scandal, but nothing was ever confirmed."

Sam chimed in, "I did some digging and found out that the church paid out a large settlement around the time the previous priest was transferred. No one knows exactly what the settlement was for, but it was enough to make people suspicious."

Jack's face contorted in anger as he processed the information. "So, they just transferred him to a new parish and swept it under the rug?"

George nodded grimly. "Unfortunately, it's not uncommon. The church tends to protect its own, even at the expense of innocent lives."

Silence hung heavily in the room for a moment before Jack spoke again. "I need to talk Father Michael. "

Sam and George both tried to join Jack, but he discouraged them. "You're both familiar with this person. I'm not. If there is something here, who do you think will be more open or guarded around?" Sam and George glanced at each other before nodding; Jack had a point. He needed to handle this on his own.

"Why don't you both hang out here. George, there are some

clean clothes in the closet, take a shower, get something to eat. You both can go over my notes while I am gone. We will meet up for Lunch at Freda's, okay?"

Jack arrived at the church where Father Michael worked and was greeted warmly by him. As they sat down for tea together, Jack explained why he was there; though at first hesitant.

"Father, I am investigating the death of Lucy," Jack began without preamble. "I know you were close with her, and I would like to ask you a few questions."

Father Michael's expression grew solemn. "Of course, anything to help find justice for Lucy."

Father Michael eventually warmed up and began telling him what he knew about Lucy, including details about a special necklace Tom had given her. She never took off until it went missing shortly before her death.

But as Jack began to ask his questions, Father Michael's answers became evasive and defensive. He claimed that he had no knowledge of any wrongdoing on the part of the previous priest and insisted that he had nothing to do with Lucy's death.

Jack didn't believe him. There was something in the way Father Michael avoided certain questions, the way his eyes flickered nervously, that made Jack suspicious.

As he left the church, Jack looked around the office, "Do you know where they moved Father Martin too?"

Father Michael hesitated, "He is no longer with us, he passed just after leaving this parish." Father Michael told Jack that he thought it was a heartache but was not sure.

"I am sorry to hear that." Jack left the church and made his way back to his car. He could feel the Fathers eyes on him as he left.

There was something not right about this, but Jack could not place his finger on it. It was nearly noon before Jack made his way to Freda's to meet George and Sam. The men sat and compared notes for most of the afternoon. They could all tell they were getting closer to finding out the truth.

CHAPTER 31

Lucy sat beneath the oak tree, expecting her father to come home soon. She could hear the dull drone of the place that was separating life and death. She could hear how quiet it was, how everything had stopped, no sounds, no movement, just the same nothingness she had heard before.

Her spirit was weary, and she knew that if she wanted to be reunited with him, she had to find him by herself. The ground beneath her had become uncomfortable and cold. She could no longer hear the laughter of children playing in the nearby meadow. Everything was changing around her, and although she didn't understand why, she knew her father would help her make sense of it all. She knew she was no longer a part of the living world, but she held onto the thought that her mother still needed her.

"Lucy, come with me." Marie appeared out of the darkness.

"I can't leave, what if dad comes for me." Lucy exhaustion had taken control of her. She was no longer full of spirit.

"I am here to try and help you one last time, please if you don't like what you see you can come back here." Marie reached out her hand to help Lucy up.

The two girls walked a short distance to a clearing, Marie told her to watch in distance she would be able to see everything.

Lucy watched as her mother danced around the living room. She was full of hope for the future. She knew about the money left by Steve's family. She watched as the connection with his family and her mother grew to a solid relationship.

"Is this really happening right now," Lucy began to smile at the knowledge her mother was happy and that she had others to hold onto.

"This is the present and the future. Continue watching there is more."

Lucy seen George with Sam and that another man, Jack, in the diner. The same place her father and her loved to go to before school. She watched as they put together notes and pictures of her. "Who is the other man?"

A TANGLED WEAVE: Death of a Child

Marie gazed at Lucy with a broad smile on her face. "Every person in the world is connected, bound together by the threads of life and death. The man's name is Jack; he was my father in life." Marie draped her arm around Lucy's shoulder. "Life is a fragile thing, but it's what makes us who we are. Even in death, the people around us will come together to make sense of it all."

Lucy could feel the warmth of Marie's embrace as they stayed in the clearing watching her mother's life go by. She couldn't believe that her death had helped bring a new purpose to her mother's life and to those around her. She felt immense joy, but also immense sorrow for the pain that was caused by losing her.

Marie continued speaking with a comforting tone, "Your death will be remembered, and it will have a lasting impact on your mother and the people around her. You are not forgotten, Lucy."

An elderly woman walked up to the pair standing the clearing, "Lucy, this is Bella, she is another part of your story." Marie took a step back allowing Bella to join them.

"My dear child, you are truly the light that shines. Your death will bring great happiness to many others. When the time is right, we will see each other again. Just remember, there are answers to every question. In heaven all the answers are within us." Bella's soft voice brought comfort to Lucy.

Lucy looked towards Marie with tear filled eyes, "But I'm gone now. I'm already part of the past."

Marie smiled fondly at Lucy and shook her head, "No you are still a part of this world in ways you can't even imagine. You have been given an opportunity to make a difference in this world, although it may not be seen until much later on down the line."

Lucy let out a deep sigh as she felt comforted by Marie's words. She realized that even though she was gone from this world, she would always remain here in spirit, and she would continue to influence people long after she was gone. "Thank you," Lucy whispered softly as tears began streaming down her face.

"What about my dad? I am ready to see him now. I am ready to go." Lucy could feel the love and the sensation of the next part of her journey.

"It will happen, I feel you have one last trip to make." Marie knew that she would go back to say goodbye to her mother. "You need to make this a quick trip. No disturbances, please Lucy, don't forget what you are learning. It is important."

Marie nodded silently and embraced Lucy tightly before taking her back to where they had first met- the edge of darkness between life and death. As they reached the entrance, Marie held out one last message for Lucy: "Know that your legacy will live on forever." With those words spoken, Marie faded away into nothingness leaving Lucy standing alone at the entrance to eternity.

It was only a brief moment later when her dad appeared, "Are you ready?" Lucy's excitement and meeting with Marie had recharged her. Lucy reached out to her father. His touch brought Lucy's strength back. She was at peace surrounded by love and light.

"Are you taking me home? Are you taking me to mom?" Lucy was excited to be able to travel again. She had not been able to be with her mom since that terrible night when she made her mother cry. It was only in her mother's dreams that she could see her.

"Yes, but only to say goodbye, Lucy. This is how it needs to be done." Tom placed his arm around his child. He would do anything to keep her safe. He knew from the moment of his death, that this was going to happen. Tom knew the pain his child was going to have to go through for the miracles to happen. Lucy nodded sadly and held her father's arm tightly as she was whisked away to the dream where she would finally be able to say goodbye to her mother.

When Lucy and Tom arrived in Teresa's dream, time had no meaning. Every sense in Lucy's body was overwhelmed with joy and sadness. She could feel her mother's presence before even seeing her. As she slowly opened her eyes, Teresa was standing there with an expression of love on her face. Tears were streaming down both of their faces, but they embraced each other one last time before Lucy had to leave again. Teresa somehow knew why they were there.

The pain in Teresa's words as they reached Lucy was palpable. She had wanted to stay, to keep her mom safe forever.

"Lucy, you are my heart and soul, I will always love you. It is okay, I am okay. It is time for you to be with your father."

"Lucy," Tom's voice echoed in her head, "Your mother has a grand mission that she cannot do while caring for you. You know that." Lucy understood - her mother would be able to save many lives because of her death. With newfound strength, she nodded and accepted it.

After a few more moments of silent exchange between

mother and daughter, Tom signaled for them to return home, but not before giving Teresa one last hug goodbye. With one final wave from Teresa, Lucy and Tom began their separate journeys to their own homes where they knew that life would never be the same again without the presence of each other.

CHAPTER 32

Teresa sat alone in the shadows, contemplating how her life had been altered. She awoke from a beautiful dream, where her beloved husband and daughter were reunited in paradise. Tom reminded her that he had a plan for her life, and Lucy reassured Teresa she was safe and content.

The violence of the world had taken away her family, leaving their lives turned upside down by the selfishness of others. Tears ran freely as Teresa tried to make sense of what had happened. She wondered why there must be so much suffering in the world and why she was being subjected to it. After a few moments of contemplation, Teresa realized that even though she may never understand why this happened to her family, she could still take comfort knowing that her beloved husband and daughter were together again in heaven.

Knowing she would not be able to go back to sleep, Teresa got up and went to Lucy's room. She sat on the bed trying to feel the presence of her daughter. The room was still and quiet, but it was filled with memories of her daughter's life. Teresa's eyes drifted to the photos of Lucy hanging on the wall. Her baby girl was growing into a beautiful young woman, full of life and promise. But she would never make it to her full potential. She would never get married or have a child of her own.

Teresa reached out to touch one of the pictures and let out a deep sigh. It seemed like just yesterday that Lucy was born, and she held her in her arms for the first time. Now, she was gone, and Teresa was left with the painful realization that she would never hold her daughter again.

As she sat there lost in thought, Teresa's mind drifted back to the day she was killed. She replayed the events repeatedly, trying to find a way to make sense of it all. But the more she thought about it, the more confused she became. The only thing she knew for sure was that she missed her daughter terribly, and the pain of losing her would never go away.

Teresa closed her eyes and took a deep breath, feeling the weight of the grief that engulfed her. She knew she needed to find a

A TANGLED WEAVE: Death of a Child

way to move forward, to honor the memory of her daughter in some meaningful way. Looking at the photographs, Teresa made a promise to Lucy that she would carry on, that her life would have meaning even without her beloved daughter by her side.

In that moment, Teresa decided to live her life to the fullest, to never take anything for granted, and to always remember the precious gift of life. And with that, she got up from Lucy's bed, wiped away her tears, and walked out of the room knowing that Lucy would always be with her in spirit. As she closed the door behind her, Teresa whispered to the empty room, "I love you, Lucy. Always and forever."

Teresa walked downstairs; her mind preoccupied with thoughts of the future. She was still trying to make sense of the tragic events that had brought her to this point. She knew that there would be tough decisions ahead, but she also knew that she could handle it. After all, she was Lucy's mother—she had been through worse before and emerged stronger than before.

As she started the coffee pot, Teresa thought about what lay ahead for her today. She was volunteering at the library for a few hours, something that provided her with some much-needed comfort and solace during this tough time. After that, she had another meeting with the lawyer and financial advisor who were helping her with the money left by Steve's family.

Teresa smiled as she thought about it—she now had a lawyer and a financial advisor! Who would have thought such things? It seemed surreal to her—just three months ago, she couldn't have imagined having any need for either one. But now they were helping guide her through the process of settling the affairs.

She hadn't spoken to Steve's family about it yet; there were too many other details to take care of first. But in her heart, Teresa knew exactly what she wanted to do with most of it—supporting causes close to Lucy's heart like the library and setting up a scholarship fund for students at Lucy's school, as well as an educational program in memory of her daughter.

By the time Teresa finished her coffee and got ready for her day, she felt more focused and determined than ever before. Even though this wasn't the life she'd envisioned for herself or for Lucy, Teresa found strength in honoring what would have been important to them both—and living life to its fullest in memory of them both.

With a heavy but hopeful heart, Teresa grabbed her keys and headed out.

As Teresa waited for Mary outside the library before unlocking the doors for the day, she had a special present in mind for the young woman whose life was in turmoil due to her divorce. Mary longed to move forward with her life, but her soon-to-be ex-husband fought for ownership of their family home—the one her grandparents had built. Her husband argued that he deserved it because he had spent his own money on all the repairs made there. Teresa had not been told about Mary's situation, only learning about it from Margaret; surprisingly, the town gossip had something positive to contribute. This brought a small smile to Teresa's lips.

"Good morning, Teresa, I hope you have not been waiting long. It was a bit of a rough start for me." Mary was doing better from when they first met but the lack of sleep was obvious in the young woman's eyes.

"Oh, no, not long at all. I was trying to get here before you. I would like to talk to you before we open up." Teresa knew she was about to make this woman's day; she was just cherishing the moment.

The two friends went inside and took a seat at a table near the window. Teresa removed some items from her purse and handed them over to Mary, who gave an inquisitive look in response. With a joyful grin on her face, Teresa explained that she had made arrangements to have an attorney handle Mary's divorce proceedings and pay the full amount of what her ex-husband was asking for. She also added that after everything was finalized and the papers were officially signed, any remaining funds would be put aside so Mary could take a much-needed vacation wherever she wanted.

Mary's eyes widened in shock as she tried to process what Teresa had just told her. Was this really happening? Was she really going to be able to move on with her life without the burden of her ex-husband and their family home weighing her down?

"Teresa, I don't know how to thank you. This is...I can't even find the words to describe what this means to me," Mary said, tears springing to her eyes.

"There's no need to thank me, Mary. I know you would do the same for me if our positions were reversed. All I ask is that when you get to where you want to go, you send me a postcard so I can live vicariously through you," Teresa replied with a chuckle.

A TANGLED WEAVE: Death of a Child

The two friends sat there for a moment, basking in the joy of the unexpected gift. Then, Mary's phone rang, breaking the peaceful silence. It was her attorney, calling to give her an update on the divorce proceedings. Mary excused herself from the table to take the call, leaving Teresa alone with her thoughts.

As she watched Mary walk away, a sense of sadness crept over Teresa. She couldn't help but wonder what her life would be like if her Tom and Lucy were still alive. Would they be happy? Would they have made different choices than she had? Teresa shook her head, trying to clear away the negative thoughts. She had made peace with the past, and she wasn't going to let it hold her back anymore.

When Mary returned to the table, she was practically glowing with happiness. The attorney wanted to see her right away to file the papers right away. This brought a small smile to Teresa's face. Teresa was excited to be able to help, it gave her a chill to know that she was doing something for others. At that moment she knew Lucy and Tom were pleased.

Alone in the library, Teresa felt the satisfaction of having a purpose: to right the wrongs that her new fortune allowed her to. Mary had become a close friend; she was so kind and generous. Doing something for her felt good and gave Teresa strength as she continued her mission to make lives better for those around her.

As she walked out of the library, Teresa felt a sense of accomplishment wash over her. She was doing something good for someone else, something that would positively affect their life forever. It felt great knowing that she could make a difference in people's lives with just a few simple steps-it gave her hope for what else she could do with this newfound fortune of hers.

CHAPTER 33

Jack and Sam were both waiting outside Teresa's home when she arrived home that evening. She was excited and nervous about seeing them standing there. It had been a good day; she was not looking forward to being pulled back into her grief.

"Hi guys, what are you doing?" Teresa tried to hold on to the happiest day she felt in a long time.

"We have a couple questions for you. We think we are making some progress just wanted to run a couple thing by you." Jack seemed a bit nervous. She was not sure if it was because Sam was with him or something else.

"Sure, come on in, coffee or tea? I can put a pot on." Teresa led the men into the kitchen.

"Coffee, please," Sam was always ready for more coffee.

As Teresa put on a pot of coffee, Jack had told her everything she learned about George and Father Michael. He was sure that Father Michael knew something about Lucy's murder but whether from the church or outside, he was not sure. Teresa was eager to find out more information and thought that maybe talking to the priest directly would be her best bet.

Sam interjected as Jack hesitated. "The necklace that Tom gave to Lucy - what can you tell us about it?" He was confused why his friend seemed so uneasy asking the question. It didn't seem like something would rattle Jack's nerves.

"Oh, Lucy loved that necklace. She never took it off. He gave it to her just before he died. It was not anything special, just a small heart with fake jewels. But for a small child it was everything." Teresa sat back and thought for a moment, it made her smile, to think about the necklace and how proud Lucy was to wear it. "She told me she lost it a few days before... before she died."

Sam went on to tell Teresa how they had discovered that Steve took the necklace away from Lucy. He told her she was no longer allowed to wear it. George knew that this hurt Lucy, and he confronted Steve. Steve promised to give it back to her, but we don't know if it happened or not.

"We are wondering if you knew where it was."

"No, I just figured she lost it. She was only twelve and it was not an expensive necklace." Teresa was wondering what this had to do with the case.

Sam's phone rang, and he got up from the table to take the call in the living room, leaving Jack and Teresa alone.

"Your face looks so different today—you look like you're bursting with life," Jack said, now no longer nervous. Sam's presence must have caused his unease earlier.

"I've come to terms with Lucy's passing and am ready to move on," Teresa replied, feeling a sense of peace wash over her.

"It suits you well," Jack replied before noticing that Sam had returned.

"We need to get going; there is something at the station that needs our attention." Jack grabbed his coat and headed for the door.

"Wait! Can I come too? If it has anything to do with Lucy, I want to know about it." Teresa was suddenly overcome with enthusiasm at the prospect of learning something new.

The three arrived at the station where Father Michael was waiting for them. "I found out a few more things about Father Martin that shed some light." Father Michael was nervous. He knew that dredging up the past discretions of the church were not going to go favorable to him. "Is there someplace we can talk in private?"

Sam looked around the station, "let's go to my office". They all made their way through the maze of desks with several police officers looking their way.

"This might have not been a good idea." Jack looked uneasy at the faces peering at them.

"You may be right, Jack" Sam stopped and looked around the room. There were questions running through the minds of all his co-workers. "Do you all not have work to do?" His voice echoed in the room. "Maybe, we go somewhere else." Sam led the group out of the station and into the parking lot.

Jack looked at his watch, it was getting late, and his stomach had started telling him he had not eaten today. "Why don't we go out to the steak house. I could really use something to eat." They all agreed, piling into cars and they drove out of town.

The steak house was empty other than a few truck drivers sitting in the back. This was much quieter than the station house with all the extra ears. Father Michael was more relaxed as he started telling the group about Father Martin.

Father Michael seemed relieved to be out of the station and away from prying eyes. He began to tell Jack, Teresa, and Sam what he had discovered about Father Martin.

"It seems that Father Martin was transferred to another church after the church discovered he had fathered a child out of wedlock. The mother passed away before the child's identity was revealed and the child went searching for answers at our church, eventually filing a claim against Father Martin."

Jack sighed heavily and shook his head. "This is why there are strict rules in place," he said. "To protect those from these kinds of scandals. But it looks like this one slipped through the cracks."

Teresa looked down at her lap, feeling embarrassed and ashamed on behalf of her church. She knew that these types of scandals were not good for business or morality, but she couldn't help but feel compassion for Father Martin as well - he must have been struggling with some problematic decisions in his life for him to make such a mistake.

Sam sighed as well, understanding both sides of the situation. He knew that this was a tricky situation with no easy solution, but he also knew that they needed to figure something out quickly before any more harm came to the church's reputation or members' wellbeing.

"We need to find out who this child is," Sam said firmly, taking charge of the conversation. "Once we do that, we can start working on making things right again."

"I don't understand, what does this have to do with Lucy? It is not like she is that child." Teresa looked at Father Michael, "Father Martin left the church before Tom and I even started attending," she added.

Father Michael's expression darkened as he continued, "This child would be in his or her late twenty's by now. But Steve did ask me about Father Martin. At the time, I didn't think anything about it." Father Michael was concerned that maybe some conversation should be left in the church. But this conversation was done in the confessional, it was just a passing conversation after a service.

Father Michael hesitated for a moment before continuing. "Steve had mentioned to me that he was meeting with the child at the park a few weeks before Lucy's death." Father Michael went on to say that Steven, and another younger man had been at the park several times when Lucy was playing with other children there. "She might have overheard something, not knowing what it was."

"Okay, then with Father Martin deceased, we need to talk to Steve." Sam, excited about what this new evidence could turn up, smiled at Teresa. "We are getting closer; this will come to an end."

Sam knew he would be the only one that could have complete access to Steve now that he was in prison. He told the group he would schedule a visit with him first thing in the morning. There would be a bit of red tape, but he would let them all know how it turned out.

CHAPTER 34

The next morning the area was blanketed in a fresh layer of snow, sparkling on the pavement as Sam took the long drive to the prison that was home to Steve Bird. The wind was still and the temperatures unforgiving. During the drive, he had plenty of time to reflect on recent years and how much this case troubled him. Lucy was just an innocent young girl who never did anything wrong; it was shocking that she had been living half her life with the man responsible for killing her father. From years in a father's loving arms to the last four years of someone only using her for money.

Driving through the locked gates of the prison, Sam knew the procedures. He had visited there several times when working cases in the city. He made an appointment with the warden first, he wanted to find out how Steve was adjusting and get a list of the visitors he had since being locked up.

When the warden was informed, he made his way to the parking lot to meet with Sam. The two proceeded to walk together towards the ward Steve had been assigned to. According to the warden, Steve had grown accustomed to the unfamiliar environment in his brief time there. He normally kept himself occupied by reading or helping in the kitchen. There had not been any reported issues between him and other inmates yet. The only snag in his settling in happened when Officer Jenkins came for questioning that day before sentencing. Apparently, it wasn't uncommon for prisoners to get anxious when law enforcement officers arrived.

The warden had Sam a list of names from the visitor log before opening the door to the interview room. "He will be brought in a few minutes. Let me know if you anything else." The warden left Sam with one of the guards and returned to his other duties.

Sam took a seat at the table; it was only a minute or two before two guards escorted Steve into the room. He looked smaller, Sam thought he had probably lost weight since the food was not what you would have been used to eating. Steve sat across from Sam with a stoic expression, his eyes cold and unfeeling. Sam could sense the disdain emanating from him, but he knew he had to keep his cool.

"Thank you for seeing me, Steve," Sam began. "I know this isn't an ideal situation, but I am here to ask you some questions."

Steve simply scoffed and leaned back in his chair. "What could you possibly want to know that wasn't already discussed? I've already been convicted, and I'm serving my time."

Sam leaned forward, his voice low and serious. "We have new evidence that suggests you and Father Martin's child had become very friendly before Lucy's murder. We believe you were involved, Steve."

Steve's face contorted into a sneer. "And what makes you think I would confess to something like that? I have nothing to gain, and everything to lose."

Sam sighed, knowing this wasn't going to be easy. "I understand your reluctance, but I am willing to help you in any way I can. Maybe there is a deal we can work out."

Steve raised an eyebrow, intrigued. "What kind of deal?"

Sam took a deep breath before responding. "You tell us everything you know about the murder, and we can work on getting your sentence reduced. Maybe even parole in a few years instead of serving out your full sentence."

Steve seemed to think it over for a moment before nodding. "Alright, I'll tell you what I know. But you have to promise me that I'll get what I want too."

Sam nodded. "Just tell me what you know, if it leads to something I will go to court. Now tell me, what do you know."

"That is not good enough." Steve folded his arms and scowl his face.

"I want some answers," Sam replied, his voice cold and steady. "I want to know who you were meeting in the park and why." Sam leaned forward; his eyes locked onto Steve's. "You do know that there's no getting out of here, right? You're facing life in prison, Steve. You might as well come clean and tell us everything. It might make things easier for you in the long run."

Steve chuckled and shook his head. "I will tell you this, look for Alice Chapman. Maybe she can answer some of your questions. Last I heard, she was living down by the old cemetery."

Sam felt a wave of anger wash over him. He had heard enough. He knew that Steve was lying and that he would never get anything out of him. He stood up and motioned to the guards to take Steve away. As they escorted him back to his cell, Sam couldn't help but feel frustrated. He knew that he was so close to the truth, yet so far away.

As Sam left the prison, he knew that he would have to find another way to find the underlying cause of this case. Who was this, Alice Chapman? Was she even a real person or was Steve just trying to get under his skin.

Back at the station, Sam pulled the records for Alice Chapman, she did exist, but she was buried at the old cemetery. Sam thought, excellent job Steve way to throw a lifeline.

Alice Chapman died of a heart ache about twenty-five years earlier. That would have been just about the same time Father Martin fathered the child. Sam needed to talk to Father Michael again. Could this be the woman that had Father Martins child? But who was the child and what happened to him or her?

Sam picked up the phone and called Jack to tell him what he had learned. "See what you can find out and meet me at the church in say an hour."

"I will be there, I can it. We are getting closure." Jack hung up the phone excited to pull all the records he could find on this woman.

Jack explored her secret, albeit illegal, avenues of research for more information than the authorities could discover. He read pages that revealed the life of Alice Chapman, including her child who would now be close to thirty years old. After her death, this child was adopted out without a father listed on the birth certificate. This meant that the man in the park with Steve had to be him.

Jack considered whether or not security cameras held onto footage from as far back as what he needed; most likely not, since too much time had passed. He didn't have time to dig, just then he needed to meet with Sam at the church.

Sam was waiting outside when Jack arrived. The two men walked into the father's office to discuss what they had both found out that day. Father Michael was not surprised although he didn't know much help he could be. It was way before his time at the church.

"Aren't there records here you could pull?" Jack knew that this would not go over well with the church, but he needed to find their information about the child.

"I just cannot go any further into this. The church records are all sealed, especially since there was a document filing." Father Michael had already stepped further into the secrets of the church than he should have. He just couldn't go further.

"Just a minute, Jack. We need to get a court order for the adoption records, and I think we have enough to present Judge Marks. She will sign it off if it can show who killed Lucy," Sam declared with confidence, knowing that the judge had refused to see him off in this case. He was right: she granted him the court order to open the file to the county records. The process only took a few minutes before he had a name in his hands. His jaw dropped as he read what he found. It was unbelievable--the man he had worked with, trusted even, could this be true?

Sam drove to Jack's motel, he needed to talk aloud but knew that the station was not the place he should be voicing his concerns on the case. He arrived at the motel and went to Jack's door, after a few knocks it opened, and a weary eyed Jack answered.

Once inside Sam began to explain what he had learned from the court records about the child of Alice Chapman, but he could not understand why he would be meeting with Steve in the park. He asked Jack for his opinion on how they should proceed in investigating this further without alerting him that they were with him.

Jack suggested they start at the church and look for any records or documents that might have more information about Alice Chapman or her child. Sam agreed that this was a good first step and took a moment to jot down some notes on where else they could look for information as well.

The two men then discussed what their next move should be if they came up empty handed with their investigations - do they keep looking or confront him directly? They both agreed that it would be best to get as much evidence as possible before speaking with him so he could not deny any involvement in Lucy's death.

In order to cover all their bases, the two men decided that one of them should also speak with Father Michael again while another checked out Alice Chapman's grave site in search of any clues she may have left behind before her death. With a plan of action in mind, Sam thanked Jack for his help and left for home, hopeful yet still uncertain of what added information may surface from their investigations.

    Before going their separate ways, they had agreed to reconvene the following morning. Jack decided that he would go to the church and talk with Father Michael; since Jack was not a member of the congregation, less questions would be asked than if it were a police officer asking them. He would make a stop on the way over to pick up Teresa, so she could distract anyone trying to get in between the conversation. Meanwhile, Sam chose to take a trip by the grave site, wondering if there was perhaps a list of visitors or any indication that someone had been tending to the gravesite recently - anything that might create a lead.

CHAPTER 35

As the sun began to climb in the sky, Jack and Sam both started on their tasks. They had agreed to come together to the steak house around noon so they could discuss what they had found. Feeling optimistic that things were about to be resolved, Sam first stopped in at the station to check in before his trip to the cemetery. Everyone was busy with their daily work and didn't take much notice as he passed through into his office. He thought it best not to leave behind any evidence of his investigation into Lucy's case since he was taken off it - he wasn't ready to make trouble with the police captain just yet.

Just as Sam sat down at his desk the phone rang, it was his captain. Sam picked up the phone not sure what he was going to be called in to do. "Can you come to my office? I need to speak with you."

"Sure, I will be right there." Sam hung up the phone, his mind was turning with the uncertainty of what to except when he walked into the office.

"Good morning, sir," Sam said, standing tall in the face of what he hadn't done wrong.

"I heard you brought a friend into the Lucy Thompson case. Care to explain?" His captain was known for his just ways but exacting rules.

"He's actually a private investigator. Teresa, Lucy's mother wanted to be more involved, so I told her about him." He hoped this answer would suffice.

"Is this investigator keeping the department informed?"

"Yes, absolutely. No concrete news yet, but you will be the first one to know when he does."

The captain nodded and Sam left the office to go back to his day job: The cemetery.

Walking back to his office, he ran into Jenkins. They both exchanged familiarities and Sam turned to walk away.

"Oh, Sam you are coming to my bachelor party, right?" Jenkins was excited. He was getting closer to marrying his girl.

"Sure, I almost forgot about that." Sam had forgotten, completely forgot he was even getting married. He was marrying into a very wealthy family. Sam was positive it was for the money but what did he know. It could be love.

As Sam arrived at the cemetery, it was strangely quiet. The snowfall had ceased, and the birds were not singing. There was a sense of peace in the air as he walked through the snowy graveyard. He was here to look for clues that may help lead him to Lucy's murder.

He searched around for Alice Chapmans gravestone. He noticed some footprints in the snow leading toward one of the grave markers. He followed them until he came across her marker. It was small and flat to the ground. Sam stood there thinking that the poor woman must have spent her last days alone with no family other than her son, there couldn't have been much money. especially not planning on a death at such an early age.

Looking down on the plate, it only read, "beloved mother". There was no mention of a husband, parents, or siblings. It was all incredibly sad to think of Sam knelt closer to the ground when he noticed a small bit of gold buried by the grass growing up around the grave site. There was the necklace.

Sam knew that he needed to keep all the evidence he collected secure. He took out his phone and snapped several pictures before putting on plastic gloves to retrieve the necklace. There was the proof he needed. Hopefully, Jack would be able to find out why.

Jack and Teresa made it to the church before many of the others had started to arrive. Jack only had a couple questions for Father Michael. They found him in the statuary preparing for the day.

"Father Michael, got a minute?" Jack spoke as quietly as he could.

"Yes, of course." Father Michael looked around and noticed Teresa standing by the door. He felt a bit less nervous knowing someone was running interference with the incoming congregation.

"I was wondering if you... if Father Martin knew who the mother of the child was or if ... well if he had multicable ladies that it could have been." Jack stumbled a bit on his words.

Jack couldn't believe that he knew about the money. "Oh, he very much knew," she said. "He was aware that the woman was entitled to a considerable amount of money from the church, but since she passed away shortly after, it never made it to her hands. I do know it's still being held in trust for her son - if he ever comes forward."

"So, as far as the church is concerned, there's no telling who this person is?" Jack asked.

"Yes, with the adoption and change in name, it would be almost impossible to trace him."

Jack told Father Michael that was what he needed. He and Sam could put the case together from this point. Jack pulled Teresa away from several ladies standing at the door and they headed out to meet with Sam.

The drive out to the restaurant was quiet. Jack and Teresa could hardly look at each other. The car was filled with anticipation and nerves as they prepared for what could possibly be their last ride together.

Teresa felt a tug in her heart, relieved that they were going to be able to catch who had killed her baby but sad that Jack would be heading back to city before long.

When they arrived, Sam was already waiting with all the evidence they had dug up. He pulled out a folder from his bag and handed it to Jack and Teresa. Inside were pictures of the necklace, birth certificate and the adoption paperwork.

Armed with a plan of action, Jack, Teresa, and Sam advanced to the final stage. Sam dialed the district attorney's number and requested a private meeting with him, the captain, and the chief. He stayed tight-lipped about the details over the phone, but he confessed that he had evidence of the murder and believed one of their own was responsible.

The district attorney assured Sam, he would put it together and set the meeting for 6pm. That way most of the office would be empty. There should not be a problem with anyone disturbing the meeting.

Sam was positive he finally had his guy. They all agreed it would be best not to return to town until after the meeting. Jack asked Teresa if she wanted to take a drive into the city, to avoid running into anyone. Jack and Teresa left Sam sitting at the restaurant putting together a presentation of all the evidence collected in the case.

Teresa could feel the weightlifting from her shoulders as Jack drove them into the city. There was so much activity, it was not what she was accustomed to. "I have not been in the city since Lucy's death. There is so much traffic." Teresa smiled as she looked on at all the cars passing by quickly. She wondered what the people in all the cars were thinking as they passed by her.

Jack looked over at Teresa sharing off into the distance. "The city is a busy place. There isn't much connection with people like there is a small town." Jack was going to miss the slower lifestyle when this case was over. But he was also going to miss her. It had been a long time since he felt a connection with anyone.

"So where are we going?" Teresa seemed to come back to reality.

"I wanted to show you something. I hope it doesn't upset you, but it is a part of my life I do not share with others much." Jack pulled off the highway and onto a small street just before the city. As he turned the corner, in front of them was a large cemetery.

"You are taking me to cemetery? I don't understand." Teresa looked at the lines and lines of gravestones.

"Yes, I want you to meet someone." Jack pulled the car over to a spot under an old oak tree. It reminded Jack of the one in her backyard.

The two got out of the car and walked a short distance to a beautiful stone with a picture of a young girl. The gravestone read, "In memory of our loving daughter. She fought until she could no long fight. May she rest in peace."

Jack sunk to his knee, brushing away the grass until he could make out the name. Marie Ellis. "This is my daughter," he said with a thick voice. "She died when she was twelve." His eyes filled with tears.

"Oh Jack, I am so sorry, I had no idea." Teresa knew this pain; she reached down to touch his shoulder. She wanted so much to take away the pain he was feelings.

"It is okay, she suffered for several years with cancer. It is terrible to say, but it was almost a blessing after the shock of it all. I know she is at peace." Jack stood up and placed his arm around Teresa, "Just think maybe our daughters are playing together right now."

"That is a wonderful thought, I hope so too." Teresa smiled at the thought they could be connected so closely to one another.

"Now, how about some shopping? We have a few more hours to kill before going back." Jack pulled Teresa back to the car.

Jack took Teresa to one of the malls that Marie loved to go to with her friends when she wasn't sick. It turned out to be a wonderful day. The two talked about their lost daughters and found that they had many things in common.

*****

As Sam walked into the district attorney's office everything was quiet. Everyone had gone home for the evening just like the plan was set. Sam was positive he had everything in place to present his case to everyone there. The DA was sitting behind his desk waiting for Sam to arrive. His captain was sitting on the couch in the corner of the office flipping through his phone. They were just waiting for the chief to arrive.

"Come on in, Sam, the chief is on his way. He should be here shortly." The DA was a young man. He had graduated top of his class at Yale, so he moved through the ranks quickly for the small town. "Why don't you go ahead and tell us why you have brought us all in here."

Sam looked over at the chief, who stood from the couch and walked to join them around the desk. "I wanted to bring everyone together because I have come across some evidence that is very disturbing in the Lucy Thompson case."

The chief spoke up quickly, "We took you off that case, and we also spoke about this early today. You could not have told me your findings then." He seemed terribly upset.

"Yes, sir but I wanted to double check the facts in the case first, I also did not want to present the case at the station." Sam paused collecting his thoughts. "Sir, some of the evidence points to one of our own."

The chief had walked in the office while Sam was in mid-sentence. "You better be 100% sure of what you are about to say before the words come out of your mouth."

"Yes, sir, I am." Sam proceeded to break down all the evidence before mentioning the name of the Alice Chapmans son. He showed the drawings of Lucy's in the park, the necklace that she never took off. He went on to tell them about the inheritance that was supposed to go to Steve and the money that had been set aside at the church for Alice's son. He showed proof of the communications between Steve and the man he was accusing. Steve had mange to find text messages between the two talking about a payout from the money from the church. He had also found evidence that Steve was investigating who the son was and how he could extort money from him. The man Sam was about to reveal had threatened Steve and his family, which would have been Lucy.

"Okay, sounds like you have put everything together, so who is this person and does he have an alibi."

No, he does not have an alibi, I know because I dropped him off at his house that is only about 6 blocks away. He could have easily made the walk to the house and back without anyone knowing it." Sam was beginning to get nervous, what if he had left something out. He was about to accuse a fellow officer of murder.

The DA spoke up, "Okay, who is it?"

Sam took a deep breath, "It is Jenkins, he is the son of Alice Chapman. Here are the adoption records. I have match them up to his employee file with the department." Sam began to relax when the entire room became noticeably quiet. He knew he had presented his case.

After several minutes, the DA spoke up, "Okay, it does seem like you have everything covered here. Why don't you leave us with this? We will go through it all together and let you know what is decided."

Sam was not expecting that, but he understood. He was accusing an officer of the law. He knew there would be plenty of Ts to cross. Sam left all the evidence on the desk, and he thanked everyone for listening.

Teresa and Jack waited patiently for Sam to come over to the house that night. The night of truth. When Sam walked in the door with no news, they were all beside themselves that the members of that meeting didn't jump on all the facts they delivered to them.

CHAPTER 36

As morning came by slowly, Teresa made way to kitchen for coffee. She had asked George to come over for breakfast. She was hoping to give the news that Lucy's killer was being arrested, but that news never came the night before. She had invited Jack and Sam to stop by as well. Jack said he would, but Sam needed to go into the station.

It was going to be ridiculously hard for him to walk in there today. She knew it would, but he was strong man the evidence against Jenkins was strong as well. Teresa was just thankful that she knew who had taken her baby from her. She knew it would not be long before she could confront him face to face.

But today, it was all about George. It was well-deserved. As Teresa began to prepare breakfast for him, her thoughts were of George and Lucy's special bond. She knew that with the money left for her, she had to do something extraordinary for him. He always put others ahead of himself, even though he was homeless. This was her chance to show how much she appreciated his kindness towards both her and Lucy.

George arrived at Teresa's home shortly after Teresa finished making breakfast. He was full of questions and wanted to know what had happened the night before. Teresa explained to George about the meeting. She was hoping to hear something this morning but nothing so far.

"George, I had a reason for asking you over today. I was hoping it would have been a celebration breakfast, but I still have good news for you." Teresa gave George a smile. She was excited to tell him but also wanted him to stir a bit.

"What is it? Whatever you need, I am here for you." George still wants to help her. Teresa gave out a small chuckle.

"No, this is about you George, I have something I want to give you." Teresa stood up and walked over, pulling open a kitchen drawer. Pulling out an envelope and handing it to George. "Inside this envelope is a new life for you. I hope you will accept it in Lucy's name."

A TANGLED WEAVE: Death of a Child

"What is this?"

"I wanted to use the money that was left me for something positive. This is the deed to a house in town. It is next to the library and is fully furnished and ready for you, George; it's something Lucy would have wanted. You are worthy of this gift, and she would have been so pleased to give you something like this." Teresa sat down and held George's hand as he stared at the envelope.

"I have no words; I can't believe you are doing this for me." George was speechless. A small tear fell from his eye. "I am not sure I can accept." George was not sure how to tell Teresa that he knew there was much to owning a house than just the money for it. George was too embarrassed to admit that he would not be able to afford the gift with the cost of utilities, maintenance, insurance. There was just so much extra that would need to be paid.

"Please, you must accept this," Teresa was confused. She thought Geroge would be excited to have a place to call home. "Am I overstepping, why won't you accept my gift."

"I am grateful for this, Teresa, I really am. But there is so much more, I am afraid of getting over my head." George knew that he would not be able to keep the house on his own.

"I understand," Teresa had another thought but was unsure how it would come across, so she just blurted it out. "How about if I give you a part time job to go with it? You can help me with setting up a community outreach program. You know the people in town that would benefit better than me."

There was a knock at the door that interrupted the conversation. It was Jack. He had got a call from Sam, asking him to meet at the house. Jack took a seat on an old, yet comfortable armchair made of woven rushes. George and Teresa joined Jack in the living room as they talked about Lucy. Jack looked up; he swears he could hear Lucy's faint laughter echoing through the walls. Taking a deep breath, Jack felt contented just being here.

Though George's heart ached at the thought of never seeing Lucy again, He couldn't help but feel awed by all these reminders that she was still here in some way - and that this house she lovingly cared for held so many special memories for them all. It felt bittersweet to be surrounded by such good friends.

The hour went by and still no sign of Sam, as the three continued to remanence about Lucy and the short life she had, Lucy's faint laughter came echoing through the walls. They all took a breath and looked at each asking with their eyes if it was just them or did, they all hear it. A comfort surrounded the house, it felt like a closure. The three friends knew that something had changed but couldn't see it with their eyes, they could only feel it in their hearts.

Jack got up from his chair and started to explore the house. The first thing he noticed was how the walls seemed to have an old-fashioned decoration that gave the place a unique charm. He passed by one of the walls and couldn't believe what he saw: it was a painting of a garden filled with colorful flowers that reminded him so much of Marie's favorite spot in the park in the city near his library.

He kept going through different rooms admiring everything he encountered: from old furniture pieces made from wood to bookshelves stuffed with interesting titles such as "Alice in Wonderland" and "A Midsummer Night's Dream." He thought back at his own daughter's death, he knew that he had made peace with it. He only wished he knew how to help Teresa make peace with her daughters. This house was a place of joy, he had been touched in a way he would never understand. He only knew that having Teresa in his life was a blessing.

Teresa walked to the backyard and looked out at the old oak tree in the backyard which had lost its leaves for winter. It was empty and still except for a few birds twittering among the trees. It had been such a special place for her and Lucy; their favorite area to play after school or just in peacefulness enjoying each other's company. She closed her eyes and smiled as she remembered fondly all the times they had spent in this spot, nursing cups of hot chocolate or reading books together under a brilliant blue sky stretching overhead like an endless canvas. S

She looked up at the sky, "Lucy, I am going to be just fine. Please find your place and be happy for me. I will work every day at making the world a better place for children just like you." Teresa thought about the friends that had brought her to this moment in time, each one of them had given her a place in their hearts.

George gathered everyone as a gust of wind swung open the living room's large window. "Come look at this!" he exclaimed. Outside, in the front yard, Lucy and Marie were standing there with Their small bodies and pale faces, beaming a cheerful smile.

"My baby girl!" Teresa cried out, running outside.

A TANGLED WEAVE: Death of a Child

"I knew they were together." Jack pulled Teresa close to him in a soft embrace. Teresa looked up into his eyes, they were glowing with warmness Teresa had not felt in a long time. Jack met Teresa's eyes; the soft embrace became more of a tug to pull their bodies closer.

"You are going to do great things mommy, I love you," Lucy said before quickly disappearing. Although she was gone, Teresa could still sense her presence; it brought her joy and tranquility. Both George and Jack were astonished at what they had witnessed. Elizabeth and Maggie also stepped out from their house next door to take in the scene too. All of Teresa's new friends now realized that peace would come to the house.

*****

Sam took a deep breath and braced himself before entering the station. He had a feeling that things were going to be hard, thinking of the meeting he had the night before. All eyes turned towards him as soon as he stepped inside, causing his hair to stand on end. Keeping his head held high, Sam made his way to his desk. The phone was ringing by the time he reached it, and with all his strength, he took the call.

"Sam, I need you to come to my office right away," said the voice on the other end of the line. Taking one last deep breath, he made his way towards the captain's office with determination in his eyes, ready to face whatever fate had in store for him.

This was it, the time of truth, Sam followed orders and walked into the captain's office. Once there, he saw Jenkins sitting in one of the chairs with a defeated expression and he knew it was done.

The captain then proceeded to tell Sam that Jenkins had been arrested for Lucy's murder and the evidence against him that linked him to her death was just what they needed. As Sam's heart jumped at this news, all he could think about was Teresa—he had promised her he would have justice for Lucy no matter what it took. Despite being grief-stricken, Sam swore to himself that Jenkins would pay for this; justice would prevail, and Lucy's memory will remain.

Sam could barely wrap his mind around the horror of it all; it was too much for him to bear. "Why, would you do this?"

A TANGLED WEAVE: Death of a Child

Jenkins twisted in the chair, the handcuffs binding to his back. "Steve lied to me, if I could have my money, he was not getting his."

"That is twisted thinking, you killed a child for the money you were not getting. You are a monster." Sam could hardly control his anger.

"Sam take the day off, go see Lucy's mother, go home, we will handle everything from here." The captain pulled Jenkins from the chair and walked him out the door.

Sam left the office moments later in a daze, having heard about someone so close being involved in such an unthinkable act. With each step he took away from there, Sam was growing more distant from this nightmare in his mind, trying to make sense of things as he walked aimlessly through the streets towards Teresa's house. He needed to give them the news.

Arriving at the house, Teresa, George, Jack, Elizabeth, and Maggie were all standing in the front yard. It only took one look to find out what had happened at the station. The nightmare was over. Lucy could finally rest.

ABOUT THE AUTHOR

K.R. Somo's family is her lifeblood and the root of her strength. She is a wife, daughter, mother, and grandmother who finds inspiration in the people closest to her. Despite the challenges that life has thrown her way, K.R. Somo has never lost her optimism or her upbeat spirit. She wakes up each morning feeling grateful for the blessings in her life- her health, her home, her family, and so much more. She knows that life is not always easy, but she refuses to let the tough times get her down. Instead, she chooses to focus on the good things in life- the moments that bring joy and make her heart sing.

She was raised in a rural area in Kansas before relocating her family to Arizona. She earned multiple full-time jobs to support them, delaying her aspirations of being a writer until now. With the help of her partner, she now has the opportunity to pursue her literary goals in the beautiful landscape that is Costa Rica.

Made in the USA
Middletown, DE
27 July 2024